Edited by Stephanie Parent
www.oliviahayle.com

brothers of paradise

SMALL TOWN
Hero

olivia hayle

EPIGRAPH

"A ship in harbor is safe,
but that is not what ships are built for."

— *John A. Shedd*

1

JAMIE

Paradise Shores looks the way it always has. I don't know if that makes me feel better or worse, that the town I grew up in is unchanged, when I so clearly am not. On some days it feels like a relief. On others a personal attack. Today? It's nerve-wracking.

I've been standing outside the Paradise Shores Yacht Club for ten minutes. My bike is locked. I have my bag. And I can't make my feet move.

The yacht club is an emblem for the town, an institution. My friends and I used to buy their famous lobster rolls and eat them on the docks in the marina, beneath the hot summer sun. The building looks unchanged from the outside. The smooth wooden slats of its roof are the same. So are the steps up to the front door. The giant anchor resting in the flowerbed.

One day of working here and the news will be out. *Jamie's back in town after a decade away.*

I desperately hope no one will care.

But I already know that's not true. My best friend moved back to Paradise a few years ago, and I haven't told her I've followed suit. Only my mom knows I'm back, and that's because I'm staying with her.

Showing up at her doorstep had been *mildly* embarrassing. But not, perhaps, as embarrassing as this. I have a job.

As a waitress at the yacht club.

I take a deep breath. And then another one. I'd been lucky to see the posting, to get this job. So I swallow my pride and walk up the steps. The yacht club has a new coat of paint, navy, and it sits overlooking the Paradise Shores marina. Row after row of sailboats and yachts lie anchored at the docks. The ocean rocks them all gently.

For years, I saw this view every day.

And for years, I didn't see it at all.

The yacht club is empty when I step inside. It's early, and the first round of sailing classes should already be out at sea. So I head toward the back office and see Neil, sitting at his desk. He's still in charge of the marina.

He sees me and gives a wave. "Hello, there."

"Hi. I'm Jamie Moraine? The new waitress?"

He runs a hand over his balding head. *Well, that's new.* "Of course! Welcome, welcome. We spoke on the phone. Thanks for coming in on such short notice."

"Thanks for having me," I say.

"Come, let me introduce you to Stephen. He's head of the waitstaff. He should have arrived by now..." Neil closes the door to the office and walks me through the lobby, past tasteful nautical decor. There are gold-framed paintings of boats at sea on the walls and in a corner is a giant statue made out of boating rope.

The place looks much better than I remember. Fresh coat of cream paint on the wainscoting and a deep blue on the walls.

"All settled in to Paradise?" Neil asks.

He had been a sailing instructor when I was young, and then head of the marina. Not surprised he doesn't remember me. I was never one for sailing.

"Yes, thanks."

The man named Stephen is wiping down a set of menus,

splayed out on a wooden table. "You're Jamie?" he asks without looking up. He might be in his forties, tall and gangly, with a mustache.

"Yes," I say, feeling underdressed. His pristine waiter's uniform doesn't fit with my sundress.

"Good, you're right on time." He hands me the rag. "Continue wiping these down while I get you your uniform."

He disappears through the staff door.

Neil snorts by my side. "He's good folk, once you get to know him."

I start wiping down the laminated menus. "I'm sure he is."

"The place looks good, doesn't it? What do you think?"

"Yes, it does," I say.

"The new boss renovated it in the off-season. The kitchen has all brand-new appliances, looks like a damn spaceship in there. These are new hardwood floors, too."

"It looks good," I say, and I mean it. Gone is the old wallpaper, yellowed after previous decades with indoor smoking allowed.

Spending the summers waitressing at the yacht club had been a rite of passage when I was a teenager. The cool girls from Paradise High did it, while the cool guys would teach sailing lessons down on the docks.

My best friend and I had stayed far away from the marina those summers.

"Well, Stephen'll take good care of you," Neil says.

And I have to give it to them, Stephen does. He tells me to tuck my shirt into my pencil skirt and makes me recite the specials on the board. It wouldn't be rocket science to a new waitress, and I've done this on and off for years.

But I understand just why he gave me such a thorough introduction during lunch. I've just served a family of six, the youngest child in that wonderful babbling age, when he stops me.

"They'll be here at four," he says in sotto voce.

"They?"

"The owner and the new chefs he's interviewing."

Now it makes sense. "Is he here a lot?"

Stephen nods. "And he always has opinions."

I bet he does, I think. The world would be a lot nicer if people stopped having so many.

The rest of the lunch service is calm. I do what I've always done, take orders and deliver food. Some ask me if I'm new, and I answer yes. I don't make much small talk.

I need the tips, but I don't have the energy.

Two young waitresses work beside me. It's clearly their summer job, and they like to whisper amongst themselves by the window, close to the heat lamp. They look like my best friend and I did at the age. Bright and happy and sharing every last thing that happens, like they're living one shared life instead of two.

It's a miracle that I don't run into anyone I know. Not an old elementary school teacher or an old classmate, and not the girl *I'd* once shared every last thing with. Lily Marchand and I haven't spoken in years, and it's entirely my fault.

It's a reunion I dread.

As the lunch service draws to a close, I watch Stephen set up a table in the corner with extra care. It doesn't take a genius to figure out it's where the owner will interview new chefs… and they'll be able to oversee the waitstaff at the same time. Isn't that just lovely?

I have one table left to wait before my shift ends. Three middle-aged men on their second round of beer, all talking louder than necessary. I've just cleared away their plates—club sandwiches, extra mayo—when Stephen stops me.

"They're here," he says with a subtle nod to the corner.

"The owner?"

"Yes. He's interviewing the first potential new chef now."

I peer around the corner at the two men shaking hands. I can't make out either of them at this distance.

So I take another lap around the room, eyes shifting over

the few guests that remain. Lunch has always been the yacht club's most popular time. People across Paradise Shores come by, often to eat before heading out on their boats. We're in May still, but come June and July, this place will be packed.

"Sweetheart!" someone calls. "Get us another round of beers, will you?"

Me?

I turn to the table with the extra mayo men. The guy who's spoken has gray at the temples, a crooked grin on his face. His eyes travel over my uniform and pause at my chest, right where the white shirt fits a bit too snug.

Anger rolls over me, tempered by a fear I hate. A fear I can't shake. So I zero in on the empty glasses at the table, speaking to them rather than the men. "Coming right up," I say, leaning past him to grab them.

A clammy hand curves around my bare thigh and slides up, under my skirt.

"Good girl," the man says. "You new around here?"

I take two steps back and away from the grip.

My heart pounds in my ears.

"Welcome to town," he says, like he didn't just touch me, and his smile widens.

I'm frozen to the spot, shame heating up my skin.

A man steps past me and puts a firm hand on the creep's shoulder. "John," he says. "I'm going to insist that you settle your bill and leave. Right away."

The voice is familiar. I stare at the short, dark blond hair that curls over the tan neck, the broad back beneath a linen shirt. If I'd been frozen before, I'm boiling now. Embarrassment crawls its way up my cheeks.

"Marchand," the creep says. "How's it going?"

"Now, John."

He sighs and gets to his feet. "Sorry, fellas," he says. "I guess someone's in the mood to play bad cop."

"Settle your bill with Stephen," Parker says, because it has to be him. "And John? I don't want to see you here again."

John's eyes narrow. "You can't be serious."

"Dead serious," Parker says. I can't stop looking at him. It's Lily's older brother.

He has to be the new owner.

The other two men mumble something and rise from their seats, eyes downcast. The three make their way over to where Stephen is waiting.

John gives Parker one last glare. It's the sort of look that promises a strongly worded email in a few hours. *Coming to an inbox near you...*

Parker stares back at him without the grin I'd always associated with him. He'd been Paradise Shores' greatest sailor, Lily's older brother, one of the shining Marchand siblings.

I haven't seen him since I'd been twenty-two. He'd been a college athlete, with sun-bleached hair that fell over his forehead and a sorority girlfriend.

Now he must be thirty-four.

Parker doesn't turn to me until John is out of the restaurant. "I'm sorry. That should never have happened, but I can promise you that he won't bother you again."

He looks at me, eyes steady. Voice sincere. Tanned from the sun and grown, hardened, in a way he wasn't the last time I'd seen him.

He doesn't recognize me.

I don't know if the crushing feeling in my chest is relief or regret.

"If you'd like to file a report I will help you every step of the way." Parker ducks his head slightly and gives me a smile. It's polite and conspiratorial and something thumps painfully in my chest. "How does that sound? Let me give you the rest of the day off, too."

I shake my head. "No, I'm okay."

He pauses. Eyes pass over my face and down to where my nameplate rests. Stephen had made it with a little laminating machine and presented it to me with a flourish. *Jamie.*

Deep blue eyes return to me. He has new wrinkles at the corners from sun and sea. "Jamie? As in, Jamie Moraine?"

I nod. "Yes. Hi, Parker."

"Hell, it's been years! I didn't know you were back in town?"

My hands shake at my sides. He's going to tell Lily, I think. And Jesus, I *work* for him. Mortification makes my voice thin. "I just got here. Sorry, I shouldn't keep you."

"That's all right," he says, his smile turning into a frown when I start to back away. "So you work here?"

I give a few nods. "Yes, and I should get back to work. Good luck with your interviews."

He looks after me, a frown between his eyebrows. "Jamie," he says. But I'm already hurrying toward the kitchen.

I knew I wouldn't be able to escape the questions in Paradise Shores. Wouldn't be able to escape the past, the confrontations. If Parker knows, it's only a matter of time before Lily will too.

I avoid the table in the corner for the rest of my shift, but I can feel the weight of his gaze more than once. I finish up the last tasks. I fill up salt in the shakers on the table and wipe down the menus again.

And by the time my shift is done, the table in the corner is empty. Parker is gone.

"Thanks for today!" I tell Stephen and change in the staff room. Biking home in a skirt won't be possible. I sling my bag over my shoulder and step out through the back entrance, into the late-afternoon sun.

I can't wait to get home, to close my eyes and breathe. To count down the days until the paycheck arrives.

But there's someone waiting for me in the parking lot. There, leaning against his dusty Jeep, is Parker Marchand. And he's looking right at me.

2

JAMIE

"Hi," he says.

I look down at the key to my bike lock. Spin it around my finger. "Hey."

"I'm sorry about earlier. About that guy."

I shake my head. "Not your fault."

"My restaurant," he says, "my responsibility."

My embarrassment bubbles over. "Gosh, Parker, I'm sorry. I didn't know the yacht club was your place now. I would never have applied if I did!"

He frowns. "Why not? I'm glad you're back. Looked like you were doing a great job in there. Was it your first day today?"

I nod. "Yes, I haven't been back in town long."

"I didn't know you were back at all," he says. "Have you spoken to—"

"No," I say. "We haven't spoken in a while."

"Ah," Parker says. He must know about Lily and me. They've always been close. All the Marchand siblings had been, a tribe of their own. I'd been fiercely jealous of that once.

"Congrats on buying this place. It looks great. I heard you've renovated?" I say, inching toward my bike. Attack with compliments, and he might not ask me about myself. Where I've been, what I've done... why I'm back.

"Thank you," he says. "I didn't know you'd applied for a job here."

"Again, sorry about that. If you want me to, I can...?" I trail off. It's not like I can quit, not really. I desperately need this job.

Parker's frown deepens. "I'm glad you're back," he says. "Jamie, we're friends. I'd have introduced you to the place myself if I knew."

"Oh. Thanks. But Stephen did a good job."

"He's a good manager," he says. "Where are you staying?"

My hands curve around the handles of my bike. "On Greene Street."

"Your mom's house?"

He remembers? "Yes."

"I can drive you. There's space in the back for your bike." He puts his hands in his pockets, a gesture I remember from our teenage years. But the Parker in front of me is a man grown. Some of the golden Abercrombie handsomeness has matured, settled into a face that's familiar, and warm, and a bit weathered.

He'll tell Lily, I think. Right after this. "Thank you, but I'd rather bike."

"Okay." He smiles crookedly, like he's trying to draw my own smile out. We'd argued a lot once. About everything, but actually nothing. Mostly over the remote. He'd watch games and I'd argue with him over how stupid organized sports was. Lily would roll her eyes.

"I haven't been back very long. It feels... kinda strange."

"I get that," he says. "Has the place changed?"

"Not particularly."

He laughs a little. "No, I suppose Paradise never really does. How have you been, Jamie?"

How do you sum up a decade? "Good, but busy."

That makes him laugh again. "You always were," he says. "Have you managed to set the world to rights?"

God, that must be how he remembers me. Idealistic and argumentative and naive. I feel a million miles away from that person.

I'm still trying to set my own world to rights.

"Not yet," I say. "How have you been? How's the family?"

"They're good, all of them. I'm an uncle now, but I'm sure you know that?"

"To little Jamie," I say. The word almost gets lodged in my throat. Lily's son is named after me. It had been a stupid pact we'd made, years ago. That our kids would be named after one another. Middle names, we'd said. She'd gone one step further.

Parker nods. "Yes, and Hazel."

"Hazel?"

"Henry's daughter."

"Oh."

"She was born a year ago now." He runs a hand over the scruff along his jaw. "Maybe a year and a half. It's hard to keep track."

"Your parents must be overjoyed."

"They are," he says dryly. "Takes the pressure off the rest of us childless bastards."

I swing a leg over my bike. It's unsettling to talk to him again. It's nice, and deceptive, because we're not who we once were. So he doesn't have kids. My eyes drop down to his hands, resting tanned and relaxed at his sides. No rings on either one.

"Thanks for today," I say.

He shakes his head, something ticking in his jaw. "Thanks for taking the job. You're a great waitress. I'm just sorry about that asshole touching you."

"Was he a regular?"

Parker shrugs. "I've seen him around town a few times,

yeah. He has his boat in the marina. Doesn't mean he has a right to eat in my restaurant, though."

"Thank you."

He smiles again. "No need to thank me, James."

I pause, a foot on the pedal. He'd called me James when we were kids, and then continued as teenagers. Back when he'd been my best friend's older brother and one of the most popular guys in our school. My name is not James. It's Jamie. He'd known, and he'd teased me about it, and I'd pretended to be more annoyed than I actually was.

Parker's eyes hold a question. *Will I remember?*

It tugs at my lips, the memory of old arguments, of jokes, of times when my heart would speed up when he walked by me in the high school hallway. How I'd sleep over at Lily's and see him in only a pair of boxers and sleep-mussed hair.

But then I remember who I am and where I am and what really matters, and the old flame dies as quickly as it had ignited.

"Well, have a good evening," I say. "See you around?"

"Yeah. Drive safe."

I leave him and the yacht club behind, cycling down familiar streets. They turn from seaside to curbside quickly, with large trees flanking the streets like quiet sentinels, watching over this suburban paradise. There are barely any cars on the roads. The season is too early for the parade of vacationers to arrive.

I stop outside my mother's house. It's nestled in between two larger ones, like the runt of the litter, and is the only one on the street that isn't white or gray. Her house is bright blue with white shutters. Macrame wind catchers hang from the porch, their sea shells in constant, audible motion. Beside it is Emma's pink bike that had once been mine.

"Mom?" I call. "Emma?"

The door is unlocked. It sends a shiver of fear up my spine. "Emma!"

Mom's voice reaches me. "Backyard!"

They're sitting on the grass, with a bucket in between them. Blowing soap bubbles.

A knot inside me relaxes at the sight. Emma is in her favorite purple dress, with grass stains on her knobby knees and a concentrated look on her face. Mom has her hair up in a bun. Her arms are streaked with dry clay from an earlier session with the pottery wheel.

A group of bubbles fly past me and one explodes, fragile and thin, right by my ear.

"Mommy!" Emma says. She shines up in a grin and rushes to dip her utensil again. "Look! We're blowing bubbles."

"I can see that, honey. Having fun?"

She doesn't answer me, face concentrated again. My mother gets to her feet and shakes out her left knee. "Hi, sweetheart."

"Hey. Did everything go okay today?"

"It went splendidly. We started with some sculpting and Emma made a snowman. A very inspired choice for the season. Oh, and we had pancakes for lunch." She takes a deep breath. "I'd forgotten how much effort it takes to watch a small child."

I feel a pinch of guilt. It's for more than I can list. For being away from my mom for so many years... and now for being back so suddenly, forcing both her and Emma into a situation they might not be ready for.

"Thanks, Mom."

She gives me a warm smile. "I'm just happy you're home. Both of you."

And cue even more guilt.

"How was your first day?" she asks.

I watch as my daughter blows more bubbles. Her brows are knitted together in concentration. Too hard an exhale and they break. Too soft and they won't form. "It was good," I say. "Waitressing is pretty similar everywhere."

And then, before I can stop myself, I add the rest.

"Parker Marchand is the new owner."

"Oh, that's right. He bought the place pretty recently, I think," Mom says. "I remember hearing about the renovations. It seemed like they went on forever."

"You knew he owned it?"

"Yes. Oh, sorry sweetheart, should I have told you? You're friends with his cousin, aren't you?"

Bless my mother's heart, but she's always lived with her head halfway in the clouds.

"His sister," I say. "Lily has three older brothers. Parker, Rhys and Henry."

"Oh, right, right."

She must be the only one in this town who can't keep track of the Marchands. The family is as well known as the yacht club itself. The famous builder and his beautiful wife, now stewards of the community.

"Well, isn't that nice?" she says. "You'll be working with friends."

I look down at my daughter's fine hair. She has my light brown color, and none of the dark curls her father has. *Mine*, I think. *Mine through and through.*

"*For* friends," I correct quietly. "Not *with* friends."

The distinction feels a gulf wide and just as important. Parker and I aren't on the same level anymore. Nor am I and Lily. She has a husband, a family, a place here. A career she's worked over a decade for—a career she always dreamed about.

I can't imagine telling her about my last few years. I can't imagine what she'll think of me.

Emma blows a huge, complete bubble that floats gently up in the summer air. She grins up at me. "See?" she asks.

Determination squeezes hard inside my chest. *Mine*, I think again. *And I'll do anything now to get us back on our feet.*

"I saw it," I tell her. "Beautiful."

3

PARKER

Jamie catapults across my sister's living room as fast as his short legs allow him. "Watch!" he screams. "Waaaatch!"

Behind him, the blanket he's tied around his neck flies out like a cape. He's in his Spider-Man pajamas. I once tried to explain to the guy that Spider-Man doesn't wear capes, but considering he's still too young to watch all the movies, he's allowed some artistic license.

"Did you see?" He's panting, having stopped abruptly in front of the fireplace with inches to spare. "I was flying!"

"Yes, I did. Very impressive," I say.

Jamie doesn't wait for me to finish before he takes off again, this time climbing onto one of the couches. His face is determined as he bends his knees, facing the armchair I'm in.

"Catch me," he says.

I have just enough time to get my arms up and stop him from careening headfirst into my chest. He laughs like a loon and wriggles like an eel, and as soon as I put him back down, he's off again. The roses on his cheeks are bright red.

"Jesus," I say to Hayden. "Is he always like this before bed?"

My sister's husband rolls his eyes. "You know he's not, but you're here. He likes to perform when you're around."

I grin. "I'm his favorite uncle."

"Don't say that when Henry or Rhys are around," Hayden says.

"Because I'm right?"

He chuckles. "Yes, because you're right."

In truth, my brothers don't live permanently in Paradise Shores, and that might contribute somewhat to my higher status in little Jamie's pecking order. But Marchands are competitive to the core, and I won't give them an inch.

"Come here, you rascal," Hayden says. He catches his son around the waist. The boy has dark hair like his father. "It's almost time for bed."

My nephew wails like he's been told it's time for the gallows.

"Yes, it is," Hayden says firmly. He spent years in the Navy. They had been dark years with him away and the rest of us none the wiser, particularly my sister. But the discipline drilled into him became a part of his very core. "No ifs or buts."

"Yes ifs!" Jamie cries, with the expertise of someone who's countered this argument many times before. "Yes butts! All the butts!"

Hayden gives me a withering look. "He has no idea what he's saying."

I smile at both of them. Hayden is holding Jamie upside down, the boy's cape dragging on the floor, and walks calmly toward the stairs. "Let's read a book," he says.

"Parker!" Jamie calls. "Help!"

"Your uncle can't help you," Hayden says, all ruthlessness.

"Sorry, kiddo!" I call. "But I'm afraid of your father too!"

I hear Hayden snort, and then they disappear up the staircase. Jamie's cry of disapproval disappears a few seconds later. He's loud, and he's determined, but he's got a one-track mind. Tempt him with his favorite bedtime story and he'll fold like a house of cards.

I lean back in the armchair and listen to the bustle my sister is making in the kitchen. Their house is close to mine, and now that we all live here again, I spend almost as much time here as I do at home. Little Jamie changed things for all of us.

"Jamie," I say out loud. It has been a long time since I'd reflected on my nephew's name.

Lily sticks her head in half a minute later. "Are you talking to yourself again?"

"What do you mean, again?"

She smiles and wipes her hands on a dishtowel. "Everything okay?"

"Yeah." I stretch my legs out and look at the expensive glass sculpture on the coffee table. Lily likes it, and Hayden is not-so-secretly hoping their son would break it. I think it looks like a blob. "I was thinking about Jamie."

"What about him?"

"Not him," I say. "About his namesake."

Lily disappears into the kitchen, puts the towel away, and joins me a minute later in the armchair opposite me. She absently fluffs the pillow behind her. "What about her?"

"Tell me about the promise again. With the names."

She laughs a bit. "We were so young when we made that pact."

"But you kept it."

"I did. Well, partly." She looks fondly toward the stairs where her husband and son went. "His real name is James. But yeah. I kept it."

"How come?" I'm genuinely curious. It must have been years since the two of them saw one another... and I haven't thought much about that. Not until *she* appeared in my restaurant.

Lily sighs. "What are these questions?"

"Tell me," I say.

She draws her legs up beneath her in the armchair. "I hadn't intended to keep it, actually. Hayden and I had a bunch of names we looked at. None really felt right. And then we came upon James. It was his grandfather's name too, did you know that?"

"I didn't."

"He was someone Hayden had fond memories of, and you know that's rare, with his family history. And I, well…" She picks at the edge of a neatly folded blanket. "I remembered the old pact. The name just fit. Jamie used to know everything about me, you know? And we hadn't spoken in years when I had the baby. It felt right, like honoring people who mattered to both Hayden and me, but who were no longer with us… for different reasons, of course." She shrugs, and gives me an un-Lily-like smile. It looks forced. "If she ever comes back, it'll be complicated with the names, but I don't think the odds are high anymore."

I scratch along my jaw. "Right."

"Parker."

"Yes?"

Her gaze sharpens. "Why did you ask me about it? What do you know?"

I sigh. "How do you do that?"

"I've been reading you since I was born," she says. "You're only a year older than me. I had to learn to if I wanted to catch up. Now spill." She leans forward, hands on her thighs. "Did you hear something?"

"You need to promise me something first."

"No way. Tell me now."

"No."

"Parker Michael Marchand, I swear—"

"You have to promise me you won't do anything rash. I don't know where Jamie's been, but she's not the same person you remember."

Lily's eyes narrow. "You've *seen* her?"

"She's back in Paradise," I say, and hold up my hands. "Don't overreact."

My sister has gone completely still. *"What?"*

"She's just taken a job at the yacht club."

"You're kidding, and it's mean, Parker."

"I'm dead serious. She started work on Monday."

"And you waited *five days* to tell me? What's wrong with you?" She reaches for a pillow, my thirty-three-year-old sister reverting back into the feral animal she'd been as a kid.

"Because you'd react like this and I didn't want you to scare my nephew."

"Excuses!"

I raise my hands again. "Look. She's back. She's been back for about two weeks. But something's changed."

"Of course it has! I haven't seen her in years!"

"No, damn it, I don't mean that. I mean…" I trail off and run a hand through my hair. How do you put it into words? The Jamie I remembered had dyed her hair pitch-black. She'd had fire in her eyes and confidence radiating from every pore. Once, she'd relished every opportunity to argue with me. She'd been on the debate team. She'd written for the school newspaper.

Timid would have been the last word I'd use to describe her. But now she seemed a shadow of herself. Docile and quiet.

"Yes?" Lily prompts.

"She's changed," I say lamely. "Look, all I'm saying is, don't come in guns blazing. Okay? Wait for her to come to you."

A fire burns in Lily's eyes. "I've waited for years. She never answered my last text!"

"Yeah. Not making excuses. But I don't think the last few years have been kind to her, that's all I'm saying."

Lily puts her head in her hands. "She's back in Paradise," she says. "Jesus."

"Living with her mom."

"And working at the yacht club?" She looks up from her hands and gives me an inscrutable glance. "I suppose we really do have to start calling my son *little* Jamie."

"Or James," I say.

"Bah, he's no James yet. Maybe when he stops wetting the bed."

I laugh at that. Hayden comes downstairs and joins us, mid-laugh. He looks between us with a crooked smile and tosses the blanket Jamie had used as a cape over the back of the couch. Lily runs a hand over her husband's back and starts to fold the cloth. Judging from her quiet expression, she's already devising a strategy.

It's *her* best friend that's back, and yet, I don't know if she'll approach this the right way.

I picture the Jamie I'd seen, standing in the yacht club uniform. The leashed anger in her gaze after that creep had dared to put his hands on her. No dark makeup around her eyes, her hair light brown instead of black. The nose ring she'd once had was gone. And then I'd watched the anger die, and sputter, and turn into embarrassment.

"Just be careful," I warn Lily again.

She gives me an angelic smile.

Right. *As if.*

————

I sit at the corner table in the restaurant. It's become mine, more comfortable than the back office, with the view of the ocean outside the windows. Seagulls trail a sailing boat motoring swiftly out of the marina and toward open water.

I watch as the sailor unfurls the main sail. The winds are good today.

My mind draws me out there, like it always has.

The yacht club is like home in the same way Paradise Shores is. I'd sailed here since I could walk. It's where I had lessons. It's where I later helped give lessons to others. It's where I trained for the regattas.

I've sailed in better waters. Bluer, calmer, warmer. But

none of it beats the deep blue of the Atlantic right here, along the coast of New England.

The figures on my screen confirm just that. The yacht club is doing as well today as it did ten years ago. Paradise hasn't seen the outflow of people like so many other small towns. It's kept steady instead. Housing prices are expensive, and zoning regulations are tightly controlled. None of us want the coastline to be overbuilt.

My father had considered my current job a downgrade. *I'm buying it,* I'd said. *I'm not working there as a busboy.*

He'd shook his head and turned his back to me, focusing on the lobsters he'd been grilling on the family porch. *You had a job in Boston. A career.*

This again. But after thirty-four years as his son, and as the younger sibling of Henry Marchand, I'd finally realized I'd never be able to make the man proud. When your oldest brother is the head architect of the newly constructed New York Opera House, well, you might as well give up the attempt.

Studying for my law degree had been interesting. Rewarding. But even then, I'd known as I sat with the thick books spread out around me, that my heart was out at sea.

So giving up my practice and renovating the yacht club instead was, for the first time in years, a project I was actually excited about. I know this place like I know my own bones. My sister and her husband, one of my best friends, live in the town. I have the ocean and the boats here, and they're better than any prestige gained professionally.

I look up from my screen again. The restaurant is slowing down after a busy lunch. With May inching toward June, the out-of-towners are increasing. Things are looking good. The new chef starts next week, and with her, I hope the menu gets a much-needed makeover.

One of the waitresses walks through the space, dishrag in hand, and sets to wiping down the tables. It's not Jamie. She's stayed mostly out of the dining room today, instead working front of the house.

I wonder if it's because I'm here.

She still hasn't said more than a curt hi or goodbye to me. There's been no repeat of the conversation we'd had in the parking lot the other week.

I watch her colleague wipe down the tables. They have no problem saying hello to me, and none of *them* avoid my eyes.

Sighing, I look back at my screen. The yacht club's website needs an overhaul. It's still using the old booking system for sailing classes, which is the incredibly high-tech honor system with Neil—you make a call, you promise to pay—and it slows us all down. I'll have to hire someone to create a new website. Re-do everything.

I'm halfway through searching for web designers online when someone calls my name. The voice is familiar. *Please don't.*

I slowly close my laptop. "Lily…"

My sister gives me her brightest, I'm-not-up-to-anything smile. I know better than to trust it. "Hi. What are you doing?"

"Working." I look over her shoulder, but I don't see Jamie. "You just happened to be in the mood for a lobster roll?"

"Not quite." She puts her bag down on the chair opposite me and looks around. "I like what you've done with the place."

"Lily," I warn. She's been here many times since the renovations ended.

But she's not having my admonitions. "Let me," she says, fast and heated. "I've waited a long time for this."

"I know that, but perhaps right here isn't the best place—"

"Then where? She won't answer my texts."

I sigh. "Don't make a scene, Lily."

"I would never."

She turns around, a hand on the table. Waiting. My teeth grind together. Something's off about Jamie, and I know that

Lily will notice it. If she had a moment to consider, she'd know what to say. But I fear she's too hurt by Jamie's silence to see past her own pain.

And right on cue, Jamie enters the dining room. Her hair is in a ponytail today. It falls soft and curved down her back, and her eyes are downcast. She's the same age as my sister, only a year younger than me, and yet there's something young and hesitant in her movements that was never there before.

I hate it. It's not her.

"Lily…" I murmur, but my sister is already moving toward her best friend. The two of them had been inseparable. Their heads always bowed together in school, the auburn and the brown, or when Jamie started dying it, the pitch-black.

Jamie's back goes ramrod straight. Her mouth doesn't move, not as Lily approaches.

I can't hear what they say, but I don't have to. Lily is the one doing most of the talking. I watch her run a hand under her eyes at one point, and at another, her voice rises. Jamie listens to all of it. She's gripping the menu in front of her tight enough that the laminated plastic curves. She nods, twice, and once shakes her head so quickly the ponytail flies.

It's too much for her, I think. I don't know why. But it is, and I can see it in the pinched set of her mouth and her cautious eyes.

I get up from the table and make my way to the two women. They're off center in the restaurant, but they're by no means hidden. And it's only Jamie's second week at work.

"Ladies," I say. "Sorry to interrupt, but there are tables to wait."

Lily looks at me like she's plotting my slow and painful death. "You run your employees ragged, do you?"

"Your brother's right," Jamie says quickly. "I'm on the clock. Sorry, Lily. It was nice to see you."

"All right," Lily says. She doesn't sound quite like my sister either. "I'll see you around?"

Jamie nods, and Lily gives a half-hearted smile. "Bye then," she says to Jamie.

She doesn't say goodbye to me, and I'm sure I'll get an earful about interrupting later, watching as my sister disappears toward the exit without looking back.

Beside me, her former best friend sighs deeply.

"I'm sorry about that," I say.

Jamie shakes her head. "I knew you'd tell her."

"I waited a week," I say, and give her a half-smile. "It took her less than three days to come here."

"I'm surprised she waited that long," Jamie says.

I chuckle. "She was always a bit impulsive."

"Yes." Jamie looks down at the menu in her hand, the plastic slowly straightening. "Thanks, Parker."

"For interrupting? No worries. You don't actually have many tables to wait, you know. Feel free to take a break."

"I think I'll keep working." She looks up at me, and there's a tiny, crooked smile on her lips. "Wouldn't want to disappoint you, Boss."

I open my mouth—what do I say to that?—but Jamie turns and disappears back toward the kitchen. I watch her go.

She'd been my little sister's friend. Off-limits in more ways than one, not least because of the giant *stay away* stamped across her face with every glance. There had been fire in her eyes. I'd seen it when she walked into school in flares when ripped jeans were trendy. In short, dark hair when the popular girls sported long, highlighted locks. In the dark eyeshadow around her eyes that, even smudged, emphasized the warm brown of her eyes.

That's gone now. The unexpected clothing. The dark makeup. But not the fire. Even with her hair braided down her back and a clean face dotted with freckles, the fire *is* there. Hidden and subdued, but present.

And I can't wait to stoke it back into a flame.

4

JAMIE

"You can stay for as long as you want," Mom says. "Maybe a year, or two…"

She's sitting in the reading nook in the living room, surrounded by pillows in a rainbow of colors. On her lap is her old laptop. A sticker for the local dive shop sits on the back, not that I think she's ever gone diving.

"I can't stay for a year," I say.

"Why not? This is your home, and it has great schools. Put Emma in line to start first grade at Paradise Elementary."

"I can't."

"There are opportunities here," she continues. "You got a job on your first week."

"That was sheer dumb luck. The yacht club needed waitresses, and I've done a lot of waitressing."

Mom shakes her head. "There's no such thing as dumb luck. You fit in here."

I draw my legs up beneath me on the couch. My head is pounding, and there's no way to make her see why I can't stay.

"I don't mind watching Emma," she says, voice softer this time. "We're getting along even better now, I think. She's not so shy around me anymore."

"She likes you," I say. My daughter is cautious around strangers, but she'd taken to her grandmother immediately. The creative streak and habit of making fluffy pancakes for breakfast had eased the way. There are few things six-year-olds like more than crafting and copious amounts of maple syrup.

At least my six-year-old.

"The school here is good," Mom says again. "One of the best in the county."

"I know."

"Please consider it, sweetheart. I just got you back."

I rest my head against my updrawn knees. Yes, we'd just gotten back. And I'm forcing myself onto my mom and her hospitality after years of too-sporadic phone calls and far too few visits. She'd only seen Emma a few times before we'd shown up at her doorstep with all of two suitcases to our name.

It's embarrassing, and not the kind that fades after a few laughs. It's the deep kind of mortification that makes me feel two feet tall, and in this town, I'm dwarfed by the wealth and success of people who hadn't let life beat them down.

I'd waited too long to take the reins of my life again, and I never thought I'd be that person. Never thought I'd lose myself. But I had. And now we're all paying the price for it.

"I can't," I say again, and my voice sounds broken. I hate hearing it. "You've already given me so much, Mom. I can't live here that long without paying rent."

"Oh, rent," she says with a wave of her hand. "If that's the stickler, we'll figure something out, if that would make you feel better. We'll talk about it. But don't you dare pick up and move on somewhere else, Jamie Elizabeth Moraine. My granddaughter deserves pancakes every day."

That makes me laugh. Emma sure does, that and so much more that I can't give her. It's all hand-me-down bikes and a mother who keeps looking over her shoulder. Right now it all feels too much—too many decisions and too much guilt.

"She does," I say. "Okay. I'll think about calling the school. But Mom, don't get your hopes up, okay? I don't know what will happen with my job at the yacht club after high season. Business slows down."

"People eat there year round," she says.

"Yes, but less often."

She smiles and looks back down at her old laptop. "We'll figure something out."

My beautiful, beautiful mother. Now it's hard to imagine how I lived without her for so many years. The times we'd fought like cat and dog when I was a teenager, over curfews, my nose piercing, my first boyfriend, the time I re-painted my room black without asking her; it all feels so far ago. And such a waste. I hope Emma and I never fight like that.

"Thank you," I say. "For everything, you know. I don't think I've said it yet."

Mom looks up at me, and she blinks twice, her eyes getting a bit glassy. "Anytime, sweetheart. Anytime."

There's still a lot we haven't spoken about. But there's time. I rest my head against my knees again and take a deep breath. It fills my lungs up completely, my chest expanding without constraint, and it's enough. For now.

"Mommy?" a small voice asks. It's thick with sleep.

Emma is standing at the top of the stairs. Her hand is clasped around her stuffed rabbit, one of his ears draping to the floor. Her feet are bare beneath the hem of her pajamas.

I'm already moving toward her. "Yes, sweetie?"

"I had a bad dream," she mumbles, hands reaching toward me. I lift her up. She's getting heavy, and my back hurts from spending the day on my feet, but I carry her up to the second floor.

"I'm so sorry. But it was just a dream."

She nods against my shoulder, eyes already drifting closed again. Her eyelashes are long against the pale cheeks. My beautiful, beautiful daughter. I have so much in this house, beneath this roof, and the completeness of it takes my breath away. "I love you," I tell her.

She doesn't answer, just nestles closer. I put her back in my bed and climb in after her. We're both sleeping in Mom's guest room at the moment. The queen bed is more than big enough, and with all the changes, I feel best having Emma close.

She mumbles something incoherent and turns over toward me, a hand settling on my chest. I tuck Mr. Rabbit away from where he'd been attacking my cheek and look at the alarm clock. It's only nine p.m., but my eyelids are heavy.

I'd seen Lily today. Looking up at the ceiling, I stroke my hand over Emma's fine hair. Lily had kept her part of the pact and named her son Jamie. I'd cried when she'd sent me the message. *Don't know if you'll read this, but...* and added a picture of little Jamie. He'd been a baby then, swaddled, with a dark mop of hair.

I'd kept my part of the old pact too. Two years before, when Emma was born. Emma Lily Moraine.

Lee had wanted her to have his last name.

But we weren't married, and I'd resisted. I don't know why, because back then I thought I was happy. But maybe some part of me had known we'd end up here.

Emma and I, together. And Lee miles away.

I hope he stays there.

Lily had asked questions I didn't have an answer to. I'd seen it in her eyes, today. I hadn't been able to give her any. She's hurt. And I'm too embarrassed to explain it to her.

Emma's breathing evens out, and the hand on my chest grows limp and heavy. I listen to the soft breathing and let my hand rest on her head.

Parker had stopped our conversation. He'd seen, somehow, and rescued me from it. That sends another pang of embarrassment through me.

As a friend of Lily's, I'd been invited everywhere with them. Asked to join family sailing trips (I'd always said no) and to hang at her house after school (I'd always said yes). Her older brothers were often away, and eventually the oldest went to college, but Parker was often around.

He'd had his annoying group of guy friends, of course. They were loud jocks and too cocky for my liking. Parker had always been annoying. Sometimes on purpose. Most often by accident.

That's the thing, really. So much of what he did and was seemed accidental and always, always effortless. The wide smile that charmed teachers. The wind-tousled hair as he leapt onto the dock or won the Paradise Shore Junior Regatta without breaking a sweat. Even falling down on the football field he looked self-assured, rising with a grin and a shrug that announced to the world *that I'm here, and I'm myself, and I know who I am. Take me or leave me on my terms.*

He couldn't be that perfect—the Marchands couldn't be that perfect, and I knew they weren't, of course. Lily never faked perfection, and we'd spent too many nights comparing our families, our upbringings, sharing stories and heartaches, for me to think her parents were idols.

But it didn't matter how close to Parker I got through her. He never became less of the golden boy, his shine never dimmed, even sprawled out on the Marchands' couch with a root beer in hand, watching the NFL.

Too golden to touch. Too popular. Too put-together.

It had made me want to needle him. To see where the limits of the façade went. He rarely cracked, even when we'd argued incessantly about the remote, the weather, politics. He rarely showed anything but the golden boy.

Now he's a man, but he's still golden… and I still want to needle him.

5

PARKER

The sun peeks out behind the clouds, shining down on Paradise, and the air outside my car window is calm. We'd caught the last of the winds this morning before the weather turned.

I tap my fingers against the steering wheel in tune to the radio. Every part of me feels light, despite the tiredness in my arms and my strained eyes. I always do after we've been at sea. Hayden and I had started early aboard the *Frida*, casting off from the marina as the day's first rays crested.

I drive past the familiar little shops on Main Street. Some have their front doors open and wares displayed outside on the sidewalk. One shop sells giant, inflatable pool mattresses. Another has sculptures made out of driftwood and wind chimes with seashells made by a local.

My siblings couldn't wait to leave this place, and I couldn't wait to return.

Henry had seen sailing as a game to win, and he'd excelled. He always did.

Rhys had seen the boat as a poetic escape. More than once in our teenage years I'd seen him read dog-eared Hemingway paperbacks on the boat, sunglasses on his face while he ignored the rest of us.

Hayden had sailed with us a lot too, perhaps as a way to fit in. After he left Paradise it became a career move. He hadn't sailed in the Navy so much as he'd been a sailor, following orders and executing them precisely.

My little sister had always loved to ride along, the wind in her hair and new freckles appearing on her cheeks from the sun. She still loves a good day on the water... If the weather is nice.

But me? I love sailing for its own sake.

I love it in good weather and I thrive off it in bad. I'd competed because it gave me more hours at sea, not more trophies. To feel the lines run in my hands and the boat speaking to me. The thrum of silent power as the wind catches ahold of the sail and the boat flies across the water without making a sound. Harnessing nature. The danger, too. The elemental nature of it.

I need the ocean like I need air.

I drum my fingers faster on the steering wheel. People are walking along the boardwalk, sundresses and shorts as far as the eye can see. The season is picking up.

The willowy shape of a familiar woman steps out of the gelato shop ahead. Her hair's not braided this time. It's loose, falling in brown waves down her back in a way I've never seen it before. She has an ice-cream cone in one hand.

And in the other, she's holding the hand of a little girl.

There's no mistaking the closeness as they walk side by side.

Stopping is an impulse decision. I find a spot and reverse park, a hand on the wheel and my eyes on Jamie. The girl is standing close, totally absorbed in her rapidly melting ice cream. She has the same color hair as Jamie.

Light brown, now that it's no longer dyed dark.

She has a daughter.

I tuck my keys in my back pocket and reach them in a couple of strides. The girl sees me first. She looks at me with unbothered eyes and takes a long lick of her chocolate ice cream. She tugs on Jamie's dress with a sticky hand.

"Yes?" Jamie says, turning. Then she sees me. "Oh. Hello."

"Hi." My gaze falls on the little girl again. She's edged closer to her mother. "You guys in town for some ice cream?"

"Yes," Jamie says. She has her own modest cone in her left hand, and places her right on the little girl's head. "I haven't had Paradise ice cream in years."

"Best ice cream on the East Coast," I say with a smile. "Look, I want to apologize for Lily again."

I hadn't planned to.

But here I am, saying just that, and looking back down at the little girl. Jamie is a mother. Where is her husband? Her boyfriend?

And why had Lily not told me about it?

"Please don't. It's not your fault," Jamie says. She looks down at the girl industriously devouring her ice cream and hesitates. Like she doesn't know what to say.

Silence stretches out between us.

"It's okay," I say. I don't know what I'm referring to, but I hate that look on her face. I shouldn't have stopped. Shouldn't have bothered her.

"This is Emma," Jamie says. "My daughter. Sweetie, this is one of Mom's childhood friends. His name is Parker."

I crouch down. "Hello," I say. "It's nice to meet you."

The girl gives a half-swallowed *mmhmm*, her lips covered in ice cream.

"Chocolate is my favorite flavor too," I say. "Next time, you have to try the toppings."

Her eyes light up and she looks up at her mother. "Yes," Jamie says. "We can try them next time."

Emma lowers her ice cream. "What kind?"

"I don't know what kinds there are. We'll have to ask Parker."

Emma turns back to me. Her eyes are shy, and the question is in them. She doesn't voice it.

I run a hand along my jaw. "Let's see here. There's coconut, chocolate, tiny Oreos, M&M's, marshmallows, cereal, rainbow. But I think I've missed some."

"Oooh," she says.

I grin at her. "Yeah. It's pretty cool. But you'll have to get your mom to agree."

"That won't be difficult," Jamie says dryly. "I'm a pushover when she gives me those eyes."

I chuckle. "I have a very hard time seeing you as a pushover, James."

"Yeah, well, times change." She looks down at her ice cream. "Are you getting some too?"

"I might, yeah. Are you gonna have a seat on the boardwalk?" I say, knowing all too well that I'm inviting myself.

"We should, yeah. I'll need a few napkins to clean this off," she says, looking down at the chocolate ice cream dripping down Emma's arm. But there's a fond smile on her face. It's one I haven't seen in the two weeks since she started working at the yacht club.

"I'll join you," I say. "If that's okay?"

Jamie nods. It's not an enthusiastic yes, but it is a yes, and I'll take what I can get. A few minutes later I grab a seat next to them on the boardwalk, a cone of chocolate ice cream in hand.

"Look what I got," I say to Emma and hold out a cup with rainbow sprinkles in it. "If you want some? Otherwise I'll have them all."

She gives a happy little squeal and then looks up at her mom again. "Yes," Jamie says. "Go ahead."

My sprinkles are quickly devoured, just as I'd hoped. I hand Jamie the extra stack of napkins I'd snagged.

"Thank you," she says. And then, quietly, "I haven't told Lily about her."

"No, I figured. Do you want me to avoid mentioning it?"

Jamie looks out at the waves, hiding her expression from

view. "Maybe, yeah. But I don't want to put you in an awkward position."

"Not possible," I say. "I'm never awkward."

She snorts. "Of course not."

"She's adorable," I say, looking past Jamie at the girl swinging her legs and munching on sprinkles. "How old is she?"

"She's just turned six."

"Does your mom take care of her when you go to work?"

"Yeah."

I lean back against the bench and stretch out my legs. There's no need to rush things. "What flavor did you get?"

"Strawberry," she says, and looks down at her almost finished cone. She's silent for a long moment. "It wasn't that I didn't care, you know. With Lily. It was that I... cared too much."

"You don't have to explain it to me if you don't want to," I say. "The relationship between you two is yours. But for what it's worth, I know she's missed you. And she'd love to be friends again."

Jamie's voice is dry. "She was upset, last week. At work."

"Yeah," I say. "But you know Lily. She can never stay angry at the people she loves. I'm walking proof of that."

Jamie gives another one of those half-laughs. "You two argued all the time."

"Mhm," I say, and take another bite of my ice cream. "About very important things."

"Who would walk Atlas, who had or hadn't completed their chores, who ate the last Coco Pops..." She trails off. "I used to think you two were so stupid. You were lucky enough to have siblings, and all you did was fight."

"We've gotten over that stage now," I say, and nudge her carefully with my shoulder. It feels like one wrong move and she might retreat back into herself. "Besides, nobody fought like you and me. Remember?"

"We did, didn't we?" Jamie says, and she sounds almost proud.

It makes me grin. "Yeah. I haven't forgotten all of our bouts, James."

"James," she says. "Gosh. High school was rough."

"You were tough, though. Lily was always lucky to have a friend like you."

It's the wrong thing to say. She turns to her daughter and carefully wipes her bare arms clean. Emma obediently stretches out one arm after the other, her cone devoured, munching on sprinkles. Her legs swing softly off the bench.

I wait for Jamie to find her words.

"The yacht club is doing well," she says finally. "I never knew you wanted to buy it."

"Neither did I, to tell you the truth. I was working in Boston up until a few years ago. Rhys sent me the link to the yacht club listing, when it went on sale, and I... well. It felt right in a way that nothing had for a very long time."

"It suits you," she says.

"Yeah, you think?"

"Yes." She looks at me, an eyebrow raised. It makes her look like the teenager I remember. "The golden son, the ultimate sailor, the pride of Paradise. It's like you've come full circle."

I laugh. "The pride of Paradise, Jesus. You used to call me a lot worse names than that."

"I hoped you'd forgotten that." She reaches up to run a hand over the back of her neck. Her ice cream is finished, too, and Emma is digging at the bottom of the cup for the last sprinkles. "It's been a long time since we were teenagers."

"Yes, but time stands still in Paradise Shores. You know that."

She snorts. "It sure seems like it. Except some things, I guess. You're hiring a new chef at the restaurant. You're not scared of inciting a rebellion by changing the menu?"

That's the Jamie I remember. "I think this town needs to be

shaken up a little bit," I say. "You know, go from one sauce with the fish and chips to *two*."

She half-laughs again. It's tantalizingly close to an actual laugh, but I haven't heard one of those yet.

"So you're modernizing?" she asks.

"Trying to, at least," I say. "I'm actually looking for a web designer and a graphic artist right now. The website needs a complete overhaul. It might actually be better to build a new one base up, with a booking system for classes as well as the restaurant."

"Oh." She scrunches the napkins into a ball. "I've done some of that in the past."

"You have?"

"Yes. I worked remotely for a while, and that was something I could do."

"Do you enjoy it?"

Jamie nods and reaches for Emma's empty sprinkles cup. The little girl is swinging her legs violently now, bored and all sugared up. "Yes, I did."

"Well, are you in the market for an extra job?"

She looks up at me. "What do you mean?"

"Do you want to design a new website for the yacht club? I'd pay you, of course. And we could reduce the hours you work as a waitress to make sure you don't work overtime."

"Oh. I don't know… Parker, I only did it for a few clients."

"But it turned out well?"

"Yes, they seemed happy."

"That's good enough for me. Think about it, okay?" I ask. The hesitation in her doesn't make sense to me, but I know better than to barrel on. "I'll ask you again at work in a few days. If you don't want to, no worries. If you start to work on it and can't finish, that's fine, too. But it would be very appreciated."

Jamie nods. A faint tan plays across her skin from her bike rides to and from the yacht club. She looks feminine, and soft, and has a smattering of freckles on her right shoulder. I look away from the bare skin. "Okay. That sounds good. Thanks, Parker."

"Anytime."

She rises from the bench and brushes off her sundress. Emma steels herself and jumps off the bench, landing with her feet together and a smile on her face. Her wispy ponytail bounces with the impact.

"Ready to go, sweetie? Grandma will have started lunch."

Emma nods and takes her mother's hand. With the other, she hands me the cup that had once contained rainbow sprinkles. "Thank you," she murmurs.

I take the empty cup with a smile. "You're very welcome, Emma. And welcome back to Paradise."

Jamie gives me a half-smile. "Thanks."

"Does it feel good? To be back?"

Her voice turns thoughtful. "I don't know."

"Well," I say. "It feels good to have you back, at least."

6

JAMIE

"This is where you work?" I stop at the threshold of the back office. It's a small room, crowded with two desks and a large map of the coastline put up on the wall with tacks. Beside it is a framed picture of a wooden sailboat, someone's autograph scrawled across it.

Parker leans back in the chair. "When I have no other choice, yes."

"It's... busy."

"And tiny," he says. "I prefer to work from home or out in the dining room, but it has its perks." He nods to a board with lists on it, rows and rows of the summer's sailing lessons. "Neil has a good overview of things."

"Everything's still analog?"

"It sure is," Parker says with a grin. "That's where you come in."

I nod. This whole thing still feels a bit crazy. It's been a year since I last did any website work. It had always been online and I didn't actually *meet* the clients. A side gig I'd started when Emma was a toddler.

"So you want a completely new website?" I ask.

"I think that would be best, yeah." He gestures to the empty chair beside him. "Neil left earlier."

I take a seat and look at the half-open door. Stephen and the other waitresses are still out there, finishing up the few evening orders. One of the younger waitresses had given me a curious look when I went into Parker's office at the end of my shift.

"Probably best with the door open," Parker says. "Is that okay?"

"Mhm, yeah. Absolutely. So... let me just find my notebook." I dig through my bag. "Right. So you want a completely new website. Do you want to keep the same graphic profile as the yacht club has now?"

He runs a hand through his hair. It's less sandy now than it once had been, darkened into a rich blond. I wonder if he went sailing this morning. "The old logo is good. I don't mind it. But do you think it needs updating?"

I hesitate. But he's never punished me for honesty, so I say it. "It could be updated, yeah."

"All right. Why don't you play around with it and show me some options?"

"Sure. What other features do you need?"

Parker lists them one by one, even going so far as to open the old website and show the parts he likes and dislikes. It looks like it was designed by a twelfth grader. Basic HTML. Perhaps that's part of the charm, but it's hampering growth.

I glance at the lists of sailing classes again. Maybe I could create an internal scheduling system for them, too. If he doesn't think the website I create sucks, that is.

"Well, Jamie..." He runs a hand along his thigh, across the fabric of his slacks. "I'm wondering if I should apologize for the other day."

I dig my teeth into my lower lip and look away from his hand. It's broad and tanned. "You were going to run into us one of these days."

"It is a pretty small town."

"It is. Really, thank you for being so nice to her. She loved the sprinkles."

He grins. "I've pulled that trick with little Jamie too. Makes me an instant favorite."

"Really?"

"Yes. She's lovely, James."

That's one thing I can agree on. "She's fantastic."

"I didn't know about her."

"No… I don't tell a lot of people." About most things. I look back at the floor, at my tennis shoes. They don't fit in with my smart uniform, with the navy skirt and the too-snug white blouse. Maybe the uniform can be changed, along with a new logo.

"You know what I'm curious about," Parker says quietly. "But I get the feeling you don't want any questions about him?"

I take a deep breath. "Not particularly."

"You're here in Paradise alone, then?"

"With Emma, but yes."

Parker nods, and there's no pity in his eyes. Just friendly curiosity, and the same steadiness that he's always had. It's comforting, like he could put out a fire, excel at any sport. In a Hollywood movie he'd be the first to enlist against an alien invasion. I don't think he's ever painted a house—the Marchands are too well off for that—but I can see him doing that, helping a friend out with his strong arms.

Maybe that's why I keep talking. "We're staying with my mom. I think I already told you that, right?"

"Yeah."

"It's weird, being back at home, especially when you have a child yourself."

"I can imagine," he says, voice steady. Not judging, and it hits me like a lode weight across the chest just how much I've missed him, and Lily, and his whole family. They'd always felt like comfort to me, even when I was a rebellious teenager. "But I'm guessing your mom is loving it. Do she and Emma get along?"

"Famously," I say. "Emma has Mom wrapped around her little finger. She's shy, but she's clever. She gets her way."

Parker laughs. "Well, she's your daughter."

"She is. Although it's funny, in some ways she's very different than me. And not like... her father, either. She's her own little human entirely."

"I've heard similar things," he says. "Seen it, too, with my niece and nephew."

"Right, you have a niece too, now. How's Henry as a father? He always struck me as a family man."

"Yeah?" Parker runs a hand over his jaw. His arm flexes with the movement, strong beneath the linen shirt he's wearing. None of his old athleticism is gone, but it's sturdier now, like clay that's been baked and hardened. "I suppose he has. He took care of us when we were younger."

"I remember. Didn't he teach you how to ride a bike?"

"Taught both me and Lily, yeah. He was a kid himself." Parker chuckles. "Well, now he has an actual kid."

"Hazel, right? That's a beautiful name."

"Yeah, she's a sweetheart. They're not here much, though. Henry and Faye finally bought a house in Paradise, but they're both too busy in New York to live here permanently."

"Oh yeah, I've heard." The Marchand name is one I've googled periodically over the last couple of years, to follow their journeys.

"Would be hard not to," Parker says dryly, but he looks pleased, too.

"What's Rhys doing?"

"What Rhys always does, which is whatever the hell he wants."

I chuckle. "That sounds about right."

"He's travelling the world with his girlfriend. They're shooting some kind of documentary, I think, while he finishes the last touches on a photography book."

"Oh. Wow."

"Yeah, it's the opposite of a settled life." Parker shakes his head. "But that's Rhys."

"Who is his girlfriend?"

"Her name's Ivy. She's awesome, actually. They argue a lot but I think they both enjoy that. She works as a model."

I nod woodenly. Once, the Marchands spent school vacations travelling to exotic locations. Now they date models and build opera houses and own yacht clubs. I think of my tennis shoes with the hole in the front and my pitiful savings account.

"I know how it sounds," Parker says, voice almost apologetic. "My siblings are off the rails."

Not really, I think. *They seem like they have it all together.*

"I'm glad they're doing well."

"Yeah, they are," he says. "Lily has an art gallery in town."

"Does she?" I ask, but in truth, I already know. I've followed her career online too.

"Yes. It's doing surprisingly well, for an art gallery, you know. She works with artists from New York and displays them here. It's a few blocks away from the gelato shop, actually."

"Oh."

"I won't tell her about this either." Parker gives me a crooked smile. "It feels fun, being secretive."

"Doesn't come naturally to you, does it?"

"She strikes again," he says, grinning. "No, I can't say that it does. And it's not like you and I used to work together."

I look at his hands, now resting on an open ledger. I make out the names of boats. "No, we didn't. Do you remember that party? At Turner's?"

"Which one?"

"When Lily and I came. You were so angry at her."

He snorts. "Of course I was. She was a minor. You both were."

"So were you," I point out, raising an eyebrow.

His smile turns crooked. "Yes, but you two were more minory."

"Lily left halfway through the party."

"Yeah, I remember that night. After graduation."

I shouldn't say anything. It's stupid, bringing up the past, and maybe I'm just wasting his time. But something about his gaze draws the words out. I haven't thought about those years in a very long time. "She had a fight with Hayden."

"I suspected they did," he says, "because he was pissed off the rest of the night and left soon after her."

"I stayed, though."

"Yeah," Parker says. "You did."

The memories are hazy, like childhood memories often are. I'd been dressed up to the nines, which for me was a tight skirt and a black T-shirt with an ironic print of a pop band I didn't listen to. My short hair had been spiky and lips coated with far too much gloss. I'd been Lily's friend, who in turn was Parker's little sister. That was my claim to fame at the party held by seniors.

And of the seniors, Parker had been the coolest.

He had the friends, the girls, the trophies. He was the one jock I couldn't hate, because while he was often annoying, he was never mean. Not once.

"You were drunk," I say. "All of you were."

"It was a sport back then. I remember trying to keep you from drinking, though."

"A valiant, but failed, effort."

He chuckles and leans forward, bracing his elbows on his knees. His skin is golden from the sun. "Yeah, you never liked doing what I told you to."

"I had a problem with authority back then."

"Oh, that's solved now?"

"I've just become more circumspect," I say.

He gives me another smile, and just like that, I'm sitting next to him on Turner's porch at two in the morning again. He's drunk and pretending not to be, his hair a mess, and giving me his best I'm-superior look. I'd been needling him about all the girls he'd meet in college. Lame, and retroactively transparent, but I'd been young and had a crush I couldn't even admit to myself.

I'm not a ladies' man, he'd said, as if there was any doubt that he might be. He was popular, sure, but we were in high school. *When I find a girl I want to be my girlfriend, I'll just... know.*

Oh? I'd asked. *And what will she look like? Tall, and blonde, with big boobs?*

Drunk, teenage Parker had scoffed. *No. I like girls with attitude.*

Who argue with you?

He'd looked at me, then. *Yes. I like them dark-haired, too.*

"I walked you home that night," Parker says. In his gaze I see the same memory. We'd never spoken about the temporary truce we struck up that night. The next time I saw him, visiting Lily's place later that summer, we'd argued over what to watch on TV with a ferocity that rivaled professional athletes.

"You did," I say. "We took the long route."

He laughs, a little self-consciously. "Yeah. Down by the boardwalk."

"I didn't think you remembered that night," I say, and tug at the hem of my skirt. It feels too short, riding up when I'm sitting.

"I remember," he says. "I think it was the only time we were actually nice to one another. You gave me a compliment."

"I did?"

"Yes. You said I was a good running back."

"Oh."

He laughs, and the sound is warm and deep. It fills the room. "I don't think you'd watched a single one of our games, James. It was an obvious lie, but I appreciated it regardless."

"Maybe I fudged the truth a bit."

"You did," he says, grinning. "It was a good night."

"Yeah, it was." My mind travels back to what happened when we stopped outside my house. When he'd brushed a hand over my cheek, and I'd wet my lips, wondering if it was happening. If he was going to do this, cross the boundary between us, the one made up of so many layers. Best friend's older brother. A grade above me in high school. Jock and misfit.

But he didn't.

He told me I was beautiful, and that it was late, and I should go inside.

"You gave me a compliment too that night."

"Yeah," Parker says. "I remember that, too. But mine wasn't an obvious lie."

"Oh," I breathe. My throat feels dry and I search for his previous words. "Well, I appreciated it regardless?"

He smiles. "I'd say it still stands, but seeing as how I'm hiring you to overhaul my website, that wouldn't be appropriate."

"Probably not," I say and reach for my notebook. I regret the words an instant later. *Stupid, stupid.*

"You know where to find me," he says. "Whenever, wherever, if you want to discuss the website. Or," he says with a wink, "which type of sprinkles are the best. I have strong opinions on that, and I suspect Emma does too."

"Oh, she does now. Thank you." I extend a hand. "Looking forward to working with you."

Parker grins and takes my hand in his. Long fingers curl around mine, calluses on the insides of his palm chafing gently. "So do I, James."

7

JAMIE

I drink my cup of coffee and look out at dawn's first rays on Greene Street. It gets light early these days, earlier than when we usually wake up. The clock in the kitchen reads just past five thirty. Emma won't be up for another hour at least, nor will my mother.

The coffee helps with my own tiredness, but actual sleep would have helped more. But it had been little and far in-between last night after Lee's calls.

I hadn't planned to pick up, even as he called a second time. And called again, and again. The last time we'd spoken he said he didn't care either way if we stayed or left. But he's changed his mind more than once before. And so I'd picked up the call.

Outside the window, a soft breeze catches the trees that line the street. Leaves stir softly. It's a beautiful morning for a run. I change into a pair of stretchy shorts and an old T-shirt. It has paint stains from the time I re-did Emma's old bedroom. Lee had hated the color I chose, so I'd re-painted it a week later.

Fuck him, I think, *and his call with polite apologies and measured speech.* And immediately after, I think *fuck me,* because the truth is that it would have worked on me two years ago. One year ago. I would have believed him, every manipulative word out of his mouth.

I hit the sidewalk outside the house in a run that sets my heart racing. I'm free now, at least. And I'm back here, with my daughter, with a job. With a future.

I reach the top of the street, right by the cul-de-sac, before my lungs start to burn. Freedom turns to torture.

I'm so out of shape.

Once, I'd been able to do this route before school. Now my lower back aches and there's a burning sensation in my chest. It's yet another thing I've let falter.

But I keep going, up the next street, and the one after that, beneath the trees and past the hedges. Birds sing happily above me, unaware of how close I am to expiring.

The streets are empty. People haven't started their days yet, and I'm grateful for it. The last thing I need is to run into anyone from high school, or my mom's friends. Or Lily. We haven't spoken since that awkward conversation in the yacht club.

But the universe isn't so kind.

I round the next street and come to face-to-face with another runner. He's heading toward me, black shorts and a white T-shirt. Strong, tanned arms move at his sides.

Because of course those are my odds.

Parker slows down when he sees me and I come to a grateful halt. My lungs pull in a few quick gulps of breath before he reaches me.

"Hey," he says. "Out for a run?"

I nod. It's safer than speaking just yet.

"I didn't know you ran."

"Not for years, now. But I just realized—" I take a deep breath—"that I have no muscle or stamina left."

Parker's eyes narrow, and I want to take back my words. "Well, you're on your feet all day as a waitress. That'll build your stamina. What you need is probably strength training."

"Strength training?"

"Yeah. Have you ever lifted weights?"

I shake my head. "Not really, no."

"Hmm," he says, and then he gives a crooked smile. His face is flushed with color, sweaty and glorious, and he's not panting at all. "I'm wondering if you'll get mad at me for what I'll say next."

"Me? Mad?"

He laughs. "Yes, you, James. You always took me to task for my jock ways."

"Well, you were very jock-y," I say.

He doesn't react like Lee would. There's no snark or mocking, no feigned hurt. He just keeps grinning. "I was. And you were very artsy."

"I had to keep up with Lily."

"Jesus, yes. Didn't the two of you try spoken word poetry one time, too?"

That makes me smile too. "We were awful."

"I don't think anyone is good at spoken word poetry."

"Oh, some are wonderful, but two high schoolers from Paradise Shores with absolutely no life experience aren't."

Parker laughs and reaches for the hem of his white T-shirt. He pulls it up and wipes his face, exposing a slab of strong, tanned stomach. With each deep breath he takes the muscles shift beneath, showing the hint of a six-pack.

I quickly look away.

"Why are you out so early?" he asks. "Most people aren't up yet."

"Couldn't sleep. Besides, I like avoiding people."

"Like me?"

I roll my eyes, even as nerves slash through my stomach. "Sure, Marchand."

He laughs again and my nerves flatten. He's not offended. "Lily, then," he says. "She lives further down Ocean Drive. You won't bump into her on the street like this."

"Oh. Thank you."

"Me, though, you'll probably see all the time," he says. "I live on Meadow."

"You do?"

He turns and points further up the street, toward a white wooden house with a wrap-around porch. An American flag hangs off one of the pillars.

"Close to the yacht club," I say, "and halfway between your parents' and Lily's?"

Parker runs a hand over his jaw. He can't have shaved yet today, and the stubble is thicker than usual. "Yes. You know too much about me."

"Well, I've known you for a great many years." I kick at a pebble on the sidewalk. "So we live close."

"Yeah, we do," he says, and there's a curious note of satisfaction in his voice. I look up to catch him smiling. "The thing I was going to say earlier, that'll make you mad?"

"I think it would take a great deal to make me mad at you," I say, and I mean it. Maybe we'd argued constantly as teenagers, but he's given me a job here. Two jobs, even.

Parker laughs, like I'm joking. "Remember that. Well, I have a gym in my garage. Lots and lots of free weights. You're welcome to use it any day. Mornings, before work, perhaps? I can show you how to lift."

I stare at him.

"Right now," he says, "is when you get mad at me, James, for suggesting you need to work out. You don't."

"But I do," I say. "I'm weak."

He stretches from side to side, chest rippling beneath his T-shirt. "Not how I'd phrase it. But if you want to tone, you know where to find the resources, okay?"

"Right. Thank you," I say, and the mental image of me in my paint-stained T-shirts, lifting tiny dumbbells while he looks on in all his glory, flashes through my mind.

"Don't overthink it," he says, still smiling.

I kick his sneaker with my own. "Idiot."

He laughs. "That's the Jamie I remember."

"She's still around sometimes," I say, and find to my surprise that it's true. She's just been buried deep down. "I have a few drafts for website designs ready for you."

Parker's eyebrows rise. "Already?"

"I have a lot of time after Emma goes to bed," I say.

"That's amazing. Anything you need me to look at?"

"Yes, just so I know which option you like before I head too far in one direction. I've been working on an updated logo, too, for you to look at."

"Terrific."

"And something struck me... well, maybe it's a stupid idea, but the yacht club is such a focal point in Paradise Shores. You know, you organize all the sailing classes, you have the restaurant, the lobster roll shack, organize the marina..."

"Yes," Parker says dryly. "Which is why I need to hire another Neil."

I give a half-laugh. "Right. Well, it's such an institution that I wonder if it would be a good idea to sell some merchandise?"

His eyebrows draw together. "Merchandise?"

Nerves surge up in my stomach. This is when Lee would have rolled his eyes or called it a stupid idea. *Worthless,* I hear in my mind. But Parker's not Lee, he's himself, and I've never known him to be cruel.

"Yes. Let's say the logo ends up going on the new linen napkins, or on T-shirts for the marina staff, or on sailing caps for the instructors. I think people might want to buy that for themselves."

"A Paradise Shores Yacht Club cap," he repeats slowly. "It's a great idea."

"You think?"

"Yeah. The waitresses could wear them when we serve on the terrace in the summer. The sailing instructors, definitely. Shoot, now I want all of this ready in time for the regatta." He grins and crosses his arms over his chest. They look larger than usual against his white T-shirt. "You came up with all of this in a week?"

"A lot of free evenings," I say.

He grins. "Good to know. Let's meet tomorrow night, then, at the yacht club and you can show me all of the designs. Does that sound good?"

"Yeah, sure."

"Great. And next week you're coming by to see my gym," he says with a wink. His voice is the one that had always needled me in the past. Strong and so sure of itself, no hesitation in it.

"So you can boss me around?"

"The day you let me boss you around," Parker says, "is the day hell freezes over." He smiles at me in goodbye and moves past me, legs breaking effortlessly into a run again. I watch him disappear down Meadow Lane and turn onto Ocean Drive. I bet he's going to run along the boardwalk, in full view of anyone who might see him.

His smile wasn't annoying. It wasn't taunting or gloating. It was warm, and looking at it, I'd felt warm too. And I wonder how different things might have been, if he wasn't who he was, if I didn't have an uncertain future and a broken past, and the memory of another man branded into my skin.

8

PARKER

We don't do dinner service on Thursdays. It's the one day of the week when the place is quiet, and the dining room is empty around me. I'm at the table I prefer, right by the windows and the ocean, when I hear Jamie's voice.

"No touching. Those are the chef's tools. They're very sharp… yes, that's it."

The door from the kitchen opens and she's there, with a laptop bag under one arm and her daughter's hand in the other. Emma looks around the room with big eyes. She steps closer to her mom when she sees me.

A slow smile spreads across my face. "Hi, you two."

"Hello," Jamie says, glancing down at her daughter. "I hope you don't mind that I brought Emma? My mother had other plans tonight. I didn't have your number to text you about it beforehand."

"Oh, the more the merrier. Hi, Emma. How are you?"

She hesitates a moment before answering. "Good."

"This is the restaurant your mom and I work at."

Jamie leads her daughter to the table next to ours and lifts her up on a chair. "Sit here, sweetheart. Now, I brought you some paper… want to color while Mom works?"

Emma nods and accepts the notepad she's handed with a

serious expression, like she's buckling down for a job, too. It makes me smile. "I have something for you," I say. "Wait a minute…"

I rummage through the back office for the giant bucket of crayons. It's been in the corner for as long as I remember, a remnant from the previous owners, given to unruly children.

Emma's eyes shine at the sight. "I can use them?"

"Knock yourself out."

She smiles a brilliant little smile, complete with crooked front teeth, and reaches for the purple crayon.

"Thanks," Jamie says. Her hair is in a braid today, but a few tendrils have escaped, framing her face. She pulls out an old laptop with colorful stickers on the back. *Flower power,* one says, and another *Paradise Dive Shop.*

"Sorry," she says as the computer loads up. "It's not the quickest."

"It's your mother's?"

Jamie nods. "But she rarely uses it."

I run a hand over my jaw and focus on the screen, not on her. A daughter, no husband, staying at her mom's. Waitressing and riding a bike. Sympathy squeezes painfully tight in my chest, along with shame at my words from the other day. *Henry, architect, opera house, models, photographer, art gallery…* Not to mention Lily with her house on Ocean Drive and me, just the other morning, pointing at the house I'd bought.

There are layers to the hesitancy in Jamie, with more secrets than I can imagine, thorns that seem stuck beneath the surface.

But I wonder if money isn't one of them.

"Parker?" Jamie says, a small smile on her face. "Are you with me?"

"Yeah, yeah. Sure. What am I looking at?"

"This is the interface I use to build websites. Here's the first potential layout… let me know what you think."

The website looks nothing like the old one. And that's a

good thing. A sleek welcome page greets me with the logo, now navy blue, a circle with a sailing boat and the yacht club's name.

"Oh," I say.

Jamie's voice speeds up. "Everything can be changed. Just tell me if you don't like something."

"No, no, I do. I like it a lot."

She leans closer, her arm reaching for the trackpad. Her hair smells of flowery shampoo. "I was thinking this could have a slideshow with inviting pictures, of the restaurant, the food and the marina."

"Paradise Shores," I read out loud. "Your slice of heaven."

"Too much?"

"It's perfect." Maybe I can get Rhys to shoot the place. He'd think it beneath him, but he owes me. And he knows this place as well as I do.

"The menu on the side pops out when you move the cursor over it. Look, here are the different functions. Sailing classes, menu, an about section, and…"

"A shop?"

She nods. "We'll keep that page internal until we actually have something to sell. What do you think?"

We spend the next thirty minutes sorting through the website options. She's thorough and soft-spoken beside me, but her voice grows in confidence as she navigates the system.

"We could have a password protected section here," she says, "for bookings or information about the sailing classes."

"God, that would save Neil so much time."

She nods. "We could start a newsletter, too, down the line."

"A newsletter?"

"Yeah. One for the sailing classes, and one for the restaurant. You know, to keep people in the community aware of new menu specials, live music events, that sort of thing. This place is such a big part of town."

"You did all of this in a week?"

She pushes a tendril of hair back. "I created a dummy website and a logo," she says. "The rest are just ideas."

"Not ideas. This is amazing."

Jamie looks down at her hands. "I think it's fun."

"Yes, and you're clearly good at it. When did you learn to do this?"

"When Emma was born." She looks at her daughter, industriously drawing colorful shapes in her notepad. "I had a lot of time at home and I wanted an income."

"Understandable. Did you have many clients?"

"Only a few." Jamie leans back in her chair, eyes far away as she looks at the computer. "But I haven't done it for a year or two."

"Well, you're a natural. I want to hire you to do all of it."

"All of it?"

"Yes. The website, the booking system, the menu, the merchandise, the newsletter."

"Parker," she says and there's admonition in her voice. "I'm not a professional."

"This looks very professional to me. Besides, my only other option is to give this job to someone outside of town. And I think this job is better suited for someone from Paradise. Don't you agree?"

She closes the lid to the laptop, with its fan working overdrive. She can't work on that old thing. "Thank you, Parker."

"No thanks necessary. It's a job." I nod at the computer. "You let me know if there's anything you need to complete it."

She gives me a smile that's textbook old Jamie. A bit cocky, a lot confident. "Less waitressing hours."

I laugh. "Already done. You'll have the same amount of hours scheduled for next week, but only half will actually be waitressing. The rest is this."

Her eyes widen, like she hadn't anticipated an actual response. "Really?"

"Yes. I want one of those caps." Driven by impulse, I give the end of her braid a soft tug. "You'd look good in one, too," I say.

Jamie smiles. She's close, and I realize I've never gotten as many of her smiles as I have this past week. Even if they're still rare. "I would?"

"Yeah," I say, letting the braid slip through my fingers. I think about the memory she brought up the other day… the night I walked her home, all those years ago. I think about her strength and her softness and her mysteries. She swallows, the movement tiny, and the noise resonates down to my very bones.

"Mommy?" Emma asks. She's standing between us, and in her hand is a drawing.

Jamie turns away from me. "You made this?"

Her daughter nods. The drawing is a child's masterpiece, in the way only theirs can be. "I copied the painting."

"The painting?" Jamie asks. The drawing has two purple boat-like figures on a thin bed of blue.

"In the crayons."

I reach across to Emma's table and grab the flyer. It must have been wedged amongst the crayons. It's a poster for the Paradise Shores Junior Regatta from six years ago. There's a picture of two sailing boats on it.

"This?"

"Yes. But I put you and me in the boats," Emma tells her mom. Her voice is tinged with excitement now, sounding more like my nephew. "Look."

Jamie obediently locates the tiny blobs. "Oh, look at that. Do we like to sail?"

"Yes. But the other ship has pirates."

"Pirates?" I ask, grinning. "Here in Paradise? I never knew."

Emma nods, and gives me a tiny smile. "But they won't catch me and Mommy."

"No, I hope not," Jamie says. She has a hand on Emma's head. "Is there a treasure?"

Emma hasn't thought that far, so much is clear from her thoughtful expression. But she points at the thin sliver of ocean she's drawn. "There."

"In the deep," I say. "Of course, treasure is always buried. Have you ever been on a boat?"

She leans closer to her mom and answers me, but keeps her eyes averted. Still shy. "No."

"Never ever?"

She shakes her head so quick her hair flies.

"There are plenty of boats here," I say. "I have one right here, in the marina."

Emma looks toward the window and the forest of masts gently bobbing. Behind them, the sun has begun its slow descent. "You do?"

"I do." It's technically my father's, and the whole family uses it, but that information doesn't feel relevant right now. "If your mom says it's okay, we can look at it after this. You can stand on board and check it for pirates."

Her eyes go round. "On board?"

"Yes." I look over at Jamie. "But only if your mom doesn't have other plans."

"Mommy, let's," Emma says, hands gripping Jamie's arm. Excitement makes her little face shine.

Jamie looks at me with eyes that are exasperated, and laughing, and I wonder again about Emma's father. Where is he? A brief pulse of anger burns below my breastbone. "If Parker is sure it's safe, then yes."

"It's safe as can be," I say. "James, the boat is anchored."

She grins. "Never stopped you from falling in before."

"That was once," I say, a slow smile spreading across my face, "and I can't believe you remember that."

"The drunken party you threw with Turner on the boat was legendary. No one could speak of anything else at school for weeks."

"I'm sure you enjoyed that."

She rolls her eyes. "I did not."

"I was grounded for a month after," I say, "and it was reckless as hell."

"And yet, I don't think you regret it." She shakes her head, but Jamie looks amused. It feels like another small victory. "Come on. Let's go."

Emma skips ahead of us outside, her drawing forgotten on the table. I'll grab it in the morning. Jamie walks beside me down to the marina, Emma in front of us. She puts one sandalled shoe in front of the other on the wooden dock.

"Stay close," Jamie calls. "And you have to stay away from the edge." Emma nods, but she peers into the blue water with every step.

I look over at Jamie. Her shoulders look slim beneath her white jean jacket, her skin clear from any makeup. Different from the person I remember… and a mother.

"You're watching me," she says.

"I'm just thinking of you, being a mom now and all."

She snorts. "Oh, great. How much I'm failing, you mean?"

"Do you feel like you are?"

"Every day."

"In my vast experience as an uncle," I say, "I think that's just parenthood."

"When did you get so wise, huh?"

"I was hit by the boom one too many times," I say. "It finally knocked some sense into me."

She shakes her head, but she's smiling. "Took one too many tackles, too?"

"Definitely."

"Hah," she says. And then, voice sharpening, "Emma, wait there!"

Her daughter slows down. She's raced past a dozen of the training dinghies.

"Mine is right over here!" I call, and point to the adjoining dock. "But come closer to us. This dock wobbles when you walk."

She comes to take her mother's hand and we walk toward the *Frida*. She lies high in the water, unloaded, her mast tall and sails rigged right.

"She looks exactly the same," Jamie says.

"Well, she's very well taken care of." I reach for her railing and tug. *Frida* inches reluctantly closer to the dock, aided by the water beneath her.

Emma's eyes are round with excitement, and a little bit of fear. "Can I?"

I wait for Jamie to say yes before I climb on board *Frida*. She's steady in the water, and too big for us to rock. "I've got you," I say, and extend my arms. "You'll just have to take one big step…"

Emma jumps instead. She lands with both feet on the deck and crashes into my left arm. "Ooooh!" she says.

"You made it on board!"

She looks down at her feet, firmly planted on the deck, and keeps one hand on my upper arm. "It's not moving."

"No, it's anchored right now. Tied to the dock here. See that giant rope?" I shift my hand to her arm, gripping firmly, and extend the other to Jamie. "Think your mom is brave enough to join us?"

Jamie rolls her eyes and puts her hand in mine, trusting me to pull her on board.

"Mommy, we're on a boat," Emma says and starts to move down the deck. She stops and frowns at my grip on her arm.

"Just one second, kiddo. There are a few simple rules when you're on a boat."

"There are?"

"Yep. You always hold on to something when you're walking. See this thin railing? I want one of your hands on it at all times."

"Oh. Okay."

"Second rule. Children have to wear a life vest."

She sighs. "Not on a pirate ship."

"Luckily for all of us, *Frida*'s days of piracy are long behind her," I say. "Come on, just slip this over your head…"

Emma stands still and lets me put on the child-size life vest we always keep on board for little Jamie. He's two years younger than her and it shows, but I adjust the straps best I can. It'll work for now.

"Third rule," I say, and this time I'm grinning. "There's a very clear chain of command on board a boat."

"Jesus," Jamie mutters.

"There is?" Emma asks.

"Yes. I'm the captain, and your mom here is the first mate. You," I say, tugging on one of the lines of her life vest, "are a deckhand."

"Oh."

"Deckhands are very important. But when they're on board a ship, deckhands always have to do what the captain says."

Emma looks at her mother. "First mates, too?"

"Yes," Jamie says, eyes dancing. "First mates too… even if they can't believe they're doing it." She raises her hand and salutes me.

"Why, look at that, James. Some obedience."

"Don't think it'll last," she says.

My grin widens. "I wouldn't have it any other way."

"Parker," Emma says.

I look down at her, my eyebrows rising. Didn't know she'd remembered my name. "Yes?"

Then she salutes me as well, her pigtails resting over her life jacket and a smile on her face.

Christ, she's cute.

"All right," I say, and have to clear my throat. "Very good. Now you can explore the boat, but only if you remember to always have one hand on the railing, and no running. Okay?"

"Yes," she says.

"Aye aye, Captain," Jamie adds.

Emma walks around, and we follow at a slower pace. She touches the sails softly, and then hurries to the very edge of the boat.

"Be careful!" Jamie calls.

But Emma is. She has both hands on the railing and looks down at the water so intently that I have to ask.

"What are you looking for?"

"Fish!"

"Are there any?"

But there's no response.

"She's ridiculously patient," Jamie says by my side. "I don't know where she got it from. Once I saw her sit quietly and look up at the sky for ten minutes, and I asked her what she was looking for, and she said a shooting star. We'd read about them the night before."

"I don't think I could sit still for five minutes at her age," I say.

"Oh, I know I couldn't." Jamie sits down on deck and tucks her hands beneath her legs. "Thanks for letting us come on board. This will make Emma's week."

"Anytime." I hesitate only for a second before I sit down next to her. The spot is narrow, and her thigh is resting next to mine. We look at Emma's small form in silence. She's lying down now, stomach to the deck, and has her head over the edge to look at the water. One of her sandals taps rhythmically against the deck.

"Captain, huh?"

I laugh. "On a much bigger boat that would be the chain of hierarchy."

"But not on a sailing boat this size."

"You remember some from your Paradise days?" I say and nudge her shoulder with mine.

She snorts. "Some."

"You're right. I'd be a skipper. But I didn't think a six-year-old would know what that meant."

A smile spreads across Jamie's face. "She'd think it meant someone who likes skipping a lot. Like her."

"Maybe," I say, smiling, "you'll let me take both of you out to sea one day."

Jamie nudges my leg with hers. "And risk getting caught by the boom?"

"Hey, it made me a genius," I say.

She laughs, full and free, and it sounds like her old self. Behind us the sun dips behind the horizon, painting the marina in gold, but I watch the woman beside me instead. Her laughter feels more rare.

9

JAMIE

I feel ridiculous, and judging by Parker's smile, I must look it too.

"I don't even know where to start," I say. The rack of weights in front of me is wide enough to stretch wall-to-wall in his garage. Parker has every weight, and with different handles, too. Some are shaped like a heavy ball with one on top. I think they're called kettlebells, but it's been years since I went to a gym.

"Start with the lightest," he says, and grabs a heavy pair himself. "You can copy what I do, or modify it to fit you. No rights or wrongs."

I look at the bench in the corner with its plate-stacked bar. "Looks like a lot of things could go wrong."

Parker laughs. It's tinged with hoarseness. He must have just woken up, like me. The speaker in the corner plays soft music from his phone. He's in the same workout clothes as last week, black shorts and a white T-shirt, and looks pristine. At least I've managed to find a T-shirt without paint stains.

"Just give it a go," he says, "and see what happens."

So I do. It's miserable, and I realize halfway through that I have no strength at all in my upper body. It's all rubber, and as I stand there panting in the corner, I wonder how the hell I became this person. Living at my mother's, working as a waitress, running from Lee and unable to do ten straight shoulder presses with the lightest of weights.

"Hey," Parker says. He puts down the giant weight he's been using and wipes sweat from his forehead. "That was great."

"Don't lie to me."

"It was, though. It's your first time. You'll have to go slow." He shrugs, irreverent, casual, and as unbreakable as always. "Come on, James. Do your squats next."

I drag myself from exercise to exercise. With a tact I never saw teenage Parker display, he doesn't look at me. Only twice does he offer pointers. I could probably use a hundred more, but I appreciate the restraint.

And watching him makes the pain in my body easier to bear.

He moves through the gym like it's his personal space, an extension of his body, a tool and a sanctuary. He lifts strong and silent, and takes the time to stretch in between muscle groups.

It makes my pathetic bicep curls a tiny bit more enjoyable, to watch his muscles flex beneath his shirt.

It's also intimate in a way I hadn't anticipated. To breathe and lift and sweat in the same space as someone else, and slowly, I surrender to that, too. He's already seen more of me in the few weeks I've been back than I had ever planned for.

And it feels good to have a true friend again. The easy conversation, the lack of poisonous subtext, the jokes that are genuine, without any mocking in them. It's like a balm to the soul after years with Lee.

I finish the last of my sit-ups with a huff and lie back on the floor. My T-shirt sticks to my skin.

Parker steps into view, using the bottom hem of his shirt to wipe his face.

Man, is he in shape.

"It's almost seven," he says. "I'm going to run down to the boardwalk and take a swim. Want to join?"

I look away from the faint line of brown hair on his stomach, disappearing into his shorts. "Thanks, but I should get home. Emma usually wakes up around now."

"Another time, then." He pulls me up to my feet. "How do you feel?"

"Tired. I'm not looking forward to the soreness later."

He grins. "Means it's working. You did great, James."

"Thanks," I say, and look him up and down, like I'm evaluating him. "So did you. I don't know if anyone's told you this, but you could play sports. Football, maybe. Or sailing."

Parker laughs. "Such flattery."

"I can be nice, on occasion."

"Oh, I'm learning that these days." He shuts the garage door behind him and runs a hand through his hair. The morning is beautiful, the air crisp. "You're welcome to come back any morning, all right?"

"When I can walk again, I might."

"It won't be that bad," he says, and gives me a wink. "Not after the first time."

My mouth falls open. In all the jokes and arguments Parker and I exchanged back in the day, they were never sexual. It was a barrier we never crossed.

But here he is, doing just that.

Parker's smile widens as he watches me process his words. "Speechless? That's a first."

"Just figuring out my response," I say. "I don't know what kind of answer you'll survive."

"Oh, really?" He jogs backwards, heels sharp on the sidewalk. "Tell me later at work, James. I can't wait to hear it."

Then he disappears down the street, his tall form heading toward the band of blue that glitters in the far distance. I watch him for a few extra seconds.

Emma is awake when I get home, but she's still in bed, rubbing her eyes. "Mommy?"

"It's me," I say. "Come down when you're ready, okay? I'll get breakfast started."

"Pancakes?"

"Not today, sweetheart."

She makes a disapproving sound and turns over in bed. Other parents talk about children who bounce out of bed, but Emma has always been a mini-teenager in that regard. She loves sleeping.

I don't start my shift at the yacht club until after lunch, so I spend the morning working on the designs for the website in the backyard. Mom's computer dies on me twice, but it gets the job done. Slowly.

Mom sits next to me and watches Emma play with the bubbles again. "She needs friends," she says. "Do any of your old high school friends have kids?"

I take a sip of my ice tea. "Yes."

"That would be great, you know. A playdate or something. Or I could take her along to the playground over by the mall some day?"

"Yeah, that's a good idea, actually. We could all go. Maybe on Saturday."

Mom makes a humming sound and looks back down at the book she's reading. But she's not quiet for long. "Emma said something interesting. Yesterday."

My hand stills on the trackpad. "Did she?"

"Yes. It was about her dad."

"Oh."

"Honey... what happened there?"

I stare at the screen. I want to sink into it, to become one with the pixels. To never hear or see again. "What did Emma say?"

"Nothing much. I opened a new pack of playing dough, you know the one I bought at the dollar store last week?"

"Yes."

"And she hesitated before playing with it." Mom shakes her head, her eyes on Emma in the distance. "She said her dad hated it… and she wanted to ask you first if it was okay."

I close my eyes. "Right."

"It didn't feel right, honey. A six-year-old isn't supposed to think like that."

"She's allowed to think any way she wants."

"Yes, of course, but… you never asked for permission."

"Well, I'm me, and Emma's Emma."

"I asked if she missed her father."

"Mom!"

She shrugs, unrepentant. "It's not a weird question. She hasn't spoken about him once since you two got here, and neither have you. Honey… I don't mean to pry… But I'll be here to listen if you want to talk about it. You know that."

I run a hand over my face. It feels damp from my post-workout shower, and I know I should get ready for my shift. Close down this monster of a computer and flee from the questions.

"Did he hurt you?" Mom asks. There's hesitation in her voice. "Hurt… Emma?"

"No. Never," I say.

"To the first? Or the second?"

"Lee never raised a hand to either of us. That wasn't his way."

She exhales. "All right. Well, that's something, I suppose. Does he know where you are?"

"He might suspect, but he doesn't know." I push back from the chair and stay for another moment, watching the sun glint off Emma's hair. She's laughing, now, as burst of bubbles rises to the sky. Last night she'd insisted on drawing another boat, and it had three barely discernible people on it this time. One of them had a funny-looking head. *It's a captain's hat,* Emma had informed me grandly.

"Well," Mom says. "You two belong with me, and if he ever questions that, he'll have another thing coming."

I put a hand on her shoulder and feel a million years old. That isn't Lee's way either. His is insidious, manipulative words and sweet compliments that turn sour in a matter of seconds. "I love you, Mom."

"I love you too, sweetie."

10

PARKER

The Junior Sailing Regatta is one of Paradise Shores' biggest summer events.

My mother, bless her heart, has been on the organizing committee for the past decade. They're a group of fearsome Paradise locals who oversee the whole thing like commanders rallying their troops.

And they've chosen my restaurant as their war room.

Stephen stops by my side, a pinched look on his face. "I just heard them mention a last-minute addition of bouncy castles."

"Oh."

"To be here, in the yacht club's parking lot."

"*Oh*. Thank you," I say, and head over to stave off this disaster. Mom is at the head of the table, her hair up in a French twist—she had informed me it was called that just a few hours earlier. Neil is also at the table, by necessity, as he manages the regatta itself. He's wearing the old sailing club jacket, logo faded on his chest.

Bouncy castles.

I clear my throat and inform them in no uncertain terms to nix that idea.

"None at all?" John McIntyre says. He's staring at me

across the table with all the ferocity of a general.

I shake my head. "My head chef needs our entire parking lot for the unloading and loading of supplies. We're manning all the food stalls out front."

He sighs, but the suggestion is dropped, thank God. The last thing we need is an unsupervised giant inflatable.

By the time they've nailed down the last details, the dinner service is almost through, and outside the rain is pouring down. It turns the ocean from a deep blue into a hazy grayness and lashes against our sea-facing windows. The group files out of the restaurant, my mom lingering just long enough to kiss me on the cheek.

"It looks great in here," she says. "I heard about the new chef."

"She's just started, and she's working on revamping the menu."

Mom pats me on the shoulder. "Can't wait to see it, *chéri*. Your father sends his love."

"Let him know I said hi."

She nods and walks with measured movements toward the exit. She's still a beautiful woman, and she knows it, carrying herself with the knowledge in every fingertip. On her way she passes Jamie. I see her, stopping and smoothing her hands over her uniform. But Mom doesn't recognize her and disappears out the door without a second glance.

Jamie looks at me, relief on her face.

I grin at her. "A narrow escape."

She pretends to wipe her forehead. "I can't believe she didn't recognize me."

"You've changed a bit since she saw you last," I say. "The hair... the clothes." I tap the side of my nose. "Your ring."

"God, the nose ring. I was edgy."

"The edgiest," I agree.

"I had to express my frustrations with the world somehow, you know?"

"Of course," I say seriously. "What better way to make a political stand than a piercing?"

Jamie pretends to aim a kick my way. "Watch it," she says. "Your big brothers aren't here to defend you."

My eyebrows nearly hit my hairline. "Defend me? Oh, the insult."

Her eyes are alight with life. "Whoops."

"Come here, you—" I don't know what I'm planning to do, advancing with my arms out. She laughs and backs away.

Then she freezes, her eyes on something behind me. I straighten and she does the same. Back to professionalism.

"Sorry," she says.

"It's my bad." I glance behind me, but all I see is Kylie, one of the waitresses hired for the summer. She looks away from us as soon as she sees me watching.

Jamie shrugs. "I should get going."

"Your shift's over?"

"Just ended."

I glance at the windows. The rain doesn't think in shifts, it seems, and it's pouring down like the sky's cracked itself wide open. "On your bike?"

"Yes," she says, and runs a hand over her thigh. "Even if I can barely move my legs."

"That sore?"

"I feel like I was just run over by a truck," she says dryly, and looks at me like I'm entirely to blame.

I laugh. "You'll feel worse tomorrow, but the day after? You'll feel better than you did before the workout. Now come on."

"Come where?" she asks behind me.

"I'll drive you home." I'm already heading for the exit.

"Parker, you don't have to do that."

"I know. But we're going in the same direction anyway," I say. As if I'd let her bike in the pouring rain.

Jamie's face is unreadable for a moment, but then she nods. "Okay. Let me get my bag."

I grab one of the yacht club's old umbrellas and put her bike in the trunk of the Jeep. By the time we make it into the car, my shoulders are wet and her hair lies damp around her face.

"Shit, it's pouring out there."

"Monsoon style." I put the car in drive and look over at her, sitting there in my passenger seat. I don't know if this has ever happened before. If old me would have believed it if it had. Her legs are bare beneath the pencil skirt of her uniform, stretched out in the Jeep's ample leg room. "How's Emma doing?"

"She's probably begging my mother to let her run around in the backyard right now," Jamie says dryly, but there's warmth in her tone.

"She loves rain?"

"Adores it," Jamie says. "Parker..."

"Yeah?"

"Thank you so much for your idea with the boat the other day. She had a blast."

I focus on the windshield wipers. "She did?"

"Yes. She drew another ship last night, and she put all of us on the boat."

"Oh," I say. It hits me right beneath the breastbone, and my hands tighten on the steering wheel.

"Yes. Don't worry," Jamie says, amusement in her voice, "she gave you a huge captain's hat."

"A captain's hat?"

"Yes. Like Captain Hook."

"Give it to me straight," I say. "Did I also get the hand?"

Jamie laughs. I savor the sound, to how it warms the entire car. "I didn't see one, but I can't actually be sure."

I don't know that I'm doing it until I turn to the right, choosing a route I rarely drive these days. Off Ocean Drive and past the gas station, through the roundabout...

"I haven't been back here in years," Jamie says.

I slow the car down to a crawl. "Does it look the same?"

She leans across the center console to get a better look. "Yes," she says. "But also smaller, somehow."

Paradise High sits right across the street. The two houses, the north and south building, the quad, the benches underneath the large maple. It all feels like an eon ago.

And also like yesterday, with her beside me, someone so strongly associated with this place.

When I turn the wheel this time it's entirely deliberate. I pull onto the parking lot. Beside it, the quad stretches out in an endless field of green, soaking up the rain.

"Remember that spot?" I say, pointing toward the bleachers.

Jamie groans. "Oh my God, I haven't thought about the Smoke Corner in forever."

"I saw you there a lot," I say, "my last year."

"Not a lot, come on. I was only there sometimes."

"You were one of the edgy kids."

"Paradise Shores didn't have edgy kids," she counters. "My nose piercing and Jonah's shaved head were about as grunge as it got."

That makes me grin. "Still, you never cared about fitting in."

"Because I didn't fit in," she says. "You had the sailing club, and football, and the Marchand name… come on, you were the school's favorite senior."

"That's not true."

She raises an eyebrow. "Isn't it? I remember standing right there," she says, pointing at the Smoke Corner, "during one of the games and hearing the entire bleacher chant your name."

"Okay, so I had a few good games. We were a terrible high school football team, if you look nationally," I say. It's the truth. Paradise High is in the business of producing academically inclined kids, not athletes, and fills their extracurriculars up with activities that'll look good on college applications. The school has every sport under the sun, including a partnership with the Sherman Riding School outside of town.

Football just happened to draw crowds.

"That might be true," Jamie says, "but that doesn't change the fact that you were a star in school."

I roll my eyes. "James."

"You, Turner and the others all had your pick of who to bring to prom," she says, eyes meeting mine. "The entire body of girls, from juniors to seniors, basically."

"Come on." I run a hand over my jaw, uncomfortable with her words. They weren't true, not really, but they had clearly felt true to her at the time.

She raises an eyebrow, and in that single second, I can almost see the nose piercing and the short, black hair, interposed on the grown woman in front of me. "Wow. Are you... blushing, Marchand?"

I snort. "No. Remind me, how come you didn't go? Neither you nor Lily went that year." I remembered, because I'd looked for her at prom, wondering what asshole she'd gone with.

"I was boycotting it," she says. "Don't ask me why. It made sense to me at the time."

"A political statement?"

"Most likely."

"Don't tell me Lily's had to do with Hayden?"

"Of course it did," Jamie says, effortlessly. "I can't believe you never saw that. Saw *them*."

"I didn't want to," I say. My windshield wipers are still going, a hypnotizing movement outside my front window. "My little sister and my best friend? No."

"But you're okay with it now?"

"Yes. It's different now."

Jamie looks down at her hands, at long fingers and bare nails. "She texted me this morning."

"Lily?"

"Yes."

I drum my fingers against the steering wheel. "What did she say?"

"Nothing I didn't expect," Jamie says, "and nothing I didn't deserve."

"Why are you worried about seeing her? You don't seem to be concerned about me, and we didn't talk for years either."

It makes her roll her eyes, just as I'd hoped. "But you and I weren't best friends. We didn't have a pact to name our kids after one another."

"So I guess you didn't keep the friendship bracelet I gave you?" I put a hand to my chest. "Ouch."

"God, I can't imagine you ever wearing one of those."

"Me neither. But tell me, if you want to."

Jamie runs a finger along the hem of her skirt. "You've already seen the worst of me," she says. "I guess with Lily, I'm just… embarrassed. And I feel guilty, and I don't know where to start."

"She'll understand," I say, and hope to God it's true, because I don't. *The worst of her?* I don't know what she means.

"She might." She shakes her head, and the tone of her voice isn't one I recognize. "I've missed her a lot."

"She's missed you too, I know that much."

"She'll be at the regatta," Jamie says. It's not a question, but I answer anyway.

"Yes, she will. Hayden should be too. Jamie…"

"Yeah?"

Something feels hard in my throat. I think of her old computer, of her daughter without a father, and the years of her life I know nothing about. My mind fills them with the worst of the worst. "I want to know about where you've been, too, but I won't ask, and you don't have to tell me. But I want you to know you can. Okay?"

Jamie's eyes meet mine. They're hesitant, and a bit soft, and a bit guarded, all at the same time. The enigma that has always been her.

"Thanks," she says quietly. And it sounds like she's thanking me for a lot more than just that.

Maybe that's why I say the next words, after pulling back out on the street. Continuing the drive toward her house and her waiting daughter. Or maybe it's just the longing inside me, stronger now than it had ever been as a teenager.

"I should have asked you to prom," I say. "Even if you would've turned me down out of principle."

Jamie's breath catches next to me. It's tiny, but I hear it. Then her voice turns smooth and teasing. "I would have said yes," she says, "even if none of your friends would have understood it."

"They never had to," I say, "as long as the two of us did."

11

JAMIE

"More?" I ask Kylie.

She nods, ponytail bobbing. "A *lot* more."

I leave the stall she's manning and head back to the yacht club, ignoring the protest in my legs. Yesterday's workout had been brutal. Parker had decided to take a more personal approach to my workout, by exchanging my light dumbbells for heavier ones.

It's your third time, he'd said. *You can handle these.*

So here I am the next day, thighs on fire, racing up to grab another box with snack-sized bags of chips. The lobster rolls are selling exactly like one would imagine in Paradise Shores at the Junior Sailing Regatta.

Which is to say, like hotcakes.

The docks are filled with activity. Boat owners have docked elsewhere for the weekend, leaving the marina free for the try-your-hand-at-sailing classes. People of all ages are enjoying the sun, waiting for the big race to begin... and eating lobster rolls with a side of chips.

I almost collide with Kristen in the kitchen. The new head chef is female, and tall, and brilliant, and she steps neatly out of my way. "Hey Jamie," she says. It had only taken her a day to learn everybody's names.

The restaurant is just as busy. Families fleeing the busy marina fill up the dining room. This event always draws crowds from outside of town.

I make it back down to the docks with the two giant crates of chip bags. Kylie and Sarah are working the stall, one accepting payment and the other making lobster rolls. I don't envy them.

"Thanks," Kylie throws over her shoulder.

I nod and reach for my water bottle, tucked behind the stall. Pull my beautiful new cap low on my head and look out at the crowd.

There will be people here that I know, walking through the crowd, minding their own business… a small part of my past and a potential part of my future. And I don't know if I'm ready to come face-to-face with it yet. But life rarely gives you things when you're ready. It gives them to you when you need to learn them.

But why couldn't the learning part be a little less hard?

The dock closest to me has a life-vest station. All kids participating in the free try-sailing sessions have to be vested up. A man is helping out, tall and broad-shouldered. He's wearing a faded *Paradise High Sailing Club* T-shirt and his dark blond hair is hidden beneath a navy cap.

It's the same one I'm wearing.

His hands move confidently over the life vest, tightening the straps, securing them on kid after kid. I can see him talking to each and every one, a steady smile on his face. The kind that lets you know everything will be all right.

If only I could be eight years old and in need of a life vest.

Parker tightens the vest on the last boy in line, who can't be more than twelve, and gives him a high five. The kids follow the younger instructors down the dock to the waiting array of dinghies. A trail of parents walk behind them, phones in their hands, ready to take pictures.

I watch as Parker walks back up the dock. He's been a

moving target the whole day. Doing anything and everything that needs be done for the regatta to run smoothly.

With his old sailing shoes, the beige shorts, the navy cap… in a second I see the teenage jock and the grown man interposed on one another. The golden boy and the golden man, the safety and the smugness. All of it blends together.

"Hey," he says. "You're hiding out?"

I nod toward the stall. "The lobster rolls are a huge hit."

"I should grab one later. Have you had lunch?"

"No, there hasn't been time."

He grins and grips the brim of my cap, tugging it down. "Are you telling me your boss doesn't give you lunch breaks?"

"No, he's an absolute terror."

"Making you work in this heat, too. I hate him for you."

I smile. It's so easy, being with him. "I don't."

"Well, your boss is glad to hear it," he says. Blue eyes dip to my lips. "You don't smile enough these days. I've noticed."

Oh. I don't know what to say to that. But his eyes don't linger on my lips and he doesn't elaborate. No, he just taps his fingers against his cap. "Brilliant job with these."

"They came out pretty good, right?" I take mine off, sliding my ponytail out the back. It's a deep navy color with white lettering on the front, together with the logo. *Paradise Shores Yacht Club.* "I'm just worried the font is a little too small."

"It's perfect," he says. "We're sticking with this design. No alterations."

"None?"

Parker takes my cap and puts it back on my head. Careful hands pull my ponytail through the hole in the back. "None," he says. "I can't believe you got the prototypes delivered on time for this."

"I'm a miracle worker," I whisper. He's standing very close.

"After seeing the new website go live yesterday, I co-sign

on that." Parker's hand falls to my shoulder, curving over my skin. "How are you feeling about being here today?"

"Great," I say, but I can hear what he's really asking, and I hate that I'm someone he thinks needs it. But I hate that he's right to do so even more.

"You can leave, you know, if you change your mind," he says. "If you want to avoid…"

His sister. Knowing how much he loves Lily, and still he would say that…

"I won't. I want to be here," I say. "Besides, my mother is joining with Emma soon. She wanted to have a lobster roll and watch the race."

He grins and drops his hand. "She'll love it."

"She wanted to take a sailing class, too, but—"

"The minimum age is eight. She'll have to wait two years."

He remembered when her birthday was. I'd only mentioned that in passing, weeks ago. "Yes," I say, a bit stunned. "She will, if we're still here then."

Parker's eyes grow serious. "Of course you'll be here then. My new newsletter won't run itself."

I run a hand over my arm. "No, I suppose it won't."

Someone calls from the docks. It's Neil, I think, and Parker turns. "Gotta go," he says. "Sorry about that. I'll see you later?"

"Yes, of course. Go," I tell him, and watch as he bounds across the dock, cutting through the mass of people. The marina is his home and these docks his streets, and it isn't long until I lose him amidst the crown. So I turn back to the food stand and the waiting line of people.

"Everything okay?" I call inside.

"We're out of rolls," Sarah says. "Can you get another box?"

And so it continues. My mother and Emma arrive an hour later, walking down the dock. Emma is holding my mom's hand, her eyes round as she looks around. Everyone is here.

Craftsmen sell jewelry, the gelato shop has a stand, there's face painting and live music. It's more than a regatta—it's Paradise's summer festival.

Emma spots me first and breaks into a run, her hair whirling around her. She bounces on her plastic sandals. "Mommy, they have face painting!"

"I know," I say. Her hand is warm in mine. "Want to try it later?"

"Yes, yes, please, can I?"

"Absolutely, but we should eat first. Hi, Mom."

Mom smiles. "Huge turnout this year."

"Bigger than usual?"

"It feels like it, yes. Must have something to do with the new leadership."

We grab three rolls and a snack-sized bag of chips to share, sitting down on the dock. Emma has a thousand questions and Mom and I do our best to answer all of them. Between the two of us, we know embarrassingly little about sailing for two people who live in Paradise.

But Emma doesn't seem to mind.

"Look!" she exclaims. It's the third *look* in five minutes.

"At what?"

She points in the distance. "It's the captain," she says and reaches for another chip. They're more interesting than her roll.

So it is. Parker is standing on one of the training dinghies, his arms moving as he rigs the sail. It must have tipped, because clinging to a dinghy next to it is a teenager in a life vest.

"Who's the captain?" Mom asks.

"Parker. He showed Emma his boat the other night," I say.

"Oh. Interesting. Lily's… brother, right? Did I get it right this time?"

"Yes, and he was kind enough to give me a job at the yacht club." I emphasize the word *kind*.

Mom's eyes glitter. "That's right. And seeing his boat,

Jamie?"

She's always been talented at writing her own narratives. Maybe that's always the case with creative types, an extra sensibility right at their fingertips. Her mind is great at putting two and two together and getting six.

"Don't," I warn her. "Please."

"I won't say a word," she says, in a tone that makes it clear she's thinking all of it anyway.

After we've eaten, I take Emma to get her face painted as Mom chats with a few of her neighbors. Half of the charm of the regatta is the socializing.

Maybe that's why I always avoided it.

"There she is!" Emma says, spotting the lady with the paint. But there's something familiar in the set of her shoulders, the auburn hair up in a bun.

"Wait—"

But Emma has already raced forwards. All her shyness suddenly forgotten, she stops in front of Lily, hands knotted in front. She rocks back on her feet.

I watch, in slow-motion, like I'm observing a car crash, how Lily leans forward. "Hi there," I hear her say. "What's your name?"

"Emma," my daughter says. She sucks in her bottom lip, suddenly remembering her personality. The girl is *always* shy around strangers. She looks over at me. *Come here*, the look says. *Now.*

"Hi Emma," Lily says. "My name's Lily. How are you?"

"Good." Her bravery forgotten, Emma takes a small step toward me. I reach her in time to put a hand on her shoulder.

Lily looks up at me. Her familiar face freezes, eyes widening. "Jamie?"

"Hello," I say.

She swallows, and looks back down at Emma. Lily blinks and blinks again, her eyes suddenly glossy. "Hello," she says quietly.

Emma curves her body into mine and looks at the paint in

front of Lily. "Do you paint?" She whispers the question.

"Yes. Yes, I do," Lily says. She takes a deep breath and blinks again. "Do you want a face painting?"

"M-hm."

"Well, come and have a seat here." Lily pads the stool in front of her. "What are you in the mood for? I can make you into a butterfly or I can paint flowers, stars."

"A butterfly?"

"Yes, like this." She points at a picture on a laminated sheet. "But I can also paint you as Spider-Man or as a tiger." Lily looks up at me, half-smiling. "I don't think she'll choose one of those, but I have to say it."

I meet her half-smile with one of my own. "Emma loves butterflies. Don't you, sweetie?"

Emma nods. "I have a butterfly bed," she says shyly.

"A butterfly bed? Wow."

"It's a bed cover with butterflies," I clarify. Over the past week Mom and I had repurposed the office she never used into a child's room again. It's a work in progress, but it means Emma has a space that's hers and hers alone. And she'd picked out her bed cover herself.

Lily smiles and reaches over to steady Emma's chin. "I see. What color is it?"

"Purple," Emma whispers, trying very hard to stay still, "and a little pink."

I watch as my old best friend, the girl I've known since I was Emma's age, and my daughter talk to one another. Watching the careful strokes of Lily's brush over Emma's forehead, drawing swirling lines of a butterfly's wings.

"How old are you?" Lily asks.

Emma takes a moment to answer. "Six. And a bit."

"I have a son that's almost your age. Well, he's four," Lily says, "and I promised to paint him as Spider-Man later." She focuses on Emma's cheek, on the pink swirl being revealed. "His name is Jamie."

"That's my mom's name!"

Lily nods, and slowly looks up at me. "Yes," she says. "It is."

It takes me a long moment to breathe. To find the movement, the words. I crouch beside Emma and put an arm around her waist. Steadying her, but really steadying me. "I saw your message last week," I say. "Sorry for not answering."

Lily shakes her head. Her eyes are trained on my daughter's face, on the butterfly that's spreading its wings beneath her talented hands. Her expression is one I know well. She's trying her hardest not to show emotion, but that's never come easy to her.

I've missed her so much, and the weight of it suddenly feels like a boulder on my shoulders, crushing me down to the dock. We'd been sisters at one point.

"I'm sorry for not answering in the past, too. For being away so long. I'm sorry for all of it."

Lily shakes her head again. It's a tiny movement, and I don't know if it means *not here* or *no need*. The brush in her hand trembles, and on her ring finger is a beautiful sapphire, the color of the ocean, resting next to a wedding band. She got Hayden in the end and I wasn't there to see it.

"Do you want to meet next week? Maybe… go for a walk along the boardwalk?"

"Yes," Lily says. "I'd love that."

There's so much to say. To apologize for, to explain. But it's a start, and something inside my chest loosens, like a rubber band expanding. Allowing me to breathe.

Emma is doing her best to sit perfectly still, but her eyes are flicking between us. I smile at her. "Sweetie, this lady is one of Mom's friends. We've known each other since we were your age."

"Really?"

Lily nods, a teasing smile spreading across her face. "Oh, yes. Your mom was a naughty one."

Emma's eyes go round. "Naughty?"

"Only sometimes," I say, and shoot Lily a look.

She laughs. "Only sometimes," she agrees, "but it was more often than me!"

When Emma is done, she bounces off the chair like she's been chained to it for days. Lily holds up the mirror and Emma lets out an *oooh* of joy. She's a pink and purple butterfly with glitter on her cheeks. Getting her to wash her face tonight will be impossible.

"So pretty," she breathes.

"Thank you," I tell Lily and dig through my pocket for money. There's a donation box next to the paints, the name of a charity on the front. "You've made her day."

"She made mine," Lily says. "Jamie... I'd love for you to meet my son, too."

Something feels tight in my throat. I think of all the years I wasted, and all the weeks I've been here without making this right. "I'd like that. A lot."

She smiles again and I leave her to the few children who are waiting for their turn. I'd forgotten, somehow, that this was something she did during the junior regattas. Something she used to do for years.

Emma skips with joy the entire way back to my mother, who'll stay with her during the race while I work.

The crowds don't let up, only settle into a hush as the race begins. Mom and Emma come to stand next to me when it starts. No one wants lobster rolls, or face paint, or gelato. Not right now.

There's fierce concentration on the faces of the junior sailers in the marina, lining up their dinghies. The race is at sea, and out in the bay, there are motorboats stationed in case of emergencies. But these sailors are in their teens, and they've been doing this since the age of eight, all across New England.

Parker had won his year.

I put my hands on Emma's shoulders when the race starts. Together we watch the boats glide out, each one quicker than the last. The boats cut through the water like butter, completely at odds with the frantic skills and hard work put in by the sailors.

Emma watches with bated breath. She's strung taut, like one of her bubbles, and I know I've lost her to the magic of Paradise Shores. We haven't lived anywhere that's had this much life and excitement.

"Look," Mom whispers by my side. She nods toward the other side of the marina. "Lily's over there."

My eyes track the group of people standing close together. Even in the distance, I can make them out.

Lily, standing tall on the dock. Hayden is beside her, his hand firm on a small boy intent on leaning over the side of the dock. Beside them is a tall man I haven't seen since he left for college, not in person, anyway. It has to be Henry. There's a dark-haired woman by his side and a small girl on his shoulders.

Henry and his wife are here, and Lily and Hayden, and Parker, coming down the dock to join them. Lily's son bolts toward him and Parker catches the boy around the waist, turning him upside down.

The sun is hiding, now, behind thick clouds that rolled in from the ocean. But I keep my cap pulled low and watch them, instead of the race. I watch Lily's son. I watch the siblings' easy conversation and familiarity.

And I let the emotion swell over me, the familiar wistfulness. I knew them all once and they're still here, still beautiful and golden, with idiosyncrasies and conflicts and love and warmth. I'd been jealous once. Now I just feel grateful.

"Mommy?" Emma asks. "Can I go sailing one day? Please?"

I bend over and kiss her cheek, once, twice, three times. She squirms with annoyed laughter and pushes me away. "Can I?"

"Yes," I say. "Of course you can."

And perhaps I should try too.

12

JAMIE

The house on Greene Street is quiet. It's the gentle kind, a soft silence rather than the uneasy ones that precede a storm. No one is holding their breath. No one is preparing their apologies in advance.

I'm sitting on the couch, legs pulled up beneath a blanket, and I'm reading a book. It's been years since I last finished one. Somewhere over the years, of Lee and motherhood and trying to make ends meet, hobbies had fallen by the wayside. Other priorities had asserted themselves, and they'd never left. Not until now.

I put the book down and look at the candles I've lit on the coffee table. Two years into our relationship, Lee had thrown my splurge of a scented candle into the trash. *Never waste my money on things like that again,* he'd said. *Are you truly that stupid?*

It hadn't been a question that invited an answer, and for years, I'd been great at not giving him one.

I shouldn't think of him, or the past. I don't want to. But with the house empty, Mom away at her book-and-wine club and Emma asleep upstairs, the thoughts find me at last. They always do.

He hasn't called or texted again, but I know it's coming. With him, something's always coming.

There's a knock on the front door.

I startle, the book falling from my lap. Has he found us? My eyes flick to the candles. *I should blow them out.*

In the next instant I hate myself for the thought. It can't be him, and I'll buy however many candles I want with my own money. Familiar guilt follows, at ever allowing him to control me.

There's another knock on the door. They bounce in a pattern, insistent, but not threatening. I inch toward the living room window and peer out.

Parker is standing on my mother's porch with a brown paper bag in hand.

My muscles relax immediately, the fight or flight response de-activated.

"Jamie!" Parker calls. "I'm leaving a special delivery for you outside!"

I hurry toward the front door. Too late I remember I'm in my pajama shorts with tiny boats on them, a cast-off from my mom, with unwashed hair. "Wait, wait…"

He turns on the steps, and a smile spreads across his tanned face. He got more color yesterday during the regatta. "Hello, James."

"Hi."

His gaze drops to my T-shirt, with the logo of a small brewery on it from out of state. I'd designed their website. "Nice outfit."

"I wasn't expecting company," I say, and nod toward the bag on the porch. "What's that?"

"That," he says, climbing the steps again, "is a feast for your palate, my friend."

"You brought us food?"

"Not just any food. Look inside."

I open the bag and take a deep whiff. The scent of spices

and something else, something that smells like cooked lobster and fried fish, fills my nostrils. "*Oh.*"

"Kristen cooked her suggestion for the new menu tonight. I brought you a sample of everything to try."

"A sample of *everything*?"

"There was enough left over," he says, and his eyes drop down to the bag. "And I want your opinion. Think you can bring yourself to eat delicious food?"

"It'll be a struggle, but anything for you, Marchand," I say. My hand pauses on the doorframe. "Do you... want to come in?"

Parker pauses on the steps. There's no grin on his face now, no teasing glint to his eyes. I wish I could inhale my words, unsay them, because I must have crossed a line. He'll say no in the nicest way possible and I'll have to move towns again.

"I'd love to," Parker says. "If that's okay with you and Emma?"

And instead I float, like one of her bubbles. "Yeah, it is. Absolutely. I mean, she's asleep."

He chuckles. "Well, I suppose it is okay with her, then. Sure I won't wake her up?"

"Her bedroom is upstairs, and that girl could sleep through an earthquake. Come on, come inside."

It feels intimate, and unexpected, to have Parker in the entryway. To watch him shrug out of the thin jacket and throw it over one of Mom's chairs. He'd worn a similar jacket all through high school, I remember. You'd see the *sailing club* written over his back as he walked through the hallways with his friends, his hair sun-bleached and longer than it is now.

"Sure it's okay?" he asks, hands curling over the back of the chair. "I can leave if you had a quiet evening planned."

"No, I'm sure. Of course. It just struck me that you've never been here before. Right?"

"Never," he says, and then he smiles. "Except the night I

walked you home from Turner's party. But I dropped you off outside."

"Yes, you were very respectable."

"I had to be," Parker says. His easy voice follows me toward the kitchen island. "You were Lily's best friend, you know."

I focus on unpacking the food onto the counter. "So if I wasn't, you'd have come inside? I'm shocked, Marchand." My tone is teasing, but there's nothing calm about my insides. I feel unmoored, adrift.

Had he really thought that?

"I might have tried to, yeah," Parker says, casting me further at sea. "This is a lovely house."

"My mom's not here to hear you," I say, looking at him over my shoulder. He's inspecting some of the drawings on the fridge.

"More boats?" he asks.

"Yes. After that day in the restaurant, she draws them all the time."

A satisfied look settles over his features. "Of course she does. She's a clever girl, like her mom."

The praise sinks into my bones, softens my movements. I survey the spread on the kitchen island. Tupperware boxes large and small.

Everything looks good.

"She really cooked the entire menu, straight through?"

"Mhm." Parker bends by one of the windowsills, inspecting an old framed picture. It's my mother and I in Antelope Canyon, one of the last trips we'd taken with my grandparents. I'd worn Doc Martens into the desert and a long-sleeved black tee.

"Did you eat all of it?" I ask.

"Some of each, yes," he says absent-mindedly. "But I wasn't alone."

"Who tasted it?"

"The family," he says.

I nod and lift the lid off a pasta dish. Of course. "I saw Henry at the regatta yesterday."

"Yes, he's in town with his family. I'm sorry he didn't see you. He would have wanted to say hi."

I doubt that, but I don't comment. "Is it rare that three out of you four are in the same place?"

"Not so much anymore, but it has been for a while, yeah." He rolls his eyes. "Rhys is impossible to pin down."

"That's always been his MO, though."

"A rebel without a cause," Parker says. "Oh, that pasta basically split the table down the middle. I want to hear what you think."

I pop it into the microwave and grab a beer for him. He settles into the same chair Emma had sat in just that morning and watches me move around the space. Long legs stretched out in front, blue eyes calm. He has the same ease here as he does in the restaurant. His hand curls around the beer bottle, and in my mind I see it tightening the straps of life vests.

"I heard about you and Lily," he says.

I look down at my plate of pasta. "We spoke at the regatta."

"Yeah. She saw Emma, too."

"Emma called her the paint lady," I say softly.

Parker laughs. "Like I said, she's a clever girl."

I swirl tagliatelle around my fork. There's clams in here, and crab, and a tomato sauce that smells spicy. "It was a quick conversation, though," I say. "We're meeting up next week."

"Mhm." Parker nods to my fork. "Tell me what you think."

I eat, and it's delicious, the sauce an explosion of tomato and seafood. And then the spice hits. It's deceptively subtle at first but soon rises in strength. I reach for my glass of water.

"Yeah, that was our reaction too," Parker says. "Dad only took one bite and said it was inedible. Faye cleared her plate and called us all pathetic."

I chuckle. "Faye? Henry's wife?"

"Yes, she's a badass. Her dad's Mexican and raised her up with a lot of spicy food. But it's good, right?"

"It's delicious. You should definitely have it on the menu, but… maybe two versions?"

"Two versions?"

"One less spicy and one more. Or maybe one with this tomato sauce and another with a non-spicy cream version." I shrug. "I'm not a chef, though."

"It's an option." He pushes a bowl of hot chowder my way. "How do you feel about meeting up with Lily next week?"

I swirl my spoon around in the creamy liquid. "What is this? Therapy hour?"

"I'm curious."

"Too curious," I say, and make my voice teasing. "Not to mention I don't know where your loyalties lie. What if you report it all to Lily?"

His eyebrows rise. "I've barely told her anything about you, you know. She asked me about you every day for a while."

"Did she?"

He nods. "I didn't tell her about Emma."

I taste a spoonful of chowder and think of the conversations they must have had. "Thank you, Parker."

His gaze softens. "Grateful you is a new version, too. Compared to the past."

"I was a brat back then."

"You were spirited," he says. "There's a difference."

I snort. "You're being generous, and this soup is delicious."

"Agreed. It's a clear winner." He pushes a piece of fried fish across the table. "What about this?"

It's half an hour later when I finally have to give up. I lean back, hands up in surrender. "I'm full," I say. "Can't stomach another bite. But it's delicious, Parker. A great new direction for the restaurant."

"The classics, but updated," he says.

"Yes. Oh, that reminds me… I added some new things to the website. Let me show you."

That's how we end up on the couch in my living room, side by side, my mom's laptop propped up across my knees. The sun has long since set outside the windows.

Parker takes up a lot of space. He always had, back in the day, too. When I'd been at Lily's and her big brother had occupied the entire couch, the loud sound of sports from the TV. Lily had always preferred their grandmother's old armchair, so I'd sat on the couch next to him.

We're sitting closer now than we ever did back then.

"So they'd be able to book through here…"

"Yes," I say. "All restaurant bookings here, and all sailing bookings… right here, if you click back to lessons."

"It'll take so much work off Neil and Stephen."

"It should, shouldn't it? I mean, some people will still call, but now there's a place to direct them toward." I return to the home page. Mom's old computer takes a full minute to make the simple shift. "But I think it'll look even better when we have new images here, for the slideshow. We should photo-graph the food, too, when the menu is set. A lobster roll, a bowl of clam chowder. Were you going to ask Rhys?"

"Already done," Parker says. "He'll do it when he finally shows back up in town. Shouldn't be long, but knowing him, it could be."

I smile. "Well, then. I think most things are done."

"Not the store," he says. "Have you ordered the other prototypes? With the new logo?"

"Yes."

"And you put it all on the company card, using the details I gave you?"

"Yes," I say, though that had made me uneasy. "They'll all arrive at the club the week after next."

Parker leans back into the couch. "Fantastic. You're a

godsend, Jamie. Now shut off that computer before it kills itself from the pressure."

I close the old laptop. It doesn't like running any programs heavier than MS Paint, and the fan slows down in gratitude. "Hey, this is an octogenarian. Show some respect."

"I have absolutely none," he says. "You know, this feels oddly familiar."

I lean back against the couch beside him. Our thighs touch. There's no reason for them to, in this three-seater, but here we are. Touching. "It does," I say. "But we're not arguing over the remote."

Parker raises an eyebrow and grabs it off the coffee table. "Come and get it."

I laugh at that. "Do you think I have a death wish? I remember seeing you tackle guys on the football field!"

"I'd never tackle you," he says, eyes oddly serious. "You should laugh more, Jamie."

"Laugh more?"

"Yes. You have a beautiful laugh."

The air feels sucked out of the room. I take a useless breath regardless. "I'll try, Boss."

That makes him smile. "Not outside the yacht club, I'm not."

"Or off a boat," I say. "You're the captain there, and everyone follows orders given by the captain."

Parker's lips tip up. "Except you," he says. "You never have to obey the captain."

"Never?"

"Never," he says quietly. "Unless you really want to."

"Oh." Something warm blooms in my chest, and he shifts from the grown version of a boy I've known most of my life into a stranger. Someone I don't entirely know, a new and foreign landscape to explore. A man with actions and words I can't predict.

"We could, um… put on the TV."

"Give us something to fight over, you mean?" His smile shifts, turning intimate. "Okay, James."

I nod. It's all I can do. The tension inside of me is rising, and I don't know what it'll do when it snaps.

"We could see if there's—what's that sound? It's raining?"

Parker looks over my shoulder at the bay windows. "It's pouring."

I fly off the couch. "Oh God. No, no, I have to take in Emma's bike. Oh my god…"

He follows me to the front door. "Isn't it waterproof?"

"Not the basket. Mom got her this beautiful wicker thing, and she stuffed it with a teddy…" I shove my feet into a pair of sneakers and open the front door. The rain is pounding outside.

I take a deep breath and rush out. She left it in the front yard, but where? I should have done it earlier, but there had been dinner, and laundry, and—

"Is this it?" Parker is standing beneath the oak tree to the side of the house. In his hands is the bike, pink embellishments dangling wetly from the handle. There's a sad-looking teddy bear stuffed in the basket.

"Yes, yes…"

He carries it to the porch and I follow, cold water sluicing down my hair. I have to wipe some away from my forehead to stop it clouding my vision.

Parker rests the bike gently against the railing, right underneath the porch. His hair is damp and looks almost brown in the darkness. Tendrils have fallen over his forehead, the way he once wore it. "It should dry," he says.

"Thank you so much." I run a hand over the teddy's fur. Soaked through. "I should bring him in."

"A few days inside will cheer him right up." Parker looks down at the small pink bike. "A new purchase?"

"It's my old bike, actually. Mom gave it a new coat of paint recently, and Emma is in love with it."

A smile spreads across his face. He looks back out at the pouring rain. "You told me she likes rain, didn't you?"

"Yes. If she'd been awake now she would be begging me to let her outside. My daughter is crazy." I tug at the hem of my T-shirt. "Why?"

He takes a few deliberate steps down the porch, back into the rain.

"What are you doing? Come back!"

Parker grins. "I'm testing her theory."

"You'll get soaked!" His T-shirt is quickly becoming the color of ink, clinging to his shoulders, arms and torso. The previously damp hair is slick against his scalp.

"I can see what she likes about it," he calls. The pouring is so loud it ricochets from the porch roof, a deafening sound.

I run down the steps to him. "You're insane. Move, Parker!"

He shakes his head. "I think I'll stay out here all night."

The water is cold, and wet, and I can't stop grinning. I wrap both of my hands around his forearm and tug. "Come *on*."

He doesn't move an inch, grinning down at me. Water runs down his jaw and gets diverted along the stubble. "Make me, James."

I'm laughing and tugging at the same time, pulling him toward the porch. But he resists, standing strong like the oak beside us.

"You've officially lost your mind," I say. "Are you still seventeen?"

He laughs. "Maybe!"

I use a shoulder to push against his back, but it doesn't make him move. So I change tactics and wrap my arms around his waist.

"You're making me wet too!"

"Yes," he says calmly, like we're not heading toward hypothermia with every second. "And don't you love it?"

I stop tugging and look up at him. "Mad man," I say, and

my hands rest against his back. The fabric of his T-shirt is soaked, molding my hands to his skin. It's hot beneath my palms.

A slow smile spreads across his face. "I get why Emma likes it so much," he murmurs.

Instinct and desire floods my system like a wave breaking, and without making the decision, I rise onto my tiptoes and press my lips to his.

They're wet from the rain and unmoving beneath mine. I pull my head back. "Sorry, I—"

Parker bends his head and kisses me, and it's wet, but it's warm, and soft, and thorough. The arms that had been solid as stone at his sides wrap around me, a hand landing between my shoulder blades.

It's a stranger's mouth I'm kissing, a stranger's hands on me. Not the Parker I'd always known, not Lily's brother. The excitement of that sends my heart into overdrive.

He deepens the kiss and runs the hot end of a tongue over my lower lip. It's been so long since anyone kissed me like that, and I come apart beneath it.

"Jamie," he murmurs, and rests his lips at the corner of my mouth. His chest rises rapidly against my own.

I keep my eyes closed and turn my fingers into claws in his shirt. If I move from this, I'll have to think about what I've done, and the wetness will go from exciting to cold.

It's safest to never move.

"Jamie," he says again, and presses a kiss to my wet cheek.

I blink my eyes open to Parker's dark blue. He's not smiling now, his lips parted, breath coming quickly. "I'm sorry," he says.

I blink again. "No… I was…"

He shakes his head and his hands, the strong, warm hands that can secure life vests on children and raise sails high, slide off my body. I let go of his T-shirt. "I'm sorry," he says again. "I shouldn't have done that."

It was me, I think. *I started it.*

I wrap my arms around myself, and I can feel my nipples, taut from the rain-soaked T-shirt and his closeness. Embarrassment sends heat to my cheeks. "No, no, it's okay," I say. "I think I like the rain too."

A half-smile from him, and the old ease is back. He's himself again, Parker Marchand, Lily's older brother. The guy I've known forever. "And you called both Emma and me crazy."

"Well, it's a bit wild," I say.

His smile widens and he takes a few steps backwards, away from the house, away from me. "You were always the wildest one," he says.

I swallow hard. "Thanks for the food!"

"No," he says. His clothes stick to him, the rain lashing on the sidewalk, and it doesn't look like it bothers him in the least. "Thank *you* for tonight, Jamie!"

13

PARKER

I take the corner too fast, tires whining against the gravel, and the Jeep protests. Henry shoots me a look from the passenger seat. I ignore it.

I've been on edge all day.

From the backseat, Hayden clears his throat. I know he's noticed it too. "So, he gave you a week to decide?"

"Yes."

"It's a good boat," Henry says, "but it will take a lot of work."

"*Hours* of work," Hayden agrees. "That's not a hobby, that's a second job."

My hands tighten on the steering wheel. I know that. Had known it since I saw the beautiful sailing boat in the ad, the wooden decks and the sleek hull. She was a boat to be honored and cared for, but she was not an easy one. And she was gorgeous.

"She's worth it," I say.

Henry runs a hand over his jaw in thought. "I don't know that I agree. It would lock you even more firmly in place in Paradise. Dad doesn't use the *Frida* that much. Why don't you stay the course?"

"Because *Frida* is all of ours," I say, and then frown at the way that sounds. "*Frida* is beautiful. And last year Rhys and Ivy took her out for two weeks along the coast, Hay and Lily want to use her for day trips from April to October, and whenever you and Faye are in town you have first dibs."

My words sound sour in the car, and my brothers don't comment. I sigh. "Look, I didn't mean it to sound begrudging. It's the family's boat, so that's only fair. But I want a challenge, a boat of my own. Dad makes all final decisions on the *Frida*. Not us."

"I get it," Hayden says from the back, and I know he means that. He has a motorboat in the marina for the days he wants to take *Lily* out for a day of swimming and lunch, without having to ask his father-in-law first.

Henry shifts in his seat. My oldest brother is, like always, unable to be anything but the voice of reason. "Why wood, Parker? It's hopeless."

"It's beautiful."

"It's impractical."

"It's challenging."

"Not everything has to be a challenge," Henry says. And then, into the stunned silence, "I can't believe I said that."

That makes me chuckle. "You okay over there, New York's youngest architect? You've never met a challenge you didn't love."

"I'm not that young anymore," Henry says, "and you're avoiding the subject."

I think about the boat we'd just seen. The sleek lines, the weathered wood, the very boat screaming out for a loving touch. For careful improvements until she could sing along with the waves again. She was expensive, and neglected, and it would be a project to take care of. To nurture. To honor.

Like Jamie.

I force my hands to relax on the wheel. To not think of her lips on mine, the sharp grip of her hands on my T-shirt. Like she didn't know if she wanted to push me away or pull me closer.

"What are you leaning toward?" Hayden asks.

They'd come with me to inspect it. Two sets of eyes are better than one, and three better still. Both of them know boats. Both of them have given me their opinion.

And yet it would be my project entirely. Evenings. Afternoons. Weekends.

I see Emma lying on the edge of the boat, Jamie sitting cross-legged behind her. But I blink the impossible image away. "I don't know," I say. "It's a stunner. She's built for speed and I want to buy her. But Henry's right, too. She's a damn inconvenient boat."

"I hate to say it," Henry says, "but you could get a newly built one. Speed, excellence, the first five years with barely any upkeep."

Both Hayden and I groan.

Henry raises his hands. "You both know I'm right."

"I know," I say. Ocean Drive is ahead, and I turn onto the road. It's a short distance to Lily and Hayden's house. Her oceanside cottage is next to it, where Henry and Faye are staying while they're renovating their new Paradise house.

"Do you want to sail long distances again?" Hayden asks. His hand is on the side of my seat as he leans forward. "Try the Atlantic? The world?"

Henry scoffs from the passenger seat. "No. He has a business now. Right, Parker?"

I drum my fingers against the wheel. The old dream is still there, burning inside my chest from time to time. Of a crew and a ship and the open oceans. The boat we'd just looked at could do much, but not that. Open ocean is a different beast entirely.

"I might," I say. "Haven't decided yet."

Haven't decided on a lot of things. The only thing I know, right in this moment, is that I might have fucked it up with Jamie that night in the rain. By pushing her further than she was ready for.

You never have to obey me, I'd told her, and I'd meant it.

Whatever had happened to put those shadows in her eyes, the jumpiness when she first arrived here, is something I can never contribute to.

I don't know a single thing about Jamie's ex. Not even his name. But I know that a man who leaves his clever, brilliant six-year-old daughter behind and her fierce, beautiful mother afraid, is a man I despise.

"I need to think," I tell them. About the boat. About whether or not I pushed Jamie too far.

She'd kissed me, but I'd devoured her in return.

"All right," Henry says. He opens the door, but pauses with a leg out. "Are you joining for family dinner tonight?"

"Yes." Little Jamie had asked me this morning if I would come and see the fort he'd built. I'd promised him I would, and I couldn't break a promise like that.

My brothers, one by marriage and one by birth, walk side by side toward the large house. I watch them disappear through the front door. Faye and Lily ate a late brunch, and while Hazel was still too young to play with little Jamie, he still adored his cousin.

I could invite myself in. But today I feel like an imposter, a puzzle piece that doesn't quite fit. They're settled, and married, and so deep in their blissful twosomes that it sometimes grates. And always, I'm the happy brother. The fun uncle. The supportive one.

The role chafes today.

My drive back takes me along the boardwalk, on Ocean Drive. Past the marina and the yacht club. I consider eating lunch there, but discard the idea with my next thought. I don't want to play the role of boss either.

There's only one person I want to impress, and until I figure out a way of apologizing for the intensity of my kiss, for crossing the line... until I know what to say to make it right, that door is closed.

———

That opportunity doesn't come the next day. It's a Sunday, and I'm not at the yacht club. I don't know if she's scheduled to work either.

No emails are exchanged. No texts.

On Monday, no one makes use of my garage, either. I leave the door open as I work out, just in case, but there's only me and my own thoughts in the gym.

All she'd wanted was a brief, impulsive kiss, and I had made it clear it wasn't impulsive at all on my part, but a slow, lingering make-out session that I'd clearly thought about for far too long.

How could she not be spooked?

I focus on my arms this morning, even if I know I'll regret it the next day when Hayden and I take *Frida* out. But the burn is good. It rivals the frustration of not having said the right thing, that night, after the kiss in the rain. Of not having found the words.

I shower longer and hotter than usual and drive to the yacht club with my cap on over the wet hair. The cap she designed, the cap we'll start selling in a few weeks.

I'd checked the shifts online. She's working today.

Stephen and Neil could manage without me. So could the staff and the new chef. But I can't stay at home, can't relax, can't wait to see her.

The club is calm when I arrive, and beyond the windows, the ocean is deep blue and calm. Last week's summer rain passed as quickly as it came. I walk past her bike, locked next to the staff entrance. Think of Emma's bike getting wet and the little teddy bear sticking out of the basket.

Stephen immediately accosts me in the hallway. One of the waiters quit after receiving a pre-season invitation for college on an athletic scholarship. Then Neil tells me one of the sailing instructors is sick with mono and he's going to have to take her place for the week. And before I've had a chance to look around for Jamie, I'm in my office and knee-deep in the new menu specifications Kristen wants.

At one point, I see a slender brunette with a long braid down her back pass by my office, but she's there and gone before I can call out.

My mood worsens after lunch. "Parker," Stephen says, sticking his head into my office. Unusually, there's a light sheen of sweat on his forehead. "We have a guest who requests to speak to you."

"Requests?"

"It's the man from earlier this season." Stephen's mouth turns down into a frown. "He got... handsy. You banned him."

I get up from the chair. "Where is he?"

"In the entryway. I've told him I won't seat him, but he won't leave."

"I'll take care of him."

John is part of Paradise Shores the same way all of us are, someone you wave at when you're filling up gas or undocking at the marina. I'd never given him much thought.

Now I hate him.

He's standing in the entryway, a salmon-colored shirt above white khakis. A set of car keys spin, over and over, in his hand. His eyes narrow when he sees me.

"John," I say.

He smiles. "Hello, Parker. It's been a while since I swung by."

"Sure has."

He leans in closer and spins his car keys one more time. "Look," he says, "your head waiter here seems to have decided I'm to be permanently punished for the little incident earlier in the summer."

"Oh, has he?"

The tension around John's eyes relaxes and he nods. "Yes, yes. An understandable mistake," he says. "I've been a customer here for decades. You know that. Hell, I sat right over there and watched you win your year's junior regatta."

"Of course. You've lived here longer than I've been alive. Isn't that so?"

"Yes, thirty-odd years or so, after I married Marie." His grin widens. "She loves this place too, and so do the kids when they come to town. My youngest went to Yale. Just like you, right?"

Reminding me of how great guests they are. He's pulling out all the stops, and a small part of my brain understands exactly why. The yacht club is an institution in this town. To be banned from it is no small thing. It means missing out on birthday dinners hosted here, retirement lunches, business meetings, lobster rolls in the sunshine after docking your boat.

"That's great," I say. "Please tell your wife and kids they're welcome to eat here any time."

His smile falters at the edges. "You're standing by your waiter's decision?"

"The decision was mine, as you might recall, and it was the least I could have done. You harassed a member of my staff. As long as I own this place, you will never be allowed past the front door." I give him a wide, conspiratorial smile. "And between you and me, John, I have no plans of selling it."

His car keys stop spinning, his fist clenched tight around these. "Parker, look here—I know you mean well, but I've been eating here since before you were *born*, and it's absolutely unreasonable—"

I let my eyes drop down over his form, to the boat shoes firmly planted on my hardwood floors. "Looks like you're trespassing, John."

He shifts closer and drops his voice an octave. It's furious. "It was a stupid mistake, okay? Do you want me to apologize to the girl? I can do that, if you insist. Won't happen again either. Lord knows she wasn't worth it."

Anger flares in my chest. *People are watching*, I remind

myself. *She might be watching.* I have to take a breath before answering or I'll say something I'll regret.

Doesn't mean my fists don't clench.

"You won't come near anyone in my employ," I say, "now or in the future. Now leave my restaurant, John. I won't ask you one more time."

A scarlet color rises up his weathered neck and cheeks. It's startling against the pink of his shirt. "You were always a good kid. I'm sorry to see this happen to you."

I take a step forward, like I'm going to force him out. He immediately backs up. "I play golf with your dad sometimes!"

"Then give him my regards." I open the door wide for him. "Now leave, and never come back, or I'll be happy to tell Marie and those kids of yours exactly why you're banned the next time they stop by."

John sighs like he's been wronged, a man infringed upon, and disappears out the front door. I watch him head toward his Land Rover.

Someone gives a delicate cough behind me. "I don't think he'll be back," Stephen says.

"Me neither," I say. "His pride won't take another conversation like that."

"And good riddance," he mutters, looking down at his ledger with bookings. "We have a big party arriving at three, I should prepare an eight-top…"

He disappears in a sharp turn of his heel, revealing who's been standing behind him. Listening to the whole conversation.

Jamie's eyes are bottomless and impossible to read.

The fire in my chest from talking to John is still burning. I resist the urge to rub my hand over the spot, right beneath my breastbone. "Hey."

"Hi," she murmurs.

"A box of merchandise arrived today," I say. "It's in my office."

She fiddles with the hem of her shirt. "Want me to take a look at it?"

"Yes, if you're not too busy," I say. Polite. Like we're strangers.

"No, I have time."

We make it into the tiny back office in silence. The box is in the corner, large, silent, a witness to our awkwardness.

Jamie pulls the door half-closed behind her.

"I'm sorry he came by," I say. "Are you okay?"

"Yes. Thank you for… saying what you did."

"I meant what I said. He's never going to come here again."

"That's good," she says, taking a deep breath. "Definitely good."

"He offered to apologize to you, but I turned that down. Maybe I shouldn't have." I run a hand over the edge of my jaw. "Did you want it?"

She shakes her head. "I'd rather not see him again."

"I figured."

Her eyes flit from mine to the box in the corner, with the merch. I look at her lips and damn, I shouldn't, because now all I can think about is their softness. "Parker, I… "

"Yes?"

"I'm sorry about the other night. I shouldn't have presumed… I mean, I was the one who started it." She shifts from one foot to the other, and I hate the words. Hate the way she's speaking them. "Can we pretend it never happened?"

I have to swallow, hard, before answering. "Of course, if that's what you want."

She nods. "Yes. I don't know what came over me."

"Consider it forgotten," I say.

I wonder if it's the first time I've ever lied to her.

Jamie's shoulders relax. "All right, okay. Thanks."

I'd been right, then. I'd pushed too hard by initiating the second kiss, by being so… into it. We work together. It's inappropriate in every way and then some, and considering she has a small daughter and a complicated past?

I don't blame her for pulling back, even if the fire in my chest feels painful.

She drops to her knees by the box, sounding more like herself. "Let's take a look at these."

I hand her a box cutter and for fifteen minutes we only talk of T-shirts and the fit of the caps and the rough linen napkins with the club's logo on them. She's tentatively convinced that if we offer them for the guests when they order seafood, people will want to bring their own set home.

There's a glow of excitement in her eyes at the ideas. I don't know why this matters to her so much, this job, beyond the salary. But I'm not going to protest or complain. Anything she wants.

"Look," she says, holding up the navy blue mug with the logo on it.

"Thank you," I say, and nab it out of her hand. "I needed a new coffee mug."

She rolls her eyes, but there's an easiness to her smile now. "This place is such a huge piece of everyone's life in town. A mug from this place is a father's day gift to the man who already owns a boat, has everything, and a bank account to buy it himself... but he won't, because he won't think of it."

I grin at her. "You're diabolical."

Jamie looks back down at the empty box, a smile tugging at the corners of her lips. "This stuff is more fun than I expected. It's creative, too."

"It definitely is. You have an eye for it. But then, you were always artsy."

She runs a finger over the rough edge of the cardboard. "Why didn't you ask Lily to help you with all this? She's artsy too."

"She is," I say. "But she also has a young son and is diving headfirst back into the high art scene. I overheard her having a conversation a week ago about the history of blue with an artist friend from New York."

"The history of blue," Jamie repeats.

"Yes. Yves Klein was mentioned, I believe, which I only know because she once wrote an entire paper in college about him and forced me to proofread it."

She chuckles. "I'd almost forgotten you went to college together, too."

"All of us did, except Rhys," I say. I don't know what happened to Jamie after Paradise, really. I don't think she and Lily kept in touch much. She'd visited Lily in New Haven once, and I'd seen her at a college party… and that had been it. The last time.

Jamie looks down at her hands. "I'm meeting her today."

"Lily?"

"Yes. We're taking a walk and talking."

"Ah." I lean back, bracing my hands against the floor. "Scared?"

She doesn't bite back, or pretend to be offended at my question. *Never, Marchand.* That would be the old Jamie.

But the new Jamie gives me honesty. "Yes."

"Don't be," I say. "She's missed you."

"Yes, and I've missed her, but I'll have to talk about things I don't want to." She rolls her neck, like she's steeling herself for a fight. "With anyone, not her specifically, you know?"

Curiosity rises inside me like a wave. She's been a closed box since she returned, under lock and key, and choosy about when she lifts the lid.

Does she talk to anyone the way she does with me? A part of me, an ungenerous one, hopes the answer is no. Wants her for myself like this, with whispered confidences and that rare smile on display.

Dinner in her kitchen and kisses in the rain.

"You can handle the conversation," I tell her. "Not to mention you don't have to answer anything you don't want to. Lily will understand."

She nods. "Yeah. Thanks."

"I'm going sailing with Hayden later tomorrow, but if you need to sweat it out in the morning… you know where to find me."

"Thank you. I might take you up on that." She rises gracefully from the floor and gives me a look that's all old-Jamie, teasing and confident. "You know, one day I'll bench more than you."

My eyebrows rise. "Oh, you will?"

"I'm determined, Marchand. Watch out."

"I consider myself warned," I say.

She smiles again and disappears out of my office, her steps echoing in the hall back toward the dining room. I stay on the floor next to the box with prototypes and, for a long few moments, let myself linger on the feeling of her lips on mine and her body beneath my hands, there in the rain.

And she wants me to forget it? I couldn't even if I wanted to…

…and I don't.

14

JAMIE

My feet feel heavier with every step I take toward the boardwalk. I'd considered biking, to feel the wind in my hair, but I'd decided the minutes of silent preparation was a smarter move. Give me time to gather my courage.

But it still feels very ungathered when I reach the spot we'd agreed to meet. Lily is already there, sitting on a bench facing the ocean. I spot her before she spots me.

Her fiery hair is pulled into a high ponytail and I watch the curve of her neck for a solid minute, taking deep breaths, before I close the distance between us.

Mommy, who are you meeting? Emma had asked me earlier. *The captain?*

That had made me laugh, and then immediately afterwards, get nervous. She's getting attached to this city, to these people.

I stop next to Lily's bench. "Hi," I say. "You're early too?"

She smiles, standing. "Yes. Things have sure changed since we were kids, haven't they?"

"So much," I say. "I actually exercise now."

Lily chuckles. "God, so do I, with yoga. I have one of those sunrise alarm clocks, you know, that wakes you up with light?"

"Don't tell me you regularly talk to a therapist and practice healthy sleep hygiene."

"I do both," she says, grinning. "Have we grown up, Jamie?"

"I'm afraid we might have." I tug at my blouse, half-smiling. "When did I stop wearing all-black?"

"A great question. I barely recognized you." Her eyes narrow, but she's still smiling. "The nose ring's gone too?"

"I took it out a few years ago," I say. "Turns out it was a phase, just like my grandad always said it was."

She laughs. "Hated proving him right?"

"Yes," I say, but my smile falters. I hadn't been here for his funeral. My mother had called, and I'd apologized and said I couldn't, not with Emma so small and Lee starting a new business.

Now I wonder how I couldn't have insisted on going.

Lily gestures to where the boardwalk winds its way toward Paradise Point. "Should we walk?"

"Yes," I say. "We have to get our steps in for the day."

She laughs again. "We've become such adults."

"Oh, I know. Filing taxes and shopping in bulk."

"Mothers, even," Lily says. Her voice softens. "Emma is lovely."

"She is," I say. "Her middle name is Lily, actually."

Beside me, Lily falls quiet. Our walk slows from brisk to ambling. Her limp from the car accident is less pronounced than when I'd seen her last. Better with every passing year, it seems, and that warms my heart.

Lily takes a deep breath. "I didn't know. Not about Emma's name, not about… her. That she existed."

I look at the ground, at the stone worn by decades of regular walking and running along the ocean. "That's on me. I chose not to share."

"Yes, that's true," Lily says, like she's commenting on the weather. She's never one for dancing around a topic, but here we are, the both of us cautious like two people on a first date. "Is her father out of the picture?"

"Yes," I say. And then, my gaze on the horizon, I add the rest. "At least I want him to be."

She makes a small humming sound. "Is he why you stayed away for so long?"

"A part of it, yes."

"I can understand that," Lily says. But the other part is evident in her voice. *But I can't understand the rest. Why you didn't answer my messages. Why you stopped answering my calls.*

I wonder if I even understand that part myself.

"You married Hayden," I say. It's a cheap change of conversation, but she doesn't comment, shining up in a smile instead.

"Yes, we got our happily-ever-after in the end."

I nudge her with my elbow. "You were always hoping for that."

"Can't deny that," she says and looks down at the ring on her finger. "Even if I'll admit it took me a while to let him in again after he returned."

"Where had he been?" Last I'd seen Lily, Hayden had been gone for a few years, having left Paradise shortly after the car accident. They hadn't remained in contact.

"Making a name for himself," she says with an eye roll. "That's the way he likes to put it. I think he was running away from the accident, and from my parents, and from his own misguided guilt."

"I can understand." I glance down at her leg. Her hip had been crushed, and I remember those fraught days right after, visiting her in the hospital. And then the entire long summer after, with all the physical therapy she had to do. I'd done a lot of the moves with her, in her childhood bedroom, while I tried to make her laugh with increasingly outlandish stories. "That was scary, Lily."

"It was," she says. "But we found our way back to one another."

"And to little Jamie."

She chuckles. "And to little Jamie. His actual name is James, you know."

Parker must like that. "He's very cute."

"Yes, he is, and he knows it. Uses those big eyes to get out of all kinds of trouble."

I play with the hem of my sleeve. "You sent me a picture after he was born. I hung it on my fridge, next to Emma's baby picture."

Lily's breath catches. "You saw that email?"

"Yes."

"But, then... Jamie, why did you never answer me? Why did you pull away?"

We curve around the benches by Paradise Point and reach the rock with the golden plaque. It's the furthest eastward point in Paradise.

"I don't know," I say, and it's not an escape, it's the truth. My words feel inadequate and dry and I have none to offer her.

Lily sits down on the bench next to the rock and gestures for me to join her. So I do. I watch the waves beat against the rocks and she watches me.

My words come out haltingly. "It was cool, not knowing what to do, you know. When I was twenty. Skipping out on college and working odd jobs in the city."

"I know," she murmurs. "I remember."

"I was living with artists, and everyone was living this life of true rebellion, you know? Against their backgrounds, their families, society. I loved it. But... what's nice at twenty isn't so nice at twenty-four. When no one in your shared apartment bothers buying soap for the shared bathroom. Impromptu parties lose their charm pretty fast." I look down at my nails, pushing down a cuticle. "You'd just graduated college, I remember, with your master's degree in art history."

Lily sits very still next to me. "Yes."

"And I started falling behind. That's what it felt like,

anyway. I'd see you and our other classmates getting jobs you'd worked for years to earn. Starting to build a future, a life, all of it. And I was still running and rebelling. Still trying to figure out who I was. It worked for a bit, but not forever. And then I met Lee."

I have to take a deep breath, and I focus on the horizon. The spot where the ocean meets the sky. Compared to that infinite distance, my mistakes are minor. "He took up so much space that for a long time I *was* him. I couldn't see or think about anything that wasn't him. I was in love, stupidly so. The kind that won't let you breathe."

"Infatuated," Lily murmurs.

I nod. "Oh yes. And he knew it."

"I never met him."

"I wanted you to, in the beginning. Spoke to him about visiting Paradise, but he made enough comments about this town, about my mother's job, my grandfather's company, to hint that I should leave my privileged past behind. It wasn't edgy enough."

Lily's hands are tightly knotted in her lap, and I look away from them, back out toward the horizon. "He was a few years older, right?"

I nod. "He got a job out of state and we moved. And then I had Emma. She wasn't planned but that never mattered to me. From the moment I knew I was pregnant, I wanted her."

"Did he?" she whispers.

"He said he did. In the beginning. And it was good for a while, Lily, I swear it was. But it didn't last, and my one solace became Emma, making sure she was happy and healthy and doing well."

"Lee?" she asks. "What did he... do?"

I shake my head. "He was never violent. But he was very good at breaking you down regardless. And I knew our one-bedroom rental in-the-middle-of-nowhere wasn't anything to write home about. I knew what people would think, the people in town, our high school friends. They'd think I failed.

And you? You'd think the same thing I did when Lee wasn't around. That I'd betrayed myself, that I'd become smaller than the person I was born to be. Smaller than the person you'd called a friend. You wouldn't let me hide from that fact… And I'd become very good at hiding."

I blink at the horizon to stop it from becoming blurry. I don't know how much more I've got in me, how many more words until I break.

I've never said any of these things out loud.

"Jamie," Lily says, "I have loved you since we were seven years old and you stood up to Billy T after he ripped my drawing in half during recess. You could become the size of a flea and I'd still consider you my best friend."

Something wet runs down my cheek and I wipe at it. Once, twice, and then my shoulders are shaking.

Lily grabs my left hand with hers. "Did you leave him?"

"Yes," I whisper. "I should have done it years ago, but I didn't… manage to."

Her low voice is fierce. "Good. And he'd better hope he never comes here, or I'll pay you back for Billy tenfold."

A broken half-chuckle escapes me. "Thanks, Lily."

"Stay here, okay? For as long as you want. Your mom must be ecstatic to have you back, and so are the rest of us." Her hand tightens around mine until it's almost painful, and I can't stop the tears from flowing down my cheeks. It's years of regret, finally acknowledged.

"I love you, you know," I say. My voice wobbles. "Even when I didn't speak to you for years. Even when I couldn't answer your texts out of guilt, and fear, and… disgust over who I'd become."

She puts an arm around me, and I marvel at the way the roles have reversed. How we're grown up and yet still the exact same, and perhaps that's all there ever is, in friendships that are more like family.

"Stay in Paradise," she murmurs. "Stay here. Okay?"

I nod, unable to find my words.

We stay there for a long time, until the sun dips behind the horizon, and it's late when I finally make it back to my house. Empty plates in the kitchen are evidence of yet another pancake dinner. Emma is getting spoiled and she deserves every single minute of it. From the stairs, I hear a murmured voice. My mother is reading a bedtime story.

I do their dishes and walk up to join them. My legs feel heavy, my heart sore, like it's taken more exercise today than it has in years. And yet my head feels crystal clear.

Mom looks up when I enter Emma's bedroom. She softly closes the book and looks back down at my daughter, who's struggling to keep her eyes open.

"Want to do the rest?"

"Sure. Thank you."

She puts a hand on my shoulder. "My pleasure, honey."

Emma smiles when she sees me. It's the sleepy, half-here-and-half-gone kind of smile only small children are capable of. "Mommy," she whispers.

I smooth my hand over her hair. Her eyes flutter as she struggles against the pull of sleep.

"Sweetheart," I murmur, "what do you think of this town? Do you like it?"

Emma's eyes open in a valiant effort. "Yes."

"Do you want to stay here?"

"Yes," Emma says again. Her eyes close for good this time, her next words barely audible. "Can we?"

"I'll try," I murmur, smoothing a thumb over her feathery eyebrow. "Mom will do her best."

15

JAMIE

I've never used dumbbells this heavy before. I have to take a deep breath before I can lift them up, resting them on my shoulders.

"That's it," Parker says. He's watching from his recline on the bench, the bar above him resting on the metal. "Back straight too."

I squat down. The first is easy. The fifth is not.

"That's it. Don't let your body drift too far in front of your knees."

"A lot of instructions," I huff out. Another squat. "Maybe you should"—another squat—"focus on your bar. It's looking"—a deep breath—"very immobile."

He grins at me. If he still thinks about that night in the rain last week, the impulsive kiss on my part and his profuse, embarrassing apology, he doesn't let it show.

"Feeling strong today, James?"

To my surprise, the answer is yes. The mornings spent in his gym have re-awakened the pitiful muscle mass I have. It's also given me a win every time I left his garage sweaty and alive.

I take another deep breath and start with lunges. "Just lift your bar, Marchand."

He chuckles and reaches for it. It's loaded with eight times the weight I can handle on chest presses. He'd showed them to me earlier, and I'd protested that I didn't need to do that exercise. *Why do I need to work my pecs?* My punishment was a five-minute lecture about the importance of core and upper-body strength.

Parker grunts quietly as he works through his set. From the safety across the gym, doing my lunges, I watch him without shame.

He's his usual self. Ignoring the kiss, just like I'd asked him to. We're back on a territory we both know how to navigate. And yet the feeling of his lips on mine is burned into my mind, impossible to forget.

My eyes drift over his arms and his long body stretched out on the bench. When he's done, he does what he always does, lifting the hem of his T-shirt to wipe his face. I watch the strong stomach and the lines that rise and fall with his heavy breathing. It's a body that's built for the strength necessary to sail, to work, to live an active life, and not to impress. No vanity muscle.

His eyes meet mine across the garage. "Done with your set?"

I nod and put the dumbbells back in the weight rack. My hands feel tingly. "Yes. I think so."

He reaches for his water bottle. "You've gotten stronger," he tells me.

"It hardly feels that way," I say, "when I'm sore all the time."

There's a flash of light in his eyes, there and gone, that tells me he heard something else in my words. A flush creeps up my neck at the innuendo.

"Right," he says, and shifts from one foot to the other.

Mirroring him, I reach for my own water bottle. It feels oppressively hot in here. "You know what I mean."

"Yes. I do." He clears his throat. "I take it your conversation went well? With my sister."

"We both survived it, at any rate."

He chuckles. "That means it went great."

"It did, yeah."

Parker raises an eyebrow. "Did she manage to get more answers out of you?"

I turn, gathering up my phone, water bottle, and keys. "Oh, I told her everything and swore her to secrecy."

"Damn it," he says, voice rough. "I'll get it out of you eventually."

"What do you think my secrets are, anyway?" I ask. His curiosity is flattering, and overwhelming, and I can feel his lips on mine again. How they'd burned.

"I change my mind every day." He goes to the garage door and pushes it open, letting in a flood of cool morning air. "Maybe you've been a government agent, a spy, and you had to return to Paradise to lie low after your last assignment went wrong."

That makes me chuckle. "And Emma?"

"Oh, she's a very charming decoy, all part of your cover story. Explains why she's so clever." He nods toward the great outdoors. "Are you finally joining me for a swim?"

It takes a few seconds to make the decision. "Okay. Sure. But I didn't bring a bikini."

His gaze drops to my chest, voice a little rough around the edges. "Sports clothes work too. Shouldn't be anyone down by the boardwalk at this hour."

"Right. Um, yes. Let's go." I tug at my T-shirt. "Lord knows I'm sweaty enough."

We don't run down to the boardwalk, the way I'd seen him do a few days ago. We walk side by side instead, his steps long, mine measured.

"Want to know something?" I ask.

"Is it about your mysterious past? Are you running from the mob?"

I knock his shoulder with mine and instantly regret it. The brief touch shoots electricity through me. "No, and no."

"Damn. Well, I'm curious about everything you say, so shoot."

"Emma wants to go out on a boat," I say. "She's asked me twice in the past few days, and every time we drive by the marina, she yells it from the backseat."

"Really?"

"Yes. I think the Junior Regatta blew her mind. Paradise has her."

I hear the smile in his voice. "Of course it does."

"Anyway, I blame you entirely."

"Me?" He chuckles. "I'll accept, of course, because in this case it's an achievement. But why?"

"She drew ships at the yacht club and learned to call you captain, and all was lost. I'll lose her to the sea."

"It's not a bad place to be lost," he says. "You know I'll take the two of you out, one day, if you want to. On the *Frida*."

I look at the horizon, the glittering band of blue getting larger and larger in the distance. "Thank you."

"No pressure, though," he adds. "I know you want us to stay professional."

To stay professional? I nod, but the word bounces around in my head. *I know* you *want us to*. My mind races through the conversation in his office, the night on the lawn, in the rain. When had I made that clear?

Parker stops at the boardwalk and stretches, tall and strong beside me.

And reality suddenly kicks me hard in the shins. I'm going to have to take off my clothes around him.

"It'll be cold," he warns with a grin and reaches down to pull off his sneakers. The dusty gold of his hair is darkened at the temples with sweat. "Ready, James?"

"I was born ready," I say. It's a lie, and he sees it too, because his grin widens. But I toe off my tennis shoes and reach for the hem of my T-shirt. Take a deep breath… and pull it straight off.

Thank God my sports bra covers enough.

Parker focuses on the tie of his workout shorts, unfastening it, and I take that opportunity to tug off my workout shorts too. My panties are black cotton and normal and not the least bit sexy. I hurry toward the ladder, desperate to get out of view from the road.

And out of his view.

"Coming?" I call.

Parker gives me a crooked smile and pulls off his T-shirt. He does it the way men do, grabbing at the shoulders and tugging it off over his head. The abs are back, but this time they're joined by a wide chest and a smattering of light brown hair.

I look down at my feet on the dock and the chipped nail polish on my big toe.

"You're going to regret this in about five seconds," Parker warns, "but give it a minute, and you'll think it's the best idea ever."

"Will I?"

He nods and stands beside me on the dock. Raising an eyebrow, he gives me a cocky grin, the picture-perfect one I remember from our childhood. And in one smooth motion he dives in, cutting through the surface of the deep blue with the skill of an athlete.

"Show-off," I mutter and take a few careful steps down the ladder. It's freezing around my ankles. A quick glance over my shoulder reveals him coming up for air, facing toward the horizon. So I quickly take the plunge to hide my body from view.

It's like entering an ice bath.

"Oh my God," I say, pushing off the ladder. "Holy moly, this is cold. So, so cold."

Parker's voice reaches me across the waves. "Did Jamie Moraine just say holy moly?"

"Shush!"

He laughs. "If sixteen-year-old you could hear you right now."

"She would have slapped me," I say. "But she also said *fuck* way too liberally for a teenager, and she didn't have a little kid around who mimics *everything.* Is it always this cold?"

"You should know," he says, easily treading water. The soft waves lap around his broad shoulders. "You're a native."

"It's been a while. I've lived inland for almost a decade." I swim out toward him, cutting through the water. It's starting to feel bearable, just almost, and the sun glints off the waves. On a whim, I dip my head beneath the surface and swim until my lungs feel like they might burst.

I break the surface and take a deep breath.

"Who's a show-off now?" Parker calls. He's behind me now, silhouetted not by the horizon but by the dock.

The water and the cold sets off a peculiar high through my veins. I feel crazy and alive and brave. It reminds me of how I'd felt getting onto that Greyhound with Emma and our two suitcases, leaving our past behind.

"The water is actually nice!"

He swims toward me, cutting through the water in a crawl. "I want to say I told you so," he says, "but I don't want to get splashed."

"Splash? Me? I would never."

He shakes his head to get the wet tendrils off his forehead, sending droplets flying around us. "You were always a troublemaker."

"Someone had to be," I say, and then I splash him. Hard. A wave of water breaks over his head and he laughs. "You Marchands were always too pristine," I say, and splash him again. "Especially you. The golden son, the winner of the regatta, a Yale legacy..."

Parker raises his arm in a sweeping motion. "You're going to get it now," he says.

I immediately duck under the surface, but a wave of water

still crashes above my head. The salt water stings in my eyes. We never did this, in the past. Lily and I would go swimming with friends, sure. And in the distance I'd see the cool kids from school do things like this. Play volleyball, have water fights, and the guys would have the *it* girls on their shoulders in the water. Parker was at the heart of all of it.

And now he's here with me.

I'm spluttering when I come up for air. "Truce!"

He laughs again. "So you can dish it out, but you can't take it? That's typical."

"Perhaps I'm just a more peaceful person."

He turns onto his back and floats beside me. One of his arms is outstretched and the hand rests only inches from me on the water's surface. "You've become more peaceful," he says toward the sky, "but you have the same fire."

Perhaps I do. Perhaps I'd lost it, but day by day, I'm finding it again. The excitement, the will to provoke, the bravery. Determination and self-confidence. So much of it had been naive and misguided when I was young, but I hadn't been scared of anything, and I miss that. The years with Lee had left me scared of everything.

There's a happy middle there somewhere.

"This is the best time of the day out here," Parker says. His voice sounds deeper, echoed across the waves. "It's too early for the families or the tourists. The damn jet-ski rentals haven't started up either."

I turn in the water. It feels warm, now, lapping against my skin. My lips taste salty from the ocean.

"I've missed this," I say. "More than I thought I did."

"Then it's a good thing you're back." It sounds layered, the words like a caressing wind. He's said that a lot. *Welcome back, Jamie.*

He gets out before me. His workout shorts seem to be perfectly capable of doubling as swimwear, falling straight and wet down his legs.

My clothes? Not so much.

I tug at the elastic of my panties, now soaked through and barely holding up. A quick look down at my sports bra reveals my nipples showing through the polyester fabric.

Excellent.

I cross my arms over my chest. "That was nice."

Parker bends at the waist and grabs the towels he'd brought. He throws one at me, a crooked grin on his face. "You should start doing it more often," he says. "Wear a bikini under your workout clothes and you'd be all set."

I wrap the towel tight around myself. "That's not a bad idea."

"I've been known to have good ones every once in a while," he says, using his towel to rub his hair. He's close and big and water droplets run in slow tracks down his wide chest, golden from the sun.

I wet my lips. "Like standing still in the middle of a downpour, right?"

Something changes in his gaze. "Yes," he says slowly. "I would say that's one of the best ideas I've ever had."

"Ever? That's a big claim." I run my hands up my arms, trying to get warm.

"It is, but I stand by it." The distance between us shrinks. "Good things seem to happen when you're standing in pouring rain. Even if I'll keep ignoring them."

My breath escapes me. "You'll keep ignoring it?"

"Yes. As requested." He lowers the towel. The dark blue of his eyes looks bottomless, a small part of the ocean behind him.

"Earlier, you said…"

"I said what?" he asks.

"That I wanted to keep things professional," I say. "But we work out together a few times a week. We just went swimming. I wouldn't say we're all that professional."

His lip curls. "No, James, I wouldn't either."

"The thing we're ignoring in the rain wasn't very professional either," I say. My words hang in the space between us.

Parker shifts closer. "I'm sorry about that," he says softly. "If that made you feel rushed in any way."

"Rushed?" I whisper. "I didn't feel rushed. I felt confused."

His eyes darken. "Well, that wasn't what I was going for."

"Not by... the kiss. But by your reaction." I shake my head. "I was the one who started it."

"But I finished it," he says, "and not briefly, either."

No, it hadn't been brief. Those seconds with him in the rain, with his hands on me and mine fisted into his T-shirt, had lasted an eternity.

Breathing feels difficult.

"Jamie, I can ignore it," Parker says quietly, "if you truly want me to. But I would much rather not."

I sway closer to him. "Is this a terrible idea?"

"It might be," he says, "but I've always been a fan of your terrible ideas."

A laugh escapes me. "Like the purple highlights."

"I loved those," he says, and it's such a blatant lie, because it had looked awful. I did it myself before school started in the fall the year I turned sixteen.

"Liar," I whisper.

"Never," he says.

"Do I have to go first again?"

He smiles, slow and wide, and lowers his head. "No," he says, and then he kisses me. It's salty and warm and water drips from his hair onto my temple, cold against my flushed skin.

My eyes are still closed when he pulls away. "There," he murmurs. "Not too little, not too much. We did it right this time."

"Don't Goldilocks this, Marchand."

He chuckles hoarsely and then doesn't make another sound, not as I reach up on my tiptoes and kiss him again. It's intoxicating being this close to him.

And just like last time, he becomes a stranger under my

lips. Familiar and yet novel, an entirely new landscape to explore. Parker and yet not Parker.

"Jamie," he murmurs, his hands finding my waist beneath the towel.

My hands settle against his chest. His bare chest. He's warm and hard under my hands, skin deceptively soft over the strong muscle beneath.

"Jamie," he murmurs again, moving his lips to my ear. He laughs softly. "We're in the middle of the boardwalk."

"Oh," I whisper against his chest.

"I don't mind, but I have a feeling you might. You know how this town talks."

"Yes." I turn my head and peek past his shoulder. An SUV drives by us on Ocean Drive. "What do we do?"

He rubs a large hand up and down my arms, as if to warm me. It sends a shiver down my back. "We'll go home," he says, "and start our days, and do this again. When we're alone."

"I like that plan," I say. My voice doesn't sound like my own.

He smiles, small and crooked. "Come on, James. You're getting cold, and I'm in danger of overheating."

16

JAMIE

My feet feel light, carrying me into the yacht club. The familiar scent of food, of browned butter and clam chowder, greets me. I nod hello to Kylie and Sarah. I give Stephen a giant smile.

"Having a good morning?" he asks me.

I attach my name plate to my shirt. "More like a great weekend," I say. Yesterday had been spent at sea. I couldn't remember the last time I'd been on a boat, and as the *Frida* cut through the waters outside Paradise, I decided it was a shame.

Emma had adored it.

She'd been shy around Lily and Hayden at first, but little Jamie had been like a rocket, zooming around, and she'd soon followed suit. Parker had been at *Frida*'s helm, a kid on either side of him, explaining things like speed, knots and steering. Both kids had been allowed to touch the steering wheel while Hayden looked on.

Lily had rolled her eyes at them. *Let them entertain the kids,* she'd said, sitting next to me. Her sunglasses had been pushed up on her head and she'd grinned at me. *It's so good to have you back.*

Parker had said, once, out of earshot from the others, that he wished we were alone. I'd let my hand brush over his on the steering wheel in response.

The high of the weekend carries me through the lunch service at the yacht club. I wait tables with a smile, suggesting some of the new dishes off the menu. And while I catch sight of Parker a few times, he's never standing still, moving from the back office out to the docks with Neil by his side. The sun glints off his hair when I catch sight of him through the windows.

I wonder why he's back here, doing this. I wonder what his parents and his siblings think. And I wonder how many things I don't know about him yet, the nuances, the histories, the questions I can now ask him. A thrill runs through me at the realization.

An opportunity presents itself after the lunch rush is over, and I duck into the back office unseen.

Parker is sitting at his computer, filling out expense reports. He looks up when I softly close the door behind me.

"Jamie?" he says, a smile spreading across his face. "Do you need anything?"

I close the distance between us. "Yes."

Parker rises from his chair and catches me against him, finding my eager lips, and he kisses me like he's waited all weekend for this, too.

My hands knot in the fabric of his linen shirt. The collar pops open and my fingers find the hair-roughened chest beneath.

"What's this?" he murmurs, lips shifting over mine. "Sneaking off from work?"

"I wanted to surprise you."

"Mmm. I like these kind of surprises." His hands stroke down my body, finding a grip on my butt, and he deepens the kiss. It's a soft touch of his tongue against my lower lip, and I open for him. He groans at the contact and pushes me more firmly against him.

I'm dizzy again, pleasurably so, like I've had too much to drink. *I'm making out with Parker Marchand*, I think. The thought is clear as fine crystal in my mind. *I wonder what we look like.* Do we fit together? Judging only by the way my body molds against his, it feels like the most natural of fits.

His hands tighten on my body. It's delicious, being held like this. Like he doesn't want to let go.

I didn't know how much I craved it.

Parker is the one to finally break the kiss and rests his head on top of mine. "Jesus," he mutters. "A *very* good surprise."

I chuckle, and the breathless sound disappears against his neck. "It was time for a break."

"I approve," he says. One of his hands drifts up to my waist, as if he's trying to behave himself, but the other stays put, like it can't bear to leave.

I smile against his skin. "Whoops."

"Don't get me wrong, I love my sister and Hayden both, but…"

"I know."

"I didn't plan for them to join us on the *Frida* yesterday."

I tilt my head back and meet his eyes. "You wanted Emma and me for yourself?"

His hands tighten, briefly and possessively, on my body. "Yeah."

"I would have liked that too. But Lily is persistent."

"She is." His eyes darken, dropping to my lips again. "Now that you two have made up, will I have to share you with her? You don't have much spare time as it is."

"Didn't your parents raise you both to share your toys?" I tease.

He snorts. "Yes. But you're not a toy, and you're far too great to share with anyone."

"Well, you'll have to learn to. Even if I don't think…"

"You don't think what?" he asks. Then, his eyes lighten. "Ah. You don't want Lily to find out about us."

I give a hesitant shake of my head. "Is that okay?"

"Yes," he says. "Sure."

"It's just, we've *just* cleared the air between us. And you know how she is, she will have a million questions, and she won't let up on either of us. It will just be easier. Is that—"

"Jamie," he says, smile widening. "Trust me, I know how my little sister gets. We don't have to tell anyone."

I relax against him, my hands flattening on his chest. "Thank you."

"I'll be your secret," he murmurs, dropping his lips to my ear. "Did you ever think about that, back in the day? What it would have been like if we'd snuck around together?"

My lips fall open. "What? You mean... you and me? Dating?"

"Yes," he says. "Right under my sister's nose, but without her knowledge."

"You thought about that," I say.

He nods, unabashed. There's a fire in his eyes. "Every time she left us alone on the couch, watching TV, I wondered what you'd do if I kissed you."

I can't find my breath. To have the old tension addressed, to hear him confirm the fire beneath our constant bickering. There had been times I'd been so sure he felt the same... and then most other times, I was convinced Parker would never see me as anything but Lily's weird friend.

Parker's grin widens. "I always wondered if you'd slap me or kiss me back."

"Both, probably," I breathe.

He chuckles. "Probably," he agrees, and dips his head lower. "Whenever you slept over at our house, in Lily's room, I'd sleep terribly."

"You would?" I whisper.

"Mhm. You were only a room away. What if we met in the hallway, going to the bathroom, late at night? What did you wear to bed?" He makes his voice teasing. "The scenarios tortured me. I was only a teenage boy, James, and you were gorgeous."

I laugh at that. "I had purple highlights and a nose ring!"

"Gorgeous," he repeats. "But I'll admit it made me feel like a pervert."

I roll my eyes. "You were only a grade older than me."

"Still. You were my sister's best friend. Still are, actually." His hand squeezes my hip.

"God, you were so annoying back then," I say, smiling. "You would take half the couch."

"Well, I wanted to be close to you."

"You insisted on watching sports, every single afternoon, and always pulled the older-than-Lily card to win the remote war."

"Because I knew how much it annoyed you," he says. "Do you think I actually wanted to watch all those games?"

My hands still on his chest. "Of course you did. Didn't you? You were a jock."

"I liked them," he says, "but I liked watching you pretend to be annoyed by me more. You'd come up with the most ridiculous arguments against organized sports. Come on, tell me you didn't enjoy our little dance?"

"I did," I say, rising on my tiptoes again. "I liked to annoy you too. Was pretty good at it, wasn't I?"

"Yes," he murmurs, and kisses me back with slow, lingering touches that promise more to come. "You always ignored me at school."

I'd laugh if he didn't have his mouth on mine. That was the other way around. He was in the glorified space *above* the cool clique, reserved for the kids who were beyond social hierarchies. He was a Marchand, the third golden son to attend Paradise High, a star athlete, and destined for great things. There was no lunch table off-limits for him.

"I didn't ignore you," I say. "You were too cool for me."

He snorts. "You were the one who wore biker boots that broke dress code and staged protests in the cafeteria. You didn't care about what anyone thought, and I loved watching you do it, all of it."

I didn't think he'd ever noticed.

He kisses me again, and it takes us several long moments to resurface for air. My head is spinning softly. "I should go," I say, my hands re-fastening the button I'd accidentally undone in his shirt. "My shift—my break, I mean, it should be over now."

Parker nudges my cheek with his nose. "When can I see you next?"

"I don't know."

He presses his lips to my neck, a warm brush over my sensitive skin. My hands slip into his hair and it's hard to concentrate. "When, James?" he murmurs again.

"Um. Soon. I want... oh. Wednesday night, maybe?"

"Wednesday," he says. "Okay."

"My mom has her book club again. You could come over. Although..."

He raises his head. "Emma?"

I nod.

"I can come over after her bedtime."

"She really likes you," I say. "You saw that, didn't you, on the boat yesterday? She hangs off your every word. But it's just that... "

"I get it," he says, stroking a thumb along my cheek. "You don't want her to get too attached. I'm not offended."

I sigh in relief. It's odd, and new, and so light to be with a man who doesn't twist my words around. Who isn't unpredictable, sunshine one day and all flames the next. Parker is steadiness itself, a contrast to the ocean he loves so much.

"Yes," I say. "I'm sorry."

He kisses me one last time. "Don't apologize. Until Wednesday, then."

"I can't wait."

"God, me neither, Jamie."

I re-fold the blanket thrown over the side of the couch. The pillows are already fluffed, a bowl of chips on the table. That might have been too much, though. Like I've prepared for a movie night with a friend.

Which I suppose I have.

I light a few candles, which leads to an immediate bout of overthinking. They make the place look date-like, and I blow them all out instead. The faint scent of smoke lingers in the air.

Upstairs, the door to Emma's room is closed. She's usually a heavy sleeper, but she's been known to wake up an hour or two after bedtime from a dream, from thirst, or something just not feeling quite right. I hope tonight isn't one of those nights.

She doesn't seem to miss her father at all. Hasn't asked me about him once since we left. But still, the idea of her getting attached to Parker, and to this town, without me knowing if we can stay here? If I can support us? Disappointing my daughter terrifies me more than Lee ever did.

There's a knock on the door.

"Showtime," I whisper to myself. Parker's standing on the other side, a bottle of wine in his hand.

"Never come empty-handed," he says with a grin.

I make a show of looking beside him. "But where's the professionally cooked twelve-course dinner this time?"

"You're a comedian," he says, and kisses me on the temple. It's a casual, affectionate gesture. I'm not sure it was even conscious. "Is Emma asleep? Your mom away?"

"Yes." I follow him into the kitchen. He sets the bottle down, hands bracing on the counter. "She passed out like a light. Summer is good like that. She runs and plays and gets enough fresh air during the days that she struggles to get through brushing her teeth without falling asleep."

Parker's smile deepens. "She likes it here."

"Loves it, more like. Do you want us to open your red wine?"

"Sure," he says.

I find two glasses and watch as he uncorks the bottle. "What wine is it?"

He rattles off the name with the ease of someone who buys and enjoys this vintage, the words round and foreign-sounding on his tongue. His mother is French, even if the influence is clearer in Rhys and Lily than the all-American could-be-model in front of me, but it's there beneath the surface.

"Do you still speak it?" I ask. Their mother had insisted on classes, and spoke to them in French whenever she could when we were kids.

He gives me a half-smile. "Only when I can't avoid it."

"You're brave," I say. Eloise Marchand is a determined woman.

"Mom's fearsome, but she's settled down some. Or maybe I've just learned to ignore her pointed demands? One of the two."

"What does she think about the yacht club?" I ask. "What does the whole family think?"

He raises an eyebrow. "One night alone, and you're diving right into the tough questions?"

I focus on pouring wine into our glasses. "Maybe. But you don't have to answer."

"They're confused," he says, "and happy in equal measure."

"Confused?"

"Do you know what I did before the club?"

I play with the rim of my glass. Lily had mentioned it, briefly, in a message a long time ago. "You were a lawyer in Boston."

"Yeah. I'd studied law and I practiced it for a few years, according to plan. I would sail in my free time, but... there was very little of it."

"Did you go pro? The summer after college?"

"Attempted to, at least."

"Oh."

"It's not a lurid story," he says with a sigh. "But there's a lot of time involved, and a lot of travelling. It didn't work with my job."

There's more to that story, I'm sure. None of the Marchands technically need jobs, from a financial standpoint. But I had overheard more than one tense discussion during my childhood visits to Lily's house. Eloise and Michael Marchand demanded nothing but excellence from their children, and it was excellence narrowly defined.

"When did you move back from Boston?"

"A few years ago now," he says. "Shortly before Lily followed suit."

"You led the way."

His smile is crooked. "I always do."

"Did you work from here?"

"Yes, I kept up my law practice. But there is something soul-destroying about reading corporate contracts day in and day out. My father wanted me to eventually work on retainer to his company, but..." He trails off and runs a hand through his hair. "This wasn't what I had in mind for tonight. I wanted to decipher your secrets, not spill my own."

I dig my teeth into my bottom lip. "Maybe you have to go first in order to get mine."

"Oh." A light sparks in his eyes. "Well, then. I lay my failings as a lawyer at your feet."

"I wouldn't consider shifting from lawyer to business owner a *failure*."

He chuckles. "Say that to my father, please."

"The yacht club is an institution in this town, and your family practically is, too. How could they not be happy?"

"They will be," he says. There's confidence in his voice. "I'm sure of it. My father loves sailing too much, and my mother the social fabric of this town, to not see how beneficial it'll be. I give it a year or two before they're asking me to host private events at the club or my mother decides to contribute with artwork."

I laugh at that. "Sounds like them."

"Besides, my license is still valid. I can practice law if I feel the need to." He nods at the glass of wine still in my hand. "You haven't tasted it yet."

I haven't had the time, I think, and keep my gaze on his as I take a sip. He is too fascinating and my stomach is too filled with nerves.

"It's good," I say, the red wine exquisite on my tongue. It's been a long time since I've had wine, too. "Should we, um... go to the living room?"

His smile widens at my awkwardness. "Sure," he says. "It's just me, James."

"Yeah, well, you're not *just you* anymore."

"I'm not?" He sets his glass down and stretches out on the couch beside me, an arm along the back and legs stretched out in front. Taking up space, the way he always has. "How have I changed?"

"Well," I say, "I didn't know how good of a kisser you were before."

His gaze darkens. "It's easy when you have a good partner."

"Oh?"

"Mhm." Parker's eyes drop to my lips. "You've changed for me too, you know."

"I have?"

He dips his chin in a single nod. "I know what you sound like, now, when I kiss your neck."

"Oh."

"That little sigh has been on repeat in my mind for the past few days."

The room feels too hot. I shift on the sofa, turning to face him. Pull my legs up beneath me. "Parker, what are we doing?"

"Right now?"

"Yes," I murmur, looking down at my wineglass. "What is... *this*? Us."

"We're spending time together, and I'm slowly discovering all of your secrets."

"I hoped you'd forgotten about that."

"Never," he says. "Where have you been living these past couple of years?"

That's a question I don't mind answering. His dark blue eyes are serious on mine, and open, like whatever I say is okay. There's no correct answer, and no acerbic comment waiting for me if I say the wrong thing.

"A few hours west of here," I say. "It was a tiny town."

"Like Paradise," he says.

That makes me laugh. "Well, in size maybe, but very much *not* like Paradise. There was no ocean close by, and definitely no lobster rolls."

"I can't believe you survived."

"It was a harrowing few years."

He smiles, arm stretching out behind my back. "Did you work?"

"Off and on, yeah. Waitressing and graphic design mostly." I tuck my hand beneath one of the pillows, the braided fabric rough against my skin. Mom is big into hemp and jute at the moment. "It wasn't very reliable."

"That's where you learned it all? The design work?"

"Some of it, yes," I say. "There are great courses online. It was trial and error, mostly. The first website I created was for a place I waitressed at."

"Same as now," he says, raising an eyebrow. "That's your trick, James? Get hired for one thing and then show your secret talents to get a second gig?"

I roll my eyes. "It's only worked twice, but maybe I should put it into practice regularly."

"There are too few places in Paradise," Parker says, "and the gelato shop doesn't need a website."

I dig my teeth into my lower lip and think about it. "That could actually work," I say. "I know you meant it as a joke, but the ice cream shop is a local institution. They could have a system where customers order pints to go, and list all flavors on their website."

Parker grins. "You're brilliant, you know."

"Gosh, that was just a stupid idea. I don't know anything, really."

"You know a lot," he says. "Own it. You're good at the business side of things."

"I have no experience with it."

"So it's all raw, natural talent." Parker shifts closer, his hand brushing my shoulder. "That's even more impressive. Maybe you should start doing this full-time, instead of waitressing. Website design, newsletters, and business strategy? Not like I want to lose one of my best employees here, though, so maybe I should shut up."

I laugh. "Not likely."

"But you could work from home with that. Stay in Paradise. Put Emma in school," he says. His voice is warm and reassuring, and I like the picture he paints. Perhaps a bit too much.

"I'm not sure about staying yet."

"Oh? What do we need to do to convince you?"

I shake my head. "Nothing, it's not... because of the town. But Paradise is expensive, and I know the cons as well as the pros. Maybe Emma won't fit in so well."

A lot of my memories of going to school here are great, but not all. The teachers were brilliant, but the kids could be ruthless, often casually so. They went on summer vacations to faraway places and spent their winters skiing in Aspen. Most weekends they'd been on their boats, docked in the marina for all to see. I'll never be able to afford that kind of lifestyle for Emma. She doesn't realize that now, but one day she will.

"She's a natural-born sailor," Parker says. "She'll fit in

beautifully. Or she'll stand out, like her mother did, and dazzle the town. Either way, she's meant to stay."

"I *dazzled* the town?"

His mouth lifts into a crooked smile. "Dazzle the high school boys, at any rate."

"I never dazzled anyone."

"Wrong," he says softly. The single word sets my heart racing. Parker shifts closer and the distance between us shrinks, inch by inch. "You've always dazzled me."

I give a tiny shake of my head. *It's you,* I think, *who've always dazzled me.* The golden boy, the golden man, confidence and ease and strength personified. Laughter that fills up a room and arms that can carry the weight of the world.

He closes the distance between us and kisses me, a brief brush of his lips, and I find my breath again.

My hands slide into his hair. The dark blond strands are soft, and just faintly salt-roughened at the ends. I wonder if he manages to get all of it out during the summer, with daily morning swims.

"Jamie," he murmurs, and one of his hands runs through my ponytail. "Let's take this out."

I help him with the scrunchie and my hair falls over my shoulders. He runs his hands through it, leaning back to watch the light brown locks spread over my tank top. It's nothing special. No real haircut, and no highlights, just light brown and mostly straight.

But his eyes are trained on it. "Your hair used to be dyed black," he murmurs.

"Do you miss it?"

His eyes rise to mine, and a smile that is entirely too charming spreads across his face. It makes my stomach flip over. "I know better than to answer that," he says. "But no, James. You're gorgeous like this. Too gorgeous."

Our kisses go from vertical to horizontal. My back hits the pillows, and then the couch itself, stretched out beneath Parker. He's always been strong, but I've never realized just how built he is until this very moment. He's everywhere, and every slow brush of his lips sends shivers down my arms. I feel like I'm coming alive again, like he's kissing me back into my own body.

Parker's attention shifts to my neck and I look up at the ceiling. I'm feeling too much, all of it at once. His lips are a feather's touch on my sensitive skin.

I want him, desperately. I want to lose myself in us, in him, and I want to be held in his arms and close my eyes and feel the strong beat of his heart beneath my ear.

But then I hear Lee's comments in my head. *Do you have to make so much noise? God, Jamie, can you buy panties that aren't for grandmothers? Hygiene is important. I'd have gotten hard if you'd showered first.*

They were always dropped casually, like things I should be aware of, instead of devastating blows. Each comment a pebble against my self-confidence. If he'd thrown boulders instead, I might've had a chance at avoiding them.

I might have seen them for what they were.

"Jamie," Parker says. His voice is hoarse, and when he lifts his head, the dark blue eyes are nearly black. There's a distinct hardness against my leg. "What's wrong?"

I tighten my grip on his shoulders. This is *everything* I've ever wanted, and Lee won't take it from me. "Nothing."

"James," he says. The arms on either side of me are solid, and I turn to look at them instead, the muscles taut as they hold his weight. "Tell me."

"I just get in my head sometimes. I'm sorry. We can keep going, it's okay, I promise."

"Hell, no," he says.

I flinch against the words. Another apology hovers on my tongue, even as I hate myself for it. For the person I became around Lee, for the person I can't seem to shake fully.

But Parker isn't him, and he pulls us up into sitting. A strong arm settles around my waist, making itself at home.

"We aren't doing anything," he says, "unless you fully want to."

"Oh, but I do, Parker, of course I do. It's just that..." My words trail off. There's no way to explain it. How things with Lee had gone from explosive to passive-aggressive, how intimacy had become another of his manipulative weapons, honed to perfection.

Something darkens on Parker's face. It's there in an instant, and it's an expression I've rarely seen on his face. He looks like he had in Lily's hospital room, all those years ago, if his devastation was matched by rage.

"It's because of Emma's father," he says blandly.

It's a statement, and not a question, but I nod.

Parker closes his eyes and a muscle jumps in his jaw. A long second passes, and then another.

"It's okay," I say.

"No, it's not. Did he hurt you?"

I shake my head. This night is spiralling, my two lives colliding. The two Jamies colliding.

"I don't believe you," Parker says.

The words tumble out, a torrent that matches the adrenaline flowing through my veins. This is it. He'll find out just how weak I've been and he'll leave. "Lee never hurt me physically. It was just... little things. Comments. By the end he would critique everything I did, all of the time, until I was walking on eggshells."

He'd tell me I was worthless, I think, *and for years I believed him.*

"He'd critique everything you did," Parker repeats slowly. His voice is monotone. "Including sex?"

I want the Earth to swallow me whole, to bury me in an unmarked grave. Mortification sets my face on fire. "Yes."

Parker closes his eyes again and the hand on my waist tightens, just slightly, the grip still soft. He turns into a statue with tightly controlled breathing.

"It's okay," I whisper. "I left him. It's just that, well, sometimes I still hear those comments in my head."

"He was wrong," Parker says, eyes still closed, "about every fucking thing he ever said. You know that, right?"

I take a deep breath. "Most days, yes. But not all."

Parker remains quiet and still, hands on me, eyes closed.

"Are you okay?" I finally whisper.

He tips forward, his forehead coming to rest against mine. Dark blue eyes open again. "I'm trying very hard to restrain myself," he says. "It's a new concept for me."

"Oh. Restrain yourself from what?"

"A great many things, most of which would land me in prison," he says. But then his lips quirk up, a tiny movement. "Or turn you off me forever."

"Not possible," I murmur.

He kisses me. It's achingly sweet, with his large hand on my cheek, and brief. When he leans back the air between us feels clear. I see none of the judgement in his eyes that I reserve for myself.

"Time, Jamie," he says. "I have all the time in the world."

"Oh."

"So whenever that bastard's words ring in your head, you tell me. What they are, or not, I don't care. But let me know so I can remind you how brilliant and beautiful you are."

Something squeezes painfully tight in my chest. All I can do is nod.

"I have questions," he continues, "and I think there are still things for you to tell me, if you want. But there's no rush. Was this enough for tonight?"

He's giving me the choice. Like Lily, he's not demanding all of it now. Where Lee is now, how I left him.

"Yes, I think it's… enough for tonight," I say. It doesn't quite feel like a defeat, with his steady gaze on me and the strength of his arm around my waist.

"Okay," he says instead. "Then let's see what movie you'll badger me into watching."

My mouth falls open. "Excuse me?"

He grins. "I remember your artsy movie taste in high school. Things had to have subtitles, remember? Or be black and white?"

"God, I was trying so hard to be alternative."

"Yes," he says, and hands me the remote. With his free hand he shifts my legs so they lie over his. "But now you can just be you."

17

PARKER

It's been three days since the conversation in Jamie's house, on that couch, and I haven't forgotten a single word she said. Nor how she looked when she said them. She'd turned inward, like a house shutting up for winter. It wasn't natural. Not for Jamie.

Not for the teenager who was afraid of nothing, and not for the woman who'd splashed me in the ocean just a week ago. Who had grown into her workouts in an impressively short period of time. The woman who is a brilliant mother to the cutest little girl.

I hate her ex.

The hatred is heavy to hold, weighing me down in bed at night. I picture him in my head, though I have no idea what he looks like, and conjure up scenario after scenario. Things he must have said to Jamie. The worst of my musings are the two of them in bed, and the comments he might have made, until I have to throw the cover back and stalk around.

Last night it had resulted in little to no sleep, and my mouth is tight when I park the Jeep outside the yacht club. I wonder what made her leave. I wonder if Emma misses him. I wonder about a lot of things that I have no answer to, and no chance to learn, not until Jamie is ready.

The restaurant is in full swing when I step inside, preparing for lunch, and I duck into the back office right away. The new website Jamie created has been a roaring success and I'm tentatively putting in larger orders for the caps, T-shirts and mugs. But when I arrive at my desk, there's something waiting for me.

Something that's lying on my laptop.

It's a large, lightly cracked chocolate chip cookie. It has M&M's in it that look an awful lot like the rainbow sprinkles I'd gotten Emma at the gelato shop.

Next to it is a scribbled note, written on a ripped-off piece of legal pad. *Captain, thank you for being so understanding. Emma and I baked yesterday. Enjoy!*

I look at the cookie for a long moment before I take a bite. A bit salty, and too dry, and perhaps the most delicious thing I've ever eaten.

Jamie's working today, and seeing her is the best kind of torture, walking through the restaurant in her uniform. Every now and then she'll send me a look over her shoulder that slays me. It's the kind of look a man would go to the ends of the Earth for. It says *hello,* and *I like you,* and *you and I are an item… but no one here knows.* It's a look that promises kisses in the dark.

Jamie passes by my office half an hour later and only stops long enough to give me a wink before dancing off toward the restaurant. The gesture makes me grin.

Time, I'd told her. I'd promised to give her all the time in the world, and I meant it, but by God I hoped we wouldn't need it.

It's past lunch when I hear a familiar tapping on the door. "What now?" I ask. "Another cookie?"

Jamie rolls her eyes, so like her old self, and smiles. "No, your brother and his girlfriend are here."

"My brother?" I say. "Do you mean Henry? Faye's his wife, but they're not meant to get back until next Friday for the White Party."

She shakes her head. "Rhys."

"Rhys is here?"

"Yes," Jamie says, smile widening. "Last time I checked he was still your brother."

My grin widens. "Sassy," I say, and get up to follow her. "Thanks for the cookie, by the way. I loved it."

She smiles at me over her shoulder, and fucking hell, there's that look again. *We have a secret*, it says, and *I like you*, and I imagine her giving it to me in bed. "Ahoy, Captain," she says.

I press a hand over my chest and groan. "You kill me."

Jamie chuckles and leads the way to the restaurant. And, lo and behold, my older brother is there. Rhys is leaning against the wall and flicking through the contents of his DSLR camera. Next to him is Ivy, her light blonde hair in a casual ponytail, looking down at the screen with him.

"That one," she says. "You have to include it."

"The light could be better," he says. Then he notices me and lowers the camera, a familiar half-smile on his face. "Hello, little brother."

I pull him in for a hug. "Only Lily is allowed to be called the little sibling."

"That's for older siblings to decide."

"Hi, Parker," Ivy says and hugs me too. She smells sweet, cloyingly so, and I can't stop the cough that escapes me.

She gives an apologetic smile. "Sorry. It's this perfume brand I'm working with. They want me to endorse them, but I wanted to test the scents first."

"They're god-awful," Rhys says.

Ivy gives a happy little shrug. "Well, I won't write that back in the email to them, but… yeah, they're not good. This one is called Spiced Honey, and now I'm stuck wearing it all day."

"I don't get your job at all," I say honestly.

Ivy laughs. "Most days I don't either!"

I take a step back and gesture toward Jamie. "Rhys, look who's back in town."

My brother looks at her for a long moment. "Jamie Moraine?"

"Yes. It's nice to see you, Rhys."

"It's been a long time," he says. "Ivy, Jamie went to school with us. She was Lily's best friend."

Was. I doubt it was deliberate, just as I doubt Jamie missed it. Ivy introduces herself with a bright smile. "It's a pleasure," she says. "You work with Parker?"

"Um, yeah. I'm a waitress here."

"She's also overhauled the website, designed the graphics for the new menu. See that?" I say, pointing to the cabinet in the entryway. It has a stack of the new caps inside, resting artfully on top of coiled rope. "Jamie's idea. We sell them now."

Ivy looks inside the cabinet. "These are so cute! I want to get one of these."

Rhys is still looking at Jamie. He must have heard some of it from Lily, but I don't know how much. The two of them always stay in contact when he's abroad. "How long have you been back?" he asks.

"Two months, now, I think. Give or take," Jamie says. "Your brother was kind enough to give me a job."

"That's all lies," I say. "I didn't have a clue she worked here until I saw her in the restaurant."

Rhys snorts. "Doesn't surprise me. He's never been particularly observant."

"More lies," I say. "Did you come to town just to insult me?"

"Oh, you know that's just a bonus." He lifts his camera up. "I came to do you a favor."

"Down from Mount Olympus to honor us mortals," I say, putting a hand on my chest.

He hits my shoulder with an open hand. "Man, do you know how much I charge per hour?"

"No, and if you send me an invoice I won't pay it," I say. "Come on, let us show you around."

Rhys and I join Ivy by the entryway. It isn't until I've opened the doors that I realize Jamie hasn't joined us.

"James," I call. "Come along?"

She hesitates, the question clear in her eyes. "Sure?"

"Yeah. You know what shots we need for the website, I've heard you talk about it several times." I grin at her. "Stephen will cover your tables, I need your brain out here."

"Okay, sure!" She smiles back and rushes into the back office to grab a notepad.

It doesn't take long before Ivy and I decide to leave Rhys and Jamie to their business. It's clear they don't need our input. As we walk away I overhear Rhys talking about *shooting it more commercial* and Jamie answering *yes, imagine magazine,* and I know I'm out of my depth.

Ivy and I talk about their recent travels instead. They've just gotten back from driving across the country, visiting national parks, and she's got a tan. She's big into fitness and health, and one topic drifts into the other, turning toward workouts.

"I just signed a new contract with a fitness brand."

"You did?"

"Yes. We'll be shooting all kinds of content—workouts, yoga, hiking, meditation, and cooking—in their workout gear and athleisure."

"That's fantastic," I say. "Congrats. But, what the hell is athleisure?"

She laughs and explains what amounts to wearing workout clothes outside of your workouts. Apparently a lazy practice I've been the master of for decades has become an entire industry. Who knew?

"How are things in Paradise?" Ivy asks. "Any updates on your bachelor life?"

I lean back on the bench. In the distance, Rhys and Jamie

are standing far out on one of the docks, facing the yacht club. Getting shots of the place from afar. The sun is shining, and the waves are soft.

It'd be a perfect day for sailing.

"No major updates," I say.

"Which means you're still enjoying it," Ivy says with a laugh. She's always been close to a laugh, quick to it where Rhys is reluctant.

Sure, they look stunning together, but it's these differences that make them work. It had taken me a while to figure it out. That her lightness where he was dark, her sincerity where he thrived on nuance, was the magic between them. And beneath it a bone-deep understanding that they *see* one another—that my brother can be unmasked in her presence in a way that he so rarely is with anyone.

Including us.

My eyes track Jamie's slim figure out on a dock. She's walking next to Rhys, her arms moving animatedly as she explains something. She's excited.

And I find myself smiling.

"I'm actually seeing someone right now."

Ivy bumps my shoulder. "Anyone special? Someone we'll see at the White Party?"

I snort. "Jesus. My parents have been badgering you guys about it too, I'm guessing?"

"Eloise only texts Rhys about it once a day or so," Ivy says. "To make sure he doesn't decide to explore a Costa Rican rainforest or something that very day."

"It's a definite possibility," I say. "With him, you never know."

She grins. "No, you never do. We'll probably be in town for it, though. I really want to go. You guys have told me enough about it to make me curious."

"Well, it's definitely a town staple," I say.

The White Party is an early August institution in Paradise

Shores. The summer kicks off with the Junior Regatta and ends with the White Party along the boardwalk, with tents and flowing alcohol and live music. Tickets are sold to locals and invited-by-locals, only.

"So I've heard, and I've had one too few lobster rolls this summer," Ivy says. "It's not okay. Besides, Rhys misses this place when we're not here. He doesn't say it, but he does."

"Well, it's in his blood, try as he may to fight it."

"He's fighting it less these days," she says easily. It's true. Rhys has been in Paradise more since he met her than he had ever had before.

We're all finding our way back here. Like a braid that untwisted after graduation, sending us on separate paths, is slowly starting to knot itself back together again. I'd been the first, and he'll be the last, but we'll all make it back. I'm sure of it.

Jamie and Rhys join us. She rocks back on her heels and shoots me a happy smile. Something squeezes in my chest.

"All good?" I ask.

Rhys nods, flicking through images on his camera. "Yes. Now I'll bother your chef by photographing the food." And then, muttered under his breath, "I can't believe I'm photographing *food*."

"I'll pay you in a lobster roll when you're done!" I call.

"Accepted," he says. "Oh, and I'm taking the *Frida* out later with Ivy. I want to shoot her at sunset."

Damn. I'd toyed with the idea of taking her out myself, but I nod. "Okay. And is Ivy okay with being shot? Because brother or not, I'll testify."

The girls laugh, but Rhys just rolls his eyes. "I'm not going to dignify that with a response," he says and turns on his heel, walking up toward the kitchen. I follow him. Together with Kristen, there'll be a bloodbath if I don't mediate.

But we get the shots, and I get my brother and his girl-friend a lobster roll, and somehow I end up in my back office with a memory card filled of images from the yacht club.

Jamie joins me to look through them. Her shift is technically over and she's back in her normal clothes, a pair of shorts that ride high on her thighs and an oversized shirt.

She's quiet as we scroll through the pictures. It's a thoughtful sort of quiet. I put a hand on her thigh. "What are you thinking?"

"These are good," she says. "They'll be great on the website, for marketing."

"Not about the pictures. You're thinking about something else, I can tell. It's not…what you told me the other night?"

The things she'd told me, about his negative comments, about her ex's voice sometimes overshadowing her own.

Her eyes widen. "Oh, no, not at all. No. I was just thinking about Rhys and Ivy. They're so cool."

"Cool?"

"Yes. I mean, Ivy and I spoke afterwards. She's a model. An actual model, and she's gorgeous. She's shot campaigns."

My smile widens. "They're normal people."

Jamie looks at me like I've lost my mind. "They're *not*," she insists. "Come on, Ivy is probably the most beautiful woman I've ever seen."

I laugh. "Wow," I say, tightening my hand on her leg. "Should I be worried here?"

"Come on, Parker, she's stunning!"

I shrug. "While I like my sister-in-law, the most beautiful woman I've ever seen is in this very room."

A blush creeps up her cheeks. "Don't tease me."

"Not teasing." Her skin is soft and warm beneath my hand. "Do you know how hard it's been not kissing you? When I see you walk through the restaurant, in your uniform? To not pull you into this very room?"

"Really?"

"God, yes."

Her lips part. "I didn't know that."

"I want you a great deal," I say. "The other night? I've thought about it. How it felt to kiss you on your couch."

It's the truth. And seeing the small, quick exhale of breath from her, I think it's something she needs to hear. I never want her to doubt herself again. I want to silence every single word her ex ever said.

I only want her to hear mine.

So I lean in and kiss her neck.

Jamie exhales shakily. "Oh."

"I want you," I say again, sliding my lips up to her cheek. Her ear. Back to her jaw. "And I won't pressure you, but I never want you to doubt that, either. I've thought about you so many times."

Her legs shift beneath my hand, widening in the chair. And then she's kissing me. It takes every ounce of my self-control to do nothing but kiss her back. I don't pull her onto my lap, I don't move my hand up her inner thigh.

I just kiss her back, pouring everything I've learned over the years into it. The slow, the steady, the teasing. When Jamie finally pulls back, she's red-faced and liquid-eyed. "I want you as well," she murmurs. "And I've thought about it, too."

The words send red-hot desire through me. My jeans feel uncomfortably tight, strained around the fly.

"I should get home," she continues, but her hands around my neck don't move. "To Emma. To dinner…"

"Good idea." I don't move either and catch her lips with my own for another kiss. "When can I see you again?"

"Tomorrow, probably, at work," she says, smiling against me.

"Jamie…"

She kisses me again, not long enough for my liking. "I know what you mean. I'm not sure. Soon. I'll try to get my mother out of the house."

"I have a house, too, you know. You're welcome to more than just my garage."

"What a gentleman," she whispers, and when she kisses me again, her chest against mine, I groan at the contact. Her body is too sweet.

But it doesn't last, and I can't help following her when she gets up. "Let me walk you to your bike."

"No bike today," she says, digging through her bag for her phone. "My mom is picking me up."

I kiss her temple while she sends a text. Being near her and *not* touching her is impossible. My hands, my head, my body, are all full of her. "I could drive you home, you know."

"Yes, but then everyone would see." She kisses me one final time. "She's on her way."

"Let's go."

Despite her protests, I walk her out onto the parking lot. It's mostly empty. Lunch is the yacht club's busiest time, not dinner.

"Jamie," I say.

She smiles up at me. It's a teasing, flirtatious smile, and it sets off something deep inside me. "Yes," she says. "What is it now?"

I raise an eyebrow. "Taking a tone with me?"

"You've always liked it when I argue."

"I always have," I agree. "It was the best part when Lily invited you over."

"Masochist," she says, and aims a soft kick at my shoe.

"Sadist," I reply.

She laughs and I pull her close. One last kiss. She lets me, her lips soft. I release her as quickly as I caught her. "Couldn't resist."

Jamie grins. "I'm that irresistible?"

"You really, really are. Come work out tomorrow morning. Come swim with me. Have dinner with me, have lunch with me."

"Wow." She presses her hands to her cheeks. "You're really not playing hard to get?"

The dirtiest of answers comes to mind. I open my mouth, ready to go for it, before I remember her hesitations in the bedroom. Old Jamie would love it. New Jamie might not.

But a flash of lights close by breaks off the convo. Jamie's mother is here. I aim a quick wave at the tinted window and nod goodbye to Jamie. *One day.*

18

JAMIE

"Mom," I say. "Please don't."

She shakes her head and keeps chopping chives. Her eyes are on the knife, not on me, but there's amusement in her voice. "He's a good man. He has a great job."

"Mom."

"I'm just saying, sweetheart. Everyone in town knows him."

I grit my teeth. "Yeah, I know."

She flips the knife over, attacking the herbs from another angle. "Not to mention he's Lily's older brother. You girls could become sister-in-laws."

"*Now* you remember who he is."

"What?"

"Nothing."

"All I'm saying," Mom continues, "is that I'm all for it. You deserve some fun and happiness, sweetheart."

I look up at the ceiling. The last thing I want is to discuss my love life with my mother, especially when it's a love life I very much want to keep quiet about.

But she'd seen the quick kiss in the parking lot and she's brought it up three times since.

"It's good that you're making yourself at home here

again," she continues. "This *is* your home, you know. People care about you here. Did you call Paradise Elementary for a spot for Emma? Summer's almost over."

I drum my fingers against the kitchen counter. "Not yet, no."

Her chopping stops. "Shouldn't you?"

Yes, I think. *I should.* There's a million things I should do. But every time I think of staying here permanently, something stops me. Fear. Guilt, perhaps. The knowledge that I'll need to rely on my mother for babysitting, for help, for everything until I finally get back on my feet.

"Jamie?"

But I want to stay, and so does Emma. "I'll call first thing tomorrow."

Her shoulders relax. "Great. And... maybe I should be out of the house tomorrow night."

"Why?"

"I don't know," she says, in a tone that makes it clear she does. "You know, just in case you want to have someone over in the evening."

I put my head in my hands.

"Or maybe you'd rather I watch Emma one evening and you go somewhere else, hmm? Out on a date?"

My first instinct is to say no. To deny it. But then I think of Parker's open eyes, the steady way he talks. He has no interest in hiding. And I draw strength from that.

"Tomorrow night, you said?"

Mom chuckles. "Yes. I can go over to Betty's. We've been meaning to catch up for ages."

"Thank you."

"I was young too, once," she says, but the way her eyes twinkle, I know she still is, inside. "He's someone from high school. Isn't he? You knew him well before?"

"He's still Lily's brother, yes," I say. "And she doesn't know about it. About... us, I mean."

"Ooh, intrigue. My lips are shut, *if* you promise to keep me informed."

I roll my eyes. *Not about everything,* I think. "All right, I will."

She grins at me over the food we're preparing. "It's a good thing you came home, honey. Life sure isn't boring anymore."

Turns out, Parker is free tomorrow night. He says that over the phone, calling me two minutes after I'd texted with the question. Through the phone I hear the sounds of laughter and something slamming. A door?

I'm at a family dinner, he says. But tomorrow night, at yours? Can't wait, James.

I spend the entire Friday in anticipation. At work, seeing him briefly in the back room, our eyes meeting. During my lunch break, when Lily and little Jamie come down to the yacht club to eat with me on one of the docks. The boy looks so much like his parents, and is as enamored with his uncle as I am, because he points at the yacht club several times and demands, *Parker!*

There's a brief pinch of guilt when I look at Lily's open face and easy smiles, our relationship healing, and know that I'm keeping another secret.

In the evening, Emma and I wave goodbye to my mom, and she gives me a cheeky wink that I pretend not to see. We eat as quiet of a dinner as is possible with a six-year-old, and I answer a multitude of questions about the TV show she'd watched earlier. Exactly how old are the dinosaurs, and were they alive when Grandma was a child?

No, I tell her, *and never repeat that when your grandmother can hear.*

Emma is giggly and tired when I finally put her to bed. She has a band of freckles across her nose from her time in the sun this summer and I pretend to count them. She swats my hand away. "Mommy," she admonishes me.

"Sorry," I say. "You're just too precious to me."

"I know," she says, "but you're supposed to *read* the book."

I look down at the book in question. It's her favorite, and I've read it twice already, cover to cover. "Right. Okay... So, Cinna woke up, and it was a day like every other day. Except for one little thing. What's that in the sky, Cinna asks?"

Emma giggles and pulls her stuffed rabbit closer. Try as she might, though, she can't fight against exhaustion, and I'm soon back downstairs. Waiting for Parker to show up.

Had it only been a week since we were here, doing this exact same thing? When I'd told him about Lee?

There's a quiet knock on the door, and then he's there, tall and familiar and strange all at once. Butterflies erupt in my stomach.

"Hello," I say.

"Hi," he says, and steps forward. Hands land on my waist and he kisses me hello. It turns into several kisses and the butterflies shift, turn into wanting.

He lifts his head. "It's been too long."

"It's only been a few hours."

"Yes, but that was at work."

I pretend to frown at him. "Yes, where you kissed me openly in the parking lot the other day. Guess who saw?"

"Your mother?" he says, smiling crookedly. "Will she ground you? Enforce curfew? Give you extra homework?"

"Very funny. No, she'll just ask me excruciatingly nosy questions."

"Hmm. Would I be interested in hearing the answers to those?"

"Maybe," I say. He walks me backward into the kitchen, hands still around my waist, and I feel like I'm soaring. "But that's privileged information."

He groans. "Don't use lawyer-speak on me."

"Bad memories?"

"It makes you even hotter," he says, and with a grunt he

lifts me up onto the kitchen counter, right next to the remnants of Emma's Play-Doh.

"You've lost your mind," I tell him, "but I hope you never find it."

Parker kisses me again. I don't know how long we make out for, the slow kisses, the steady ones, his hands working in my hair. I slip my fingers inside the collar of his linen shirt and feel the warm smoothness of his skin.

His hands dip to my waist. One of them finds the hem of my T-shirt and strokes the skin on my lower back.

It scrambles my thinking.

"I had lunch with your sister today," I say.

Parker shifts to my neck. "I know," he says.

"She asked me about this weekend."

"Mhm."

"About the barbecue on Sunday."

"She told me she would invite you," Parker says. His hand slides clean under my shirt and curls around my bare waist. "You should come."

"You sure?" I say. "It'll be your entire family."

"You've met them all before." His lips trail down to my collarbone, and a quick tug of my shirt exposes it to his lips. "Bring Emma."

"Emma," I whisper. "She'd like that."

"So would little Jamie. Henry's daughter isn't old enough yet for him to play with, and he can't understand why," Parker murmurs.

We kiss for another eternity. It's impossible not to agree when heat spreads through my limbs, my stomach. "I'll tell her yes, then."

"Good." Parker's hands settle on my thighs. "Jesus, I really love touching you."

I laugh. "You really do?"

"Yes, and I'll tell you all the time if you need to hear it." His hands tighten over my shorts. "I could kiss you for the rest of the night, but...?"

He doesn't want to push.

"I think I might be amenable to that," I say, smiling.

He grins back. "*Might* be? And *amenable*?"

"Uh-huh."

"You're terrible," he says, but he doesn't sound like he means it. "What did you have planned for us tonight?"

"Well… do you like building things out of clay?" I ask, looking down at the Play-Doh next to me on the counter. I feel light, about to float away, the smile etched on my face. "Or drawing? We do a lot of both in this household."

Parker chuckles. "Tempting, but no."

"Then we could watch another movie."

"True. But I'd spend most of the time trying to learn more about you." He tips my head back and kisses the spot beneath my jaw. "You told me a lot of things last time that I've been thinking about."

"Uh-huh," I say, my hands closing around the collar of his shirt. "I can imagine. But I still have questions for you."

"For me?"

"Yes. Why are you single? I half expected you to have a litter of kids by now."

He leans back, laughter in his deep blue eyes. "What? Have you been talking to my mother? My grandmother? Where did this come from?"

"I don't know. It's just, you're… you. Golden and handsome and a catch. How come you aren't off the market?"

It's easy to imagine the beautiful, statuesque wife that would match him. She'd be athletic too. Maybe a former swimmer or track runner. They'd play tennis on Sundays and go running in the mornings, and they'd have three cute kids who never threw tantrums.

I hate her.

He chuckles. "I'm a catch, James?"

"Come on, it's a serious question," I protest, unable to stop smiling. "Tell me, Marchand."

"Are you asking to figure out what's wrong with me?

Because I'll never tell you. I have no flaws." His hands tighten around my ribs, fingers fluttering.

I shriek. "Parker!"

"Is that it?"

"No," I say, laughing. "Stop it. You're a grown man!"

"Yes, and I have to spend many hours a day being one. Here with you I just want to relax." His hands relent, smoothing down my sides. "James, there's no big secret behind it."

"Behind your single life?"

"I've dated," he says evenly, "and I had a serious relationship back in Boston. But there hasn't been anyone serious in Paradise."

"Because you know everyone?"

"Because I didn't find anyone I wanted to seriously date," he says. "Maybe because the person I wanted hadn't moved back yet. Does that satisfy you, your honor?"

My breath catches in my throat. Words are beyond me, and I pull him toward me instead. Answer him with my lips.

He groans low in his throat when I deepen the kiss. My legs brace against his hips, and I'm drowning in sensation. In his words and his touch, and then I try not to think at all beyond the hungriness of his kisses and the strength of his hands on my body.

My hands tug his shirt up and, caught between our bodies, I trail my fingers over the tautness of his abdomen. Muscles tighten instinctively beneath my touch.

"Christ," he mutters against my lips. "I love it when you touch me."

My hand pauses. "You do?"

"There's nothing you can do that I wouldn't like. No mines hidden in this, in *us*. You know that, James."

I do. I do, because it's him, and it's me, and this has never been anything but safe. And I surrender to him completely. His kisses deepen, and large hands slide down to tug me toward the edge of the counter. I'm flush against his chest.

"God, yes," he murmurs when I wrap my legs around his waist. "Isn't this so much better than Play-Doh?"

I laugh and he switches to my neck, kissing a trail down to the neckline of my shirt. "Marginally," I tease.

His left hand slides up along the side of my chest, brushing past the swell of my breast, and I take a shaky breath. There's a fire in my stomach that hasn't burned there for months. Years, probably.

"Okay, a lot better," I murmur, "even if you don't know what you're missing out on."

His lips pause at the neckline of my shirt, right there, halfway down my chest. I thread my fingers into his thick head of hair. "I'll take my chances," he says, speaking the words into my skin, right above my heart.

So will I, I think, and reach for the hem of my shirt.

But even deep in the fog of desire, with the man I'd never thought I'd see again, my mom ears haven't signed off from duty. I register the telltale creak of small feet on the stairs.

I push Parker away.

"Mommy?" a thick voice asks. Emma walks into the kitchen in her purple pajamas, and in her left hand is Mr. Rabbit.

I jump off the counter. "Honey, did you just wake up?"

Emma nods and looks at the man beside me. "You're here?" she asks. It sounds like an accusation.

"Yeah. I came over to help your mom with something," Parker says. His voice is only slightly rougher than usual.

"Oh," Emma says. She blinks at us, eyes sleepy. Then she smiles. "Did you like the cookie?"

"I did, yes. Very much. Did you bake it?"

"Yes, with Mommy and Granny. Mommy said she would bring you one."

"She did. It was very good. Was it your idea to put M&M's in it?"

Emma shifts from one foot to the other and yawns so large

I can see her tonsils. It makes me smile, and beside me, Parker chuckles.

But she manages a nod.

I bend to smooth her hair back. "Ready to go back to bed, honey?"

"Mm. I'm thirsty."

"Let's get you something to drink, then," I say. But when I turn around Parker is already on it, filling up one of the clean glasses drying by the sink.

Emma drains half of it and yawns again. I bend to lift her up. "Come on, sleepyhead. Let's go upstairs."

She rests her chin on my shoulder. "Read the book."

"Again? We read it before."

"Again," she says. We're halfway through the living room when a request stops me in my tracks. "I want the captain to read it."

The captain in question—he's never going to get over being called this, I think—hears her.

"You sure?" he asks Emma. His eyes are blue and serious on hers. "I might not be as good at it as Mom."

Emma buries her head in my neck, bravery forgotten. "I'm sure," she mumbles.

Parker looks at me. There's hesitant surprise in his eyes.

"Only if you want to," I mouth.

He nods. "Let's go upstairs."

That's how I find myself standing in the doorway to my daughter's new bedroom, watching Parker sit down on the very edge of Emma's purple bed. It makes me smile to see how he tries to make himself small, the gentle way he moves in her space. "This is the book?"

"Yes. It has a funny name." Emma pulls the comforter up past her nose, muffling her voice. "Seg id."

"Huh?"

"Say it."

"Oh." Parker flips the book over. *"Cinna and the Flying Cinnamon Buns,"* he says.

Emma erupts in giggles beneath her comforter.

"You're right. That is a funny name." Parker opens it to the first page. I watch as he reads words that are too familiar to me now, a script I've stopped reacting to, and hear them for the first time. He's warm and gentle with her. He emphasizes words that make her laugh, and when he notices she's starting to drift off, he lowers his voice. It's deep and soothing in the room.

I could fall asleep to it too.

And when she's out like a light, he gently puts the book down on her night table, and puts her beloved bunny next to her on the pillow.

"Thank you," I tell him. He pulls me close and presses his lips to my forehead, and I close my eyes, hoping this isn't just a dream.

19

JAMIE

"Who will be there?" Emma asks, for the third time. She's walking beside me on the sidewalk, putting one sandal after the other in an attempt to walk in a perfect line.

I tell her again, starting with the people she knows. Lily, little Jamie, Hayden, and Parker.

"Jamie is very small," she says.

I smile at that. "He's only two years younger than you, sweetie."

"I was a baby two years ago."

"Well, you were smaller than you are now, yes. But not quite a baby."

She drags her feet when we pass the gelato shop, but after a short discussion, we decide to postpone ice cream to tomorrow. Saying *tomorrow* instead of *today* really is the hallmark of great parenting, I've learned.

"Why was the captain at our house the other night?" she asks.

I reach for her hand as we cross the street. "Well, you know we work together."

"At the restaurant."

"Yes."

"But, that's there. Not at our house."

"No, that's true, but I help him with other things. Like building a website for the restaurant so people can find out what's on the menu before they come."

"Why?"

"Well, some people like to know in advance."

She frowns. "Why?"

"Some are allergic. Others aren't sure they'll like the food and want to make sure before they go."

"Oh," she says. She's quiet for a long time, face lost in thought, and not for the first time I wish I could read her mind. We pass mansion after impressive mansion on Ocean Drive. Most are more window than wall, all to make the most of the ocean view.

"Mommy? I've been thinking."

The tone in her voice makes me smile. Absolutely anything could follow that statement. "Oh? What about?"

"I don't miss Daddy anymore."

It takes me a deep breath to hide my shock. "You don't?"

"No," Emma says. There's only calm in her voice, a child's easy self-confidence. "I did before. But he never played with me and he hasn't come to visit us."

"No," I murmur. "No, he hasn't."

And thank God for that.

"I like Granny more. And I like it here. Can I learn sailing this fall? In my new school?"

I have to swallow. "Um, not yet, honey. You have to be eight to start sailing. Remember? We've spoken about that."

"The captain can teach me. He said so last weekend on the boat. Well, he promised little Jamie too, but he's too small." She tugs her hand out of mine and climbs onto the small ledge cornering off Lily and Hayden's front yard, arms out to keep her balance. "So don't feel bad, Mommy."

"Feel bad?"

"About Daddy," she says. "Do you miss him?"

There's a time when dishonesty is okay with your kid. Ice

cream tomorrow instead of today, Mommy didn't bring her wallet so we can't go to the toy store.

This doesn't feel like one of those times.

While I wish I could undo Lee, that I could shelter her from this, that I had a perfect father to give her... I don't have any of those things.

And so I don't lie. "No, honey. I don't."

"I didn't think so," she says, sounding satisfied with herself. Then we've arrived, and she asks me about who'll be here again, and the conversation slips away from me.

We're not the first to arrive, but we're not the last, either. Hayden, Lily, Parker, and Henry are sitting in the backyard together with their parents. The grill is already going and on the ground is a small bubble machine. Little Jamie is sitting in front of it, happily swatting at them.

Emma immediately forgets her shyness. She rushes forward and starts to catch them, her favorite activity.

"Parker brought it," Lily says, by way of greeting, and looks at her brother. "Are you a child yourself? Sometimes I wonder."

He rolls his eyes and turns to me. "Hi, Jamie."

"Hello," I say, and struggle to hide my smile.

The rest of the introductions are swift. Their parents, Michael and Eloise, are like they've always been. One is curt where the other is verbose, and both know how to wield words well. Both love their family, too, with a fierceness I've always admired, even when I know their children have some-times resented the pressure that accompanied it.

"Where's your lovely wife?" I ask Henry.

He nods toward the house. "With the baby. She's teething, and I don't know if it's worse for the baby or for her parents."

"Tough stage," I say. "It seems like it lasts forever when you're in it, too."

His eyes light up. "How long did it last for you and Emma?" he asks, and just like that, we're adults who can have an adult conversation, with the awkwardness I'd always felt around Lily and Parker's older siblings melting away. We're not teenagers anymore.

Ivy and Rhys are the last to arrive. I watch them all interact and feel the same warm envy settle in my chest, watching the large family. It's not intrusive, the feeling, and it's not malicious. I'm grateful to be here.

Emma sits next to me when we eat. Michael has cooked lobster tails on the grill, and there's potato salad, watermelon, lamb skewers and dinner rolls. A veritable surf and turf feast.

Parker sits on Emma's other side. When she stares at her lobster roll he's there, helping her crack it open, and is rewarded with a giggle when the shell snaps.

"Feel like trying it?" he asks. "It tastes pretty good. My restaurant sells thousands of these."

"Thousands?"

"Oh, yes. Maybe *millions.*"

And my fussy little daughter, who is a picky eater on the best of days, pops the thing into her mouth. "It tastes like the sea!" she says, and reaches for a second bite.

Lobster. Figures.

After dinner I find myself sitting on the grass with Lily, watching as our kids race across the lawn. There's a hula hoop and a loosely defined game that involves chasing it as it rolls. The sun is setting and there's a light summer chill in the air, and I think about how much I love my life.

How grateful I am to be back here.

Lily leans against my shoulder, and I wonder if she's thinking the same thing.

"They're good together," she comments, nodding to our kids.

I snort. "When they're not trying to kill each other, yes." I'd appreciated the bubble machine, but they'd managed to headbutt each other as they fought to pop bubbles.

Lily chuckles. "They'll grow out of it."

"Do you know what I did yesterday?" I ask.

"No? Tell me."

"I called the school to see if they had a place for Emma this fall."

Her eyes widen, and then she bursts into a smile. "You did?"

"Yes. They had space." I echo her smile, feeling light, so light. "It'll be hard to stay. I'll be leaning on my mother *a lot*. But I really want to, if I'm able."

"Oh, Jamie, that's wonderful. You know you can lean on us too, right? I'm happy to watch Emma whenever."

"Thank you. Truly. I don't..." I shake my head, knowing there are no words. "Thanks."

Emma crawls across the grass to me. There will be stains on her dress, and I won't begrudge her a single one. "Mom?"

"Yes?"

She puts a hand on my knee. "Can you ask the captain to come read Cinna again tonight?"

"Um, I'm not sure if he's able to, honey. He has his own life to live." I focus on her inquisitive eyes and not on those of my best friend, which have no doubt sharpened.

"He did good voices," she says. And then, remembering herself, "But you're very good too, Mommy."

"Thank you," I say.

She turns back toward the hula hoop. Little Jamie is struggling to get it rolling and she launches to her feet, off to the rescue.

I avoid looking at Lily.

She won't have any of it, of course.

"Jamie," she says. "Did I just hear what I *think* I heard?"

"You heard nothing."

"Pretty sure I did."

"Pretty sure you didn't."

A pair of boat shoes and tanned legs step between us. I recognize them both, and close my eyes. Damn.

"You ladies need any more lemonade?" Parker asks.

"No," his sister says. "But I'm about to demand some answers."

"What?"

She pats the grass beside her. "Have a seat, my dearest brother."

Parker recognizes her tone of voice immediately. He's had more practice with it than me. "And if I say no?"

"No is not an option."

With a sigh, he sinks down beside us. "Never have a sister," he tells little Jamie. The boy doesn't pay us any attention, but it makes Lily snort.

"He should be so lucky."

"Lily," I say.

Her gaze shifts to mine. "I have to ask. You know I have to ask. Parker, why were you at Jamie's house the other night, reading a goodnight story to Emma?"

I groan and look up at the sky. This is it. When she finds out and she tells us both off for it. When she pulls back her forgiveness for my years of silence.

How could you keep this from me?

"I was spending time with Jamie," is Parker's measured response. "We're friends."

Lily's green eyes narrow. There's speculation there, and like a dog with a bone, she's not going to let it go. I know that.

So I come clean. "I'm sorry for not telling you, Lily."

She bursts into a squeal. "Oh my God. Seriously? The two of you? *Together?*"

"Jesus," Parker mutters. "Scream it louder, why don't you? The neighbors didn't hear you."

"It's very new," I say, "and I don't think either of us know exactly what it is yet. Please don't be angry."

"Angry?" Lily asks. She turns to Parker with a grin. "You're helping me make sure Jamie stays in town?"

He snorts. "Yes, I'm dating your best friend as a favor to you."

"Really?"

"Of course not."

"This is wonderful," she says, looking between the two of

us. "I mean, unexpected. Although maybe not. You always squabbled as teenagers, didn't you? There was definite chemistry there. Hmm. This could become something serious. Oh my God. Our kids will be *cousins*, Jamie."

Both Parker and I open our mouths to protest, I'm sure, but she cuts us off.

"Oh, don't worry, I won't jinx it. I won't embarrass you either. No one else needs to know while the two of you figure it out. But oh, I'm so excited!"

Parker lies back in the grass and puts a muscled arm over his face. "Lily," he says. "Know when to be quiet."

She makes a small sound of outrage and turns to me for backup. I don't know what she sees in my expression—I'm still half expecting her to be upset—but she shuts her mouth. And puts her hand on my arm.

"I get it," she says. "I won't push."

I release the breath I'd been holding. "Thanks, Lily."

"But you know I'm on both of your sides, right? And I can help and listen to either side. I'll be neutral. I'm like Switzerland!"

I laugh. It intensifies when Parker, still stretched out beside us on the grass, says in a dry voice, "I've never once needed your help with my dating life, Lily. Not about to start now."

"All right, all right," she says, holding her hands up. She's grinning. "He's prickly today, isn't he?"

I don't get a chance to answer her, because her son comes barrelling between us. He's seen his uncle prone on the ground and takes the opportunity to attack, throwing himself over Parker's torso.

Parker lets out a pained *oof* and turns in the grass, little Jamie shrieking. I watch them roughhouse with an almost painful feeling in my chest.

Emma comes up beside me and I wrap an arm around her waist. She's watching Parker and his nephew intently.

"Want to join in?" Lily asks. She's leaning back, resting on her hands, and gives my daughter an encouraging smile. "The big one is really ticklish, and the smaller one loves to play tag."

Emma looks at Lily for a long moment. And then, decision made, she runs out of my arms and into the fray.

Lily leans closer and we watch them together. They're tackling Parker to the ground, and he groans, feigning defeat.

"He's a good man," Lily says softly.

Yes, I think, watching him, and watching Emma. *He's the very best.*

20

PARKER

She's in my garage gym the next morning, being distracting as hell, and I wouldn't have her anywhere else.

"Like this?" Jamie asks. She's deadlifting with my weight bar. It's got the lightest plates. Today's goal is just to nail the form.

"Yeah, keep your back straight… yes, like that. Knees just lightly bent. Don't lock them out."

She's gotten stronger, has thrown herself against my weights like they're another challenge to conquer. Jamie does a set of ten and sets the bar down. "That one hurts."

"It's great for your back," I say and put a hand on the body part in question. Just to make my point clearer. She's working out in a tank top today and the fabric is thin beneath my hand.

She smiles up at me. It'll never stop warming me, seeing just how easy the expression comes to her face these days.

So I kiss her. It's not the first time today. Won't be the last either. Jamie turns in my arms and puts her hands on my arms. Her fingers flex, gently, and I want to feel them all over.

"You're sweaty," she murmurs, sliding them up to my neck. "I like it."

"You do?"

"Mhm."

I turn to kiss the side of her neck. She smells so good, the scent of warm skin, soap, faint sweat, and something else, something that's only her.

"Our workouts are getting longer," she says, "but we're working out less."

I chuckle. "It's the only time of day I can get you alone."

Her hands tighten around my neck. "Is that okay? I know I'm not as available as most women you've dated."

I lift my head. "Of course it is. You're a mom, Jamie. That comes first."

Her eyes turn serious. "Yes, and that's never going to change. Emma and I are a package deal. I have to put her first, and after Lee, my child's my main focus."

I smooth my thumb over her cheek. "Jamie," I say. "We don't have to see one another every day to know where we have one another."

"No," she says, "we don't."

"I want you, and I like you, and we're seeing where things go. Right?"

A smile warms her lips. "Yes. I think you might be the best thing that's happened to me all year."

I raise an eyebrow. "Is that so?"

"Yes." There's a vulnerability in her eyes, but there's happiness there too, and I can't believe we're here. At this point together, the two of us. We don't need old arguments or banter to tie us together. We're not hiding behind any facades.

"You coming back to Paradise is the best thing that happened to me this year, too."

"It is?"

"Yes." I bend to touch my lips to her ear. "You've been invaluable to my business."

Jamie laughs and pushes me away, pretending to swat me. "You're impossible."

I catch her around the waist and kiss her, to show her just how much I'm joking. The kisses deepen, and like always, the fire of desire inside me flares. The constant make-out sessions have put me on edge. I don't think I've made out this much before seven AM in... ever.

Not that I'm complaining, only it's the most non-sex contact I've gotten since high school or college, probably, and my body is taking notice.

But nothing matters more than her comfort levels.

So I'm surprised when her hands tug at the hem of my T-shirt. I lean back and ask her with a glance, *Really?* She nods, so I pull it off and toss it into the corner.

Her eyes fall over my chest, a look of quiet appreciation on her face. And that, right there, is enough to make me feel ten feet tall. When we kiss again, her hands roam free. And I hadn't realized how good it would feel. How much I've craved it.

She runs them over my back and I groan against her mouth. Thank God for the elastic waist of my workout shorts tucking my erection flat against my stomach, or she would realize just how much I want her.

Jamie's hands come to rest on my chest. "Take off mine too," she whispers.

My hands still on her waist. "Are you sure?"

"Yes."

So I find the hem of her tank top and slowly inch it up over her smooth skin, over the sports bra, until it joins my T-shirt in the corner.

"You're so beautiful," I murmur, smoothing my hands down her waist. All I see is skin, and the soft swell of her breasts beneath the elastic. "Stunning."

Jamie shakes her head, almost like she wants to protest, and kisses me again. We end up against the long wall of my garage. My foot hits a kettlebell but the pain barely registers.

Her breasts flatten against my chest and I've never hated fabric more than I do with this piece of elastic.

"Parker," she whispers, hands knotted in my hair.

I nod. Words are too hard to form, and my hand stills on her rounded hip. She's still wearing shorts.

Can we take those off too?

"Are you in your head again?" I ask.

"A little bit," she confesses.

I try to think through the haze of desire. Identify the things she's told me. But it's hard, so I just lean my forehead against hers and speak the truth. "There's nothing you can do wrong here, Jamie. Nothing that would turn me off. I'm so hard for you, it's stupid. I'm like a teenager with a boner." I laugh at the confession, at the widening of her eyes. "And if you wanted to stop I'd do that in a heartbeat, too. No wrong decisions. But, James? If a single thing in that head of yours is about me and my wants, or doubts about yourself... banish them. You're all I want."

Jamie digs her teeth into her lower lip. "I should probably get going. Emma will wake up soon."

I close my eyes. Struggle against the wave of desire. "Of course, baby."

"But maybe I should shower first."

"Yeah."

"Do you want to join me?"

It takes me a moment to process her words, to open my eyes. She's looking at me, and there it is again. The mixture of the strong and the vulnerable.

"Yes," I say. She's never been inside my house. Somehow that's escaped us, and I should give her a tour. But my mind is clouded.

Soap. Skin. Water. And I want her beneath my hands so badly.

"This place is so you," she says, voice teasing, as we walk through my living room.

"It is?"

"This style of couch, the giant TV. Are those your trophies? Is that from the Junior Regatta trophy?"

I lead her away from the bookcase. "Don't comment."

"I never saw you win it," she says. "Did you lift it high above your head on the docks?"

"Shush, you."

"Did all the girls swoon?"

"Not you, clearly," I say and hold the door open to the bathroom. "Are you stalling?"

Jamie looks at me. In her shorts, her sports bra, her braided hair... I can't fucking wait to touch her again.

"Absolutely not," she says and steps past me into the bathroom.

I don't know what happens, exactly. Only that at the end of it I'm standing beneath the hot spray of water in my workout shorts and watching Jamie gently unbraids her hair. It falls in waves around her face. The freckles have intensified, and they stretch across her chest, too. Small, intoxicating patterns I want to trace.

"Parker," she says.

I swallow. "Anything you want to do. Anything you don't want to do. It's all okay."

She smiles a bit, and nods, and steps into the shower with me. It dampens her hair and turns it dark brown.

It darkens her sports bra, too, the soaked fabric revealing hard nipples. Need explodes in my stomach. I need to get the thing off. And yet I force myself to go slow, to shield her from the spray and kiss her thoroughly... but I can't stop my hands from roaming. She exhales softly into my mouth and I'm lost, wet skin beneath my palms.

Her fingertips trace my chest. My biceps. Down my forearms. I don't know that anyone's ever studied me like this before.

Jamie reaches for the bottle of body wash and it slips out of her fingers, the cap twisting off. We both laugh at it, breathless and heated. And then she's using her lathered up hands on me. "You're bigger up close," she says, running a slow palm over the side of my chest.

"You're stroking my ego?"

"Maybe," she says. "You've stroked mine plenty already."

It's safer to look down, to watch her hands on me, than to watch her own wet body. But even that is sensual. Her hands with the short clean fingernails, long fingers, no rings. They look pale against my skin—she's not out in the sun enough—as they trace across my abs.

"Jamie," I say. I don't know if it's a plea to stop or to continue. The bulge in my shorts looks obscene against the wet fabric and feels just as painful.

She lets her hands drift to her own chest, and to the band of her sports bra. "Maybe you should wash me."

"I can do that." My voice comes out hoarse. And then I see the hesitation in her eyes, remember the things she's told me. And a sharp tendril of hatred toward her ex cuts right through my dizzying need.

I find her hips and curl my hands around them, the wide hipbones and the soft indents above her waist. No one's skin should be as soft as hers.

"Don't be scared, James," I say. "Not of me, and not of us. You've got all the power here. You can see how turned on I am, right?"

Her lips twist, and there's the flash of fire in her eyes that I love. That I'm used to. She glances down at my workout shorts. "You're big there too?"

"Whatever you want to do, I'm game. And if you want to stop? Just let me kiss you here in the shower? I'm okay with that too," I say. Even if my balls might be bright blue by the time we're done.

Her smile stretches into a grin. "And let you be braver than me? No way."

She reaches for the hem of her sports bra and tugs it up, over the roundedness of her tits. They pop free beneath the band and I groan at the sight. Perfectly rounded and topped with pink, rosy nipples that point directly at me.

Jamie struggles to get the wet fabric over her head and I help her. "There," she says, tossing it to the side.

Standing in front of me in only her wet panties and glistening droplets, travelling down the curves of her body.

"You're staring," she says.

"It's impossible not to." My thumbs dig into the groove right next to her hipbones. "You're so beautiful."

She laughs and reaches for the body wash. "Right," she says, cheeks heating. "Come on."

I don't need to be asked twice. My hands slide easily across her wet skin, aided by the soap, over the grooves of her spine, the roundedness of her hips, and brushing beneath the heavy weight of her breasts.

"Jesus," I murmur, letting myself finally cup them. Enjoy the feel of her hard nipples beneath my thumbs, smoothing back and forth. They're a perfect handful.

She shivers at my touch and turns her face up. The kisses aren't soft and hesitant now. They're heated, and when she presses herself against me and I feel the soft roundness of her breasts flatten against my chest, I have to think about famine and expense reports and an incorrectly tied knot to stop myself from erupting.

Especially when my erection is still trapped in my workout shorts, and pressed against her stomach, giving it delicious friction.

It's not a conscious thing, the way we end up. Her against the tile wall of my shower and my hand on the back of her knee, lifting her leg up to my hip. The way my hips grind between her legs.

"Parker," she whispers, and it's the most beautiful thing I've ever heard. "*Parker.*"

I find her nipple with my mouth and suckle hard. The rosy bud tautens and I cup the other with my free hand. Can't get enough. Will never get enough, and between her legs, my hips are softly thrusting. Every brush of friction feels like the sweetest hell.

Her hand knots in my hair. "Parker," she says again. "Let me feel you."

Yes. I reach for the edge of her dark underwear. They're luscious on her, the high-cut fabric holding to her body, but she stops my hand. Her eyes are liquid on mine.

"No. Like this…" she says, and slides her hand inside the tight elastic of my shorts.

The first brush of her fingers has me groaning. It's a tentative swipe across the head, sending molten heat up my shaft. She murmurs something that sounds like *wow*. Her hand lies flat against the length, still tucked against my stomach, and I can't take it. I reach for the elastic of my shorts and tug them down. Kick them off.

"Jamie," I say. "I haven't been this hard in forever."

A wicked smile spreads across her face and she leans back against the tile wall, her hand tightening around my cock. "Really?"

"Yes," I grind out. She starts to stroke, lazy movements of her hand, aided by the soapy water. Lightning rackets up my spine.

I can't look away from her. The excited, teasing look in her eye, the length of her neck, her beautiful tits with their rosy nipples, her soft waist, the damp fabric of her panties and her long legs. Leaning against the wall… and stroking me.

It's my ideal fantasy come to life.

I brace my hands against the tile wall on either side of her and widen my stance, letting her get acquainted with me. She can do whatever she wants.

Her hand speeds up and I groan in response.

"You like this," she murmurs. "How about when I do… this?" Her fingers form a tight ring that passes over my head and I curse, my hips bucking once. She laughs and does it again, and again, and I have to close my eyes to keep from coming too soon.

Goodbye, beautiful tits. You're too good.

She adds her other hand to my base, and then down below to cup my balls, tight with need, and I can't think anymore. No rational thought at all. It's left me, disappeared right down the drain.

"Tell me what you like," she says. "I want to make you…" Her words trail off, like she's oddly shy to say the last bit. I shift down to my forearms, on the tile, and let my hips guide the motion.

"Like that," I mutter. My own hand grips her smaller one, tightens it slightly around me. "Near the end I need it faster. Right there… fuck yes, baby. The head is the most sensitive. You can squeeze here—"

And then she does, and I have to kiss her, have to have her, have to get closer. My hips buck into her tight grip and with her mouth beneath mine I come, lighting flaring up my spine, my legs, through and out my cock. I groan against her lips, my whole body tightening with each release.

Her hands grow slow, and soft, and I shiver at the pleasure-pain across my too-excited skin. I open my eyes to find her smiling up at me in victory, and it's the hottest thing I've ever seen.

I need this woman in my life, I think. It's such a hit of post-orgasm clarity that I grip her to me. Only then do I realize I've marked her thighs and stomach.

"Shit," I murmur. "I was supposed to clean you up."

Jamie wraps her arms around my neck. "This was better."

"Well, you know I agree." I kiss her deeply, and thoroughly, and think about ways to persuade her to come to bed with me. Let me return the favor slowly and methodically.

She rests her head against my shoulder beneath the warm spray and lets me soap her down, washing away my pleasure.

"You just blew my mind," I tell her. "I can't believe that just happened."

"I live to impress, Marchand."

"Well, you succeeded." I run a finger along the edge of her underwear. "I want to reciprocate, you know. Feels ungentlemanly of me not to. But if you want to save that for the future…?"

She nods, a note of shyness entering her voice. "Yes. You can think of ways to do it."

"That's a challenge," I say, stunned. "One I accept."

She laughs again and I reach for her hair, running the wet tresses through my fingers. "Come with me to the White Party this weekend," I surprise myself by saying.

She lifts her head from my shoulder. "Really?"

"Yes. We could go together, enjoy the open bar, and swipe some of the catering to bring back to Emma."

Her eyes are open on mine. No makeup, just wet eyelashes and cheeks flushed with the heat. "But your family will be there."

"Yes," I say with a shrug. "But Lily already knows about us. The others won't comment."

I'll make sure of that.

"Besides, we won't show up with a giant sign above our heads that says we're dating. But I'll know, and you'll know, that we came together." I bend my head, speak the next words in her ear. "Let me be your date, Jamie."

I don't know why this matters. But it feels like it does, another puzzle piece in Jamie's return to Paradise.

She looks at me for a long time. Then she smiles, and it feels like the sun emerging after a rainy day. "Okay," she says. "I'll go with you."

I grin, and kiss her, and when we finally make it out of the shower and she sees the time she has to run back home.

Best workout ever.

21

JAMIE

I'm waiting by the porch of my mother's house. The late summer air is hot and thick with late-blooming flowers, the sun is unchallenged by any clouds, and I'm giddy with nerves.

Emma and my mom aren't home. They'd left a few hours earlier for the beach. My mother hadn't been interested in attending a White Party for years, doesn't share the same circle as Eloise and Michael Marchand, and Emma was excited about her new sandcastle equipment.

She'd *oohed* about my outfit before she left. *You look so pretty!* The white dress was a splurge, with all of my earnings earmarked for my savings account, and here I took a little bit out. But it had been on sale and I'd been unable to resist and here I am, standing on the porch of the house I grew up in and waiting for a man to come pick me up.

I feel like I'm living out an alternate reality, like I'm sixteen again. Like the past decade-plus never happened.

What would it have been like? If we'd done this a lot earlier? If I had my bad decisions in front of me instead of in the rearview mirror.

He comes walking up the street toward me and I lean against the porch, watching him. He's wearing navy chinos and a white linen shirt. The dark blond hair is darker. Still a bit wet from his shower. I can identify it, even from this distance.

I can't stop my excited smile.

Parker sees it, and an answering grin spreads across his own face. He bounds up the stairs in his old sailing shoes and stops in front of me. The same man I've known almost all my life, and yet brand new.

"Hi, gorgeous," he says. "You look stunning."

"You cleaned up pretty well yourself."

His lips lift. "I've been known to wear a shirt once or twice. Now, James, I'm planning on kissing you hello. But is this door about to be opened by a six-year old?"

I shake my head. "She's by the beach."

"Perfect," he says, and lowers his head to kiss me. Warmth travels through the simple, considerate touch all the way down to my feet.

We walk toward the boardwalk and the park with the gazebo that houses the yearly White Party. With each step, nerves rise in my stomach. There will be people from high school there, old teachers, friends of my mother's, friends of my grandparents.

Parker puts a hand on my lower back and bends to speak in my ear. He smells like soap and cologne and I think of his groan in the shower earlier this week, when he'd looked at me like he might die if he couldn't have me. "If you want to leave at any point, you just tell me," he murmurs. "Okay?"

"Okay," I say, and bump my elbow into his side. "But I was promised food first."

He chuckles. "I've heard the restaurant catering is excellent."

A live band is playing music in the gazebo, and beneath the marquees are tables filled with food, courtesy of the yacht club restaurant. I see the familiar kitchen staff. They'll see us, too, I realize. Me and Parker together.

Everyone will.

It doesn't take long for Parker to draw the attention of party-goers. He knows everyone, I realize, as the third couple stops us.

"Great job on the renovation," a man says, slapping Parker on the shoulder. "The place somehow looks the same but ten times better."

Parker smiles. "I'll take it."

"We tried the new menu last week," his wife says. "The chowder was divine. A cheat meal, perhaps, but a hundred percent worth it."

The same kind of small talk continues with person after person. I remain by his side and try to scan the crowd for Lily and Hayden.

"We even signed up to the newsletter!" a person says. "I heard there might be live music Fridays?"

"Yes." Parker motions to me beside him. "That was Jamie's idea. She's the new graphic and web designer for the club."

Five pairs of eyes turn to look at me. "Is that so?" one of them asks.

I clear my throat. "Yes. You can reserve a table online, too, now."

A man I vaguely recognize nods. "About time. You've got a great head on your shoulders, Parker, to surround yourself with talented people."

That's how Michael Marchand finds us, with his son congratulated on a business endeavor he himself hadn't originally supported.

"You made it," he says to us both. "The food is good, Parker. You hired a new chef?"

"I did, yes."

"My son, the restauranter," Michael says. "Well, there's no denying it. Your changes are popular."

"That's been my impression too," Parker says. His voice is so smooth, so at ease, it's hard to imagine him as anything but unbothered. But I can see as he puts on the smile, like when I pin my name tag to my shirt at work.

Lily and her mother join us, and then Hayden arrives and gives Parker a half hug, and the party becomes a Marchand family reunion.

"This is as good a time to announce it as any," Parker says to us all. "I've bought a boat."

Lily is the first to react. "What?!"

Eloise grabs her son's arm. "Tell me it's not to sail around the world. Non, I won't have it."

Parker gives her a half smile. "She could, but she would need a lot of work before getting to that stage."

Michael's eyes are sharp. "Tell me about her."

They connect, as they always have, about sailing. It's always been a cult in this town and them the most devoted of disciples. At one point Hayden chimes in and immediately attracts Lily's ire.

"You knew about this?" she accuses.

He grins at her. "Yes."

"I swore him to secrecy," Parker says, hands up. "Didn't want to jinx anything before the seller accepted my offer."

Michael grills his son about the boat. They step aside, and speak in nautical terms I have no hope of understanding. Lily drags me away, and the following hour is spent in a daze of good food, nice company, and copious amounts of small talk.

Lily insists on introducing me to our old friends in town. There weren't many, but some are left, and she's clearly gotten closer with them over the years.

It's a dizzying amount of names and incredulity. Is it really you, Jamie? Yes, it really is. Are you back, for good? Yes, I am. Where are you staying? What are you doing? *What, where, how, who, why?*

My eyes note the perfectly blow-dried hair, and dresses ten times the price of mine, as they share a laugh about the PTA at Paradise Elementary.

A cold sweat breaks out across my back when they start

talking about their husbands. *What's my official story about Lee?* Avoidance has been the one so far. But if I'm staying here, it won't be good enough, not when Emma starts school.

Lily has always known my moods better than I have myself. She excuses us after a particularly lengthy discussion about mortgages—*I am so far from being a home owner*—and walks us toward the drinks table.

"That was a lot," she says.

I nod. "Yeah."

"They're nice, and they mean well. But they're sometimes best consumed in small doses."

I laugh weakly and accept another glass of white wine. "Yeah, I can see that. But you eat brunch with them? Have playdates with your kids?"

She shrugs, looking almost embarrassed. "Yes. They're not you, Jamie, or how we were, but it's a community. I think you can like them. If you were to give them a chance."

That makes me nod. Once, I'd been quick to judge everyone. Life has taught me better than that. "You're right. I will, I promise."

She nods, but her eyes quickly sparkle with interest. We're alone and she can ask the question she's been dying to. "So you came as my brother's date?"

I take a deep sip of the wine. "I plead the fifth."

She laughs. "He gave me an earful after the barbecue."

"He did?"

"God, yes." Lily rolls her eyes. "He was so protective of you, it was silly. Don't put any pressure on her, don't force her to label anything. Don't tell anyone. And Lily, don't you dare ask for any intimate details."

She parodies Parker's voice with the skill only a younger sister has and I can't help but smile. "He said all that?"

"Oh, yes. It was like he was afraid you'd get spooked or something if I added any pressure. I told him, very sternly I might add, that you're not made of glass. Whatever you've gone through, I know you, Jamie, and you've got a spine of steel."

I have to swallow. "Thank you. I don't know about all that, though. I think I forgot who I was for a few years."

Her gaze softens. "It's a good thing you're home, then, and surrounded by people who can remind you of it."

We're joined by an old high school teacher and the party spins ever onwards, conversation after polite conversation. I'm aware of where Parker is throughout. My eyes are drawn to him. I can see him across the crowd, holding court, a glass of red wine in his hand. At ease even here. The same golden steadiness radiates from him wherever he goes. If an accident happened, if a guest fell into the water, the yacht club ran out of food, I know exactly who'd take the lead. Him.

And he'd do it all without complaining.

The group Parker's with all laughs at something he says. Effortless, I think. Life beside him would mean more of these events. Would mean everyone talking to him, to us, all the time.

He would constantly have to justify being with me. Others wouldn't understand. He could have anyone.

My gaze snags on a woman standing by the buffet. Her profile is strikingly familiar, and suddenly I'm back in high school, watching Blair Davids.

She was in the same grade as Parker and I'd always suspected they'd dated for a while. She looks like a polished version of her eighteen-year-old self, with beautiful blonde hair and a happy smile. And as I watch she waves to Parker.

He gives her a smile back and they talk, exchange a half hug. It's nothing special. Just friendly.

But they look so good together. The kind of woman he should be dating.

"Jamie, dear," Eloise Marchand says, bringing me back into the conversation. "Spotted someone you know?"

Dear. Lily's mother had always called me dear, and my artistic pursuits *inspired*, even when I was clearly not her first

188

pick of friends for her daughter. She'd hated my nose piercing and she'd once called my hairstyle a travesty. But she had never once been disrespectful of me as Lily's best friend.

Would I be good enough for her son?

"Yes, I'm sorry," I say. "Most of the town is here. It's a beautiful event—even better than I remember them."

She preens, and above her glass of wine, Lily winks at me. I haven't forgotten the way to her mother's heart.

I excuse myself a few minutes later to check my phone. It's late afternoon, and my mother and Emma should be back home by now. My mom is brilliant at check-ins. As if she knows just how nervous I am about Emma, she sends me updates all the time.

The latest one is in, making me grin. *We have sand everywhere. I'm going to have to scrub our scalps.*

But the second message on the screen melts my smile right off my face. It's from Lee.

You went back to the town you grew up in, didn't you? And here I thought you were serious about being independent. That town sounded like nothing but safety nets and money. Everything you once said you hated. Think you'll fit in now? Or that I'll let my daughter grow up in a place like that? She's too good for it, and you've sunk too low for it.

I read the words again. And again. Every sentence is a carefully designed dagger, my mind reading it in his voice, and dread unfurls its night-black wings in my stomach.

He's right.

I'll never fit in. This summer has been one long game of pretend. Who do I think I am? To show up at the White Party with Parker?

I start walking down the boardwalk, away from the party, fighting the urge to run. Emma is my first instinct. The next is the ocean. If I swim far enough I'll disappear, and so will my problems.

A gust of wind sweeps in from the waves. It catches my hair and untangles the careful curls I'd made in front of the mirror earlier. I take a deep breath and let the salty air wash away the dark haze of his text.

Lee is wrong.

I know that.

It takes me another minute to shake off the yoke of the message, of his words, of his voice in my head.

And then real terror kicks in.

He knows where I am. And he won't let his daughter grow up here. Which means it's only a matter of time before he's here.

22

JAMIE

I make it to Paradise Point, to the bench right at the outcrop. The late-afternoon sun is starting to drop, hinting at a warm evening to come. I'm far enough away now that I can't hear the music.

And they can't hear me.

Panic rises in my chest like a tidal wave. Lee can't come to this town, with these people, with me. With Emma. The scenarios build upon one another until they tower around me, a wall I can't look over. I'm trapped.

I sink onto the bench and focus on my breath, drawing it into my lungs with heavy inhales. Something wet is running down my cheeks and I wipe at the tears. I can't believe he can do this to me with just one text.

I thought I was stronger than this. That I'd come further.

"Jamie?"

I look down at my shoes and try my best to ignore the voice. There's a golden buckle around each of my ankles.

"Jamie, my God, are you all right?" Parker's voice is closer, and the bench creaks softly beneath me. "Do you need help? Are you hurt?"

I shake my head and a half-crazed, half-sobbed laugh escapes me.

"Okay, baby. Just breathe, then." He puts a large hand on my back, rubbing it in circles.

I do what he says, several long breaths, and then my sobbing breaks out in full force. It feels ridiculous. And the ridiculousness of it, of crying here, in front of the ocean, next to *him* of all people, makes me cry even harder. What if everything I've built here has been a dream?

"Jamie," he murmurs and draws me into his arms. He does it effortlessly, folding me against his body. I grip onto the collar of his linen shirt and smell the soap on his skin and it makes me cry harder.

"What happened? Was it something at the party?"

I shake my head against his neck. We sit like that until I can control myself, until my tears have slowed to a drip instead of a waterfall.

"Hey," he murmurs and uses his thumb to wipe beneath my eye. "What happened?"

"Maybe I don't fit in here. At the party, with all these people..."

His eyes sharpen. "Where is this coming from? Absolutely not. You're as Paradise as I am, as any of us."

I laugh at the absolute impossibility of that. It comes out like a half-sob. "No, I'm not. No one I spoke to would understand what I've been doing the last couple of years. I have no career. No car. No house. No husband, no father for my daughter. I don't even have a proper savings account. I'm an absolute failure."

"Jamie, Jamie..." he says, both hands cupping my face now. "Where's this coming from? These aren't your words."

"Yes, yes they are. They're true," I say. "And Lee just texted me."

Parker grows still. "He did?"

"Yes. He's figured out where I am. I wasn't sure he even remembered the name of Paradise Shores, but he did. And he said he doesn't want his daughter to grow up where I did, and I can't take that, can't… I have to leave with her again. And she loves it here. And I love it here." I shake my head and look down at my hands. "I sound half insane, and I can hear it, and I know you can hear it… You're probably thinking it right now. That this isn't the Jamie you grew up with, the Jamie you remember. Maybe you're even thinking, *she's changed so much. What a shame.* You are, aren't you? I can't bear it. I can't bear to be anything less than what I was, but I'm reminded how much I fall short every single day in Paradise Shores."

"Jamie," Parker says. His voice is steady. "Do you assume I'm thinking it, because that's what you believe about yourself?"

"Yes."

"All right. Well, it's absolute bullshit," he says. "I don't think any of those things. Not a single one of them. I think you're still one of the strongest people I know. I think you're a fantastic mother—no failure in sight there—and I've seen how you and Emma are together. You spend every single hour you're not working with her, and you've done your best to make this summer her best yet. I've seen you do all of that. Is that a failure?"

I swallow. "No."

"No," he says. "Exactly. And I couldn't have done what I've done with the yacht club without you. You have all the necessary skills to start working as a freelancer, you know. Offering graphic design, website design, and newsletter services. Does that sound like someone with nothing to offer?"

I shake my head.

His eyes darken, and something tightens along his jaw. "You do not have to leave this town because your ex knows you're here. If anything, he should be the one to stay away."

"I don't know how I'll react," I whisper. It feels like a terrible thing to admit. But his influence had once been so strong, and I so weak to believe his words. *Worthless*, I think. It had been his favorite word.

"Will you tell me about him?" Parker asks. His hand shifts from my cheek to my shoulder. "Emma's father? How did you leave him?"

I take a deep breath. What do I have left to hide? "He'd been growing more distant. He did that, sometimes. He'd freeze me out when he was displeased about something. I don't even know what he was angry at me for the last time. Not frying his bacon the way he liked it? Talking to the neighbors down the street who he thought were too nosy? It changed all the time."

Parker exhales sharply. "He'd ice you out?"

"Yes. Not talk to me, ignore Emma, make little comments about how I could never do anything right. It had gotten worse over the years. Wasn't like that in the beginning. And this last time... I couldn't take it any longer. Not when he froze out Emma too, when he refused to answer her quiet questions, punished her as a way to punish me. She's big enough to take notice."

"Of course she is," he says, voice hard.

I take another deep breath. "So I packed a suitcase for me and Emma. Took out all the money I had in my account. He had access to it." I shake my head, shame acidic in my stomach. "I can't believe I gave him that. But I wrote a note and left it on the kitchen counter. I wrote that if he didn't want us anymore, we didn't want him. And Emma and I left to the bus station."

"Just like that."

"Just like that," I murmur. "He was working odd jobs, and he didn't always like me working. We had to get away."

"He's not paying child support," Parker says slowly.

"No, he most certainly is not. But I don't mind. I don't want him to have any claim on Emma, no more than he already does. I'd revoke even that if I could."

"So he has custody, legally speaking?"

"Yes," I say. The thought sweeps a wave of nausea through me. If he were to exercise it…

A thoughtful, calculating look comes into Parker's eyes. The one I'd seen often enough at the yacht club, or back when he'd been sailing. He's so much more than a jock. Always was, even back when I tried to only see him as that. "Have you saved text messages? Between the two of you?"

"Um, yes. I think so. Everything's automatically saved, right?"

"Yes. Don't delete anything," he says.

"Do you think… it might be necessary?"

"I don't know," he says, and his mouth tips up in a reassuring smile. "But if there is, you have a lawyer in your corner. Emma isn't going to go anywhere without you. He was emotionally abusive and manipulative, and a judge will hear your case."

I lean back on the bench and wipe at my face. My outburst has left me empty and restless. "Thank you."

"Anytime. You have people here, James. People who care about you." His hand lands on my knee, curving over my bare skin. "People who can remind you who you are."

I take a deep breath. "You're way too good for me, you know."

He snorts. "That's ridiculous."

"You are, though. I felt like I was watching you at prom, back there. With your group of cool friends, lighting up the room."

He runs a hand through his hair and faint color creeps up his neck. "Come on."

"You're popular, and likeable. You know that, right?"

"Yeah," he says. "I can make people like me, surface-level. What's the big deal?"

"It's not a skill everyone has."

"Sure. But I don't want a lot of people to like me surface-level." His hand tightens around my knee, and the blue eyes get serious. "I want one person to like me on a deep level."

My heart stutters in my chest. The quick throws of the past hour have left me drained, and open, and I feel paper thin. Life is all around me, only a heartbeat away. "Oh," I say.

His smile curves. "Yes."

"If this person is who I think she is…" I start.

"Jamie," he murmurs.

I smile. "Well, *if* she is, then she already likes you on a deep level."

"She does, does she?"

"Yes. She likes you so much, in fact, that she's a little bit scared of it."

Parker leans closer on the bench. "It scares her?"

"Well, liking people hasn't always gone well for her, and if she were to let someone in… hypothetically speaking, of course?"

"Of course," he says with a grin.

"Things could go south again. It's a question of being brave enough to open herself up to it again… It's weird to talk about yourself in the third person."

He chuckles. "Yes, but you're doing it very well."

"I don't want to live in the past," I say. "I want to live here and now. Not being afraid, not living in my head."

Not living with my fears.

His arm tightens around mine. "You're well on your way to do just that," he says. "What do you want to do now? To kickstart your new attitude? Because there's no way we're going back to that party."

"Are you sure? I didn't mean to take you away from it."

He rolls his eyes. "Come on, I'd rather be with you any day of the week than talk to my old coach."

"Oh," I say, and smile. "Right."

"I can walk you home? Emma must be home from the beach by now. How does that sound?"

I take his hand. It's warm and large around mine, and as we walk back toward my house, I experience a warped sense of déjà vu. A glimpse into what might've been, what could still come to pass. My teenage self would never have believed I'd be walking hand-in-hand through Paradise with Parker.

I want to act on that feeling, and I want to chase away Lee's text, the thoughts, the return of the Jamie I'd tried so hard to bury. That's in the past.

This is the present… and maybe also my future.

So when we reach my street, I keep walking.

"Jamie," Parker says. His voice is teasing. "Have you lost your sense of direction?"

"No." I release his hand and turn, walking backwards up toward the cul-de-sac. "But your place is on the other street."

"Yes, that's true."

"Well, I figured… what if this was our do-over on prom? Do we really want the night to end yet?"

His eyes are blank on mine. And then they narrow in understanding, a whole new kind of focus transforming the tanned face. "Oh."

"Yes," I say. "*Oh.*"

We make it into his house. The front door shuts behind us, and Parker locks it, and I mentally vow to pay my mother back in dinners and laundry for the extra babysitting she's doing.

Parker's hands are steady on my waist, but the mouth kissing mine is hungry. *He* wants me, he *wants* me, he wants *me.*

I peel off his shirt and he tosses it away, groaning when I trace my hands over his chest. I hadn't gotten my fill in the shower the other day. I don't think I ever will.

"Jamie," he murmurs, reverently running his hands down my dress. I raise my hands up and he lifts it over my head.

And we're still in his hallway.

I laugh and take his hand, breathless, pulling him toward

the giant couch in his living room. But he shakes his head. "My bed," he murmurs. "We're doing this right, James."

"Fancy."

He rolls his eyes again and bends at the waist. The movement is so quick I don't realize what he's doing until I'm hoisted up in his arms. He carries me through the back of the house, and my smile feels like a physical thing, etched into my face. Because of course this is fun with him, too, effortless with a man who doesn't know how else to be.

He puts me down on his bed and I stretch out on the navy sheets. His bedroom is dark and simple with wooden accents.

Parker's smile slowly fades as he watches me on his bed.

"What's wrong?" I ask. My body is okay. It's nothing special, and with faint stretch marks after my pregnancy, it's not what it was before Emma.

"I can't really believe you're here," Parker says. "In my house, in my bedroom."

"That's what you're thinking?"

"You're so fucking beautiful." He reaches for the buckle of his belt. "It feels like I've waited a lifetime for this. For you."

It does, I think. Like the twists and turns of life led us to this moment, a winding road that took us far away before bringing us back together again.

And he doesn't feel like a stranger at all. Not after the shower, the make-out sessions, the kisses we'd snuck in his office. He feels like Parker, my best friend's older brother. Parker, the man who'd become my friend and confidante since I returned. And Parker... the man who looks at me like I'm a wave he can't wait to sail.

He climbs on to the bed next to me, and somewhere in the deep kisses and smooth hands, my bra comes off. He tosses it aside and returns to my arms, hitching my knee to his hip.

Parker holds his body against mine like space is the enemy. I don't complain, not when his skin is warm and dry and taut, his chest and lower stomach smattered with light brown hair. The hand he smoothes over my outer thigh has callouses from pulling ropes at sea.

He rests his head against my neck. I'm on my back, eyes closed, and keep my hands tight on his wide shoulders.

It feels so good to be held like this. To feel the need rising up in him and the answering want in me.

"Jamie," he says. The voice against my neck is hoarse. "Jesus, I need you so bad."

He's hard against my leg. The outline is clear through his pants and I take a deep, shaking breath. There's no artifice here. No games, no manipulation.

"I need you too," I whisper.

He groans, moving the scruff of his cheek over my chest, and closes his lips around my nipple. I close my eyes as sensations sweep through my chest. He licks, and bites, worrying it between his teeth.

"Oh," I whisper. "*Oh.*"

"You have to tell me what you're feeling," he says, a large hand moving down across my stomach. "Talk to me, okay?"

"Yeah."

The hand pauses between my legs, cupping me through my underwear. "I'll listen to whatever you tell me, through your words or your body." He presses down with the heel of his hand and a shaky breath escapes me.

It's been a long time since I've felt like this. Since desire was a physical thing, a source of red-hot emotion coursing through my limbs.

Parker uses a hand to gently push my knees apart. He teases me through the fabric, and I keep my arm firmly placed over my head. Try to focus on nothing but my pleasure.

"You're wet," he murmurs. "So at least one of you is talking to me."

"Parker," I mutter.

He chuckles. "There she is. What do you want me to do, baby?"

"I don't want to say it."

"Why not?"

"I can't hear it aloud."

"One day," he promises, but he takes pity on me, long fingers hooking around the elastic hem of my panties. And then he waits a few seconds, but hearing no protest, he tugs them down my legs. They only make it to my knees before he curses.

"Jamie, fucking hell... You're going to make me last all of two seconds tonight, look at you. You're so pretty."

"Oh my God," I whisper. He blows over my exposed skin and I wrench my arm away to find him grinning. "Parker!"

"Yes?" He puts his hands on my hip bones, long fingers curling down toward my center. "What do you want me to do, huh? Tell me, baby."

"I hate you," I whisper.

His grin widens. "No, you don't. But let me show you what I want to do..." He bends forward and kisses the inside of my thigh. Kisses the top of my mound, my other leg. "This. And then I want to do this..."

He kisses me softly, open-mouthed, right *there*, and I'm so grateful I didn't have to use my words. Grateful that he's treating this with a smile and a laugh and with darkened desire in his eyes. Calloused fingers help spread me and all I can do is breathe deeply, chest rising and falling in tune to his mouth on my skin.

Lee never liked doing this. He made it seem like a favor, a sacrifice on his part, and it made me feel bad for wanting it. For liking it. It had stopped being a part of our sex lives years ago.

There's no comparison to the man now between my legs.

It's too much, and my nerve-endings are too sensitive. I need this to end. I need... but as I reach down and run a hand into his hair, prepared to stop him, he flicks his tongue. And my thought process short-circuits. I tug him closer to my skin instead.

And then I'm barreling toward an orgasm.

It surprises me with the unexpected force that sweeps through me. My legs straighten and I tighten my hand in his hair, breathing becoming difficult. And he doesn't stop. Not until I tug at his hair, breathless, does he look up. Dark blue eyes meet mine with a desire that makes my heart clench.

"I want to do that again," he murmurs. "All day, all night."

"Your employees would have something to say about that."

He grins, the crooked, victorious smile. And I've never wanted anything like I want him in this moment. "The yacht club will never stand a chance pitted against you."

I have to swallow hard. "Come here."

He climbs up my body, kissing it all the way. He goes still when I reach for the zipper in his pants.

"You sure?" he asks. "We can stop with this. I'm happy to go slow, Jamie. Whatever you—oh, fuck. Jesus."

I tighten my grip around him and watch as his expression pinches, eyes closing. The square jaw sets beneath the stubble and he breathes sharply out of his nose. This large man, tanned and glorious, is stretched out beside me... completely unmanned by my touch. His erection is like solid stone in my grip and already weeping.

And the last of my fears melt away.

This is Parker. This is me. Letting him in will hurt, but so will letting him go. There's no safe option anymore.

Maybe there never was.

I kick my panties off from their spot around my ankles. He'd never gotten them down any further.

Anticipation flutters through me. "Do you have...?"

He nods. "One second."

When he returns, condom on, I open my arms to him. He covers me like a warm blanket, all hot skin and warm kisses and a need that makes the arms on either side of my head tremble. "Jamie," he mutters. It sounds like an admonition and a prayer, his mouth drifting down to my neck. "Dear God…"

I bend my legs around his hips and feel the blunt head of him resting on my stomach. The blue of his eyes looks almost dark in the dim light, throwing shadows across his tan skin. "Jamie," he murmurs.

"Yes?" I whisper. Any louder and the moment would shatter, float away. I tilt my hips to welcome him in. It feels like I've been waiting a lifetime for this.

"I want to go slow," he says, a hand drifting down to my hip. He grips himself, aligning us with measured strokes.

I don't need slow. I just need him. "You can go at whatever pace you'd like," I say, "as long as you *go.*"

He gives a hoarse chuckle and pushes in. My body protests for a second before I relax and he sinks in, and in, and *in.* It's a delicious pressure.

"Jesus," he mutters.

I don't talk. I just hold on to his shoulders, my fingers digging into the muscles, and raise my hips to his. He drives into me again with powerful rolls of his hips that send me gasping every time he bottoms out. The movement leaves no room for thought beyond the present. No sensations except those our bodies provide, and I'm here, with him, in his bed, and nowhere else.

He rises up on his arms and looks at me. It's intimate, our eyes meeting while we're doing this. A flush creeps over my face and he smiles as he sees it.

"Getting shy on me, James?"

"Never," I say, and pull him down for a kiss.

His body grows more frantic, the skin beneath my hands damp with sweat. I wrap my legs around him and hold him when the movements crescendo into a snapping of hips. He groans when he comes, just like he had in the shower, the sound deep and honest. Just like him.

He's always been honest in his feelings.

Afterwards, I keep him on top of me, my forehead against

his shoulder. I don't want to break away from the bliss of the now.

Parker is the one who finally pulls away, disposing of the condom. Afterwards he tugs me against his side like it's the most natural thing in the world. I rest a hand on his chest and feel it rise and fall beneath my palm, thinking that maybe, just maybe, it could be.

23

PARKER

I wake up early. It's a habit, ingrained after years of morning sailing lessons. The blinds aren't drawn in my bedroom and summer light filters across my bed, gilding the woman lying next to me.

Jamie's hair is a light brown cascade across her pillow and her left shoulder, mussed at the temples. Her cheeks look rosy with sleep.

She's still here, and as I watch her, a deep sense of satisfaction sweeps through me. Last night had been everything I'd ever wanted and more, but this? This is just as good. To have mornings with her in my bed, with Jamie's guard down. To be the person she trusts.

She blinks her eyes awake to the sunlight, and then immediately closes them again. Stretches out.

"Mmm. Parker?"

"Yes?"

"Oh," she murmurs. "*Oh.*" She laughs, burying her face in the pillow. "I slept here last night."

"Sure did." I put a hand on her bare back, the skin silky to the touch. She looks up at me from beneath her hair and I can't stop my wide smile. "I'm glad you did, too."

"So am I," she says. "Gosh, I almost can't believe we… but we did. And it was great."

I raise an eyebrow. "You sound almost surprised."

"I was, a bit."

"I've always known you and I would have the best sex."

She laughs. "You did not."

"Of course I did. You think I haven't thought about it? Back in the day, or in the weeks since you've been back?"

She slaps my chest and I catch her hand, pulling her across me.

"I know you did too," I say. "Come on. Tell me."

Jamie pushes her hair back and admits the truth. "Fine, I did. Of course I did."

My grin widens. "I knew it. I was your friend's hot older brother, wasn't I? And you couldn't stop thinking about me. Had my name in your diary."

"You should shut up while you're ahead."

"That's never been my strong suit," I say, and I'm rewarded by another eye roll. But she's grinning, and her breasts are flattened deliciously against my stomach. Sleeping naked with Jamie is something else.

"Then why was it better than you expected?" I brush a tendril of hair off her face. "You and me, together?"

Her face is open and soft, but she looks away from my eyes. Traces a finger down my chest instead. "Well, you know who I last…"

"Yes," I say, because do I ever.

"This was very different. So much better. I didn't expect…" She shakes her head. "It doesn't matter."

"You can tell me," I say, sweeping my hand over her back. *Give me more reason to hate your ex.*

"Well, I didn't think you'd go down on me."

A slow smile spreads across my face at the memory. "Baby, I'll want to do that every time. All the time."

She swallows. "Wow. Well, he didn't."

"He didn't deserve you." My hand curves around her hip,

and then across the twin dimples on her lower back. "Were you in your head at all? Last night?"

She shakes her head. "No. I didn't have the space to think about anything but us. You took it all."

"So I did," I say with a grin, and she chuckles. But then I sober, looking at a lock of her hair I'm twining around my finger. "Any man who would criticize you during sex lost his mind a long time ago. You know that, right?"

She smiles, a finger tracing through my chest hair. The touch is light and teasing. "So you don't think my nipples are a bit too big?"

"What? Of course not."

"They changed size after my pregnancy. So did my hips. Not too wide, then?"

My hand drifts to her round hip and tightens. "Fuck no."

Jamie's smile widens. "And I wasn't too loud? Or too wet? Or too needy, or clingy, and I shouldn't have taken a shower before, or worn nicer underwear for you?"

Gently, but with hands that I have to work to keep soft, I turn her over. Run a hand over her body, across all the spots she'd mentioned. She's still smiling, in a teasing mood.

I'm not. "He said these things?"

"Yes, interspersed over the years. That was just in bed. Other days I was worthless, or a failure, a terrible girlfriend and mother." She gives a little laugh. "Once it was over how I'd cooked his bacon. I can't believe I ever listened."

"I hate him," I say. "I don't care that he somehow fathered the cutest girl in the world. I fucking hate him, and he'd better not set his foot in this town."

Jamie's smile softens, settling into an expression of trust. It soothes the jagged edge of rage inside me. "He's in the past," she says. "His words don't hurt me anymore."

I vow to myself that they never will again. Dropping my head, I kiss one of her pink nipples. "Perfection," I say. "The best fucking size."

She laughs and slides her hand into my hair. "I've never heard you swear so much."

"You've got me worked up," I say. In my mind, I'm thinking a lot worse about her ex. Words I wouldn't say around her or anyone I loved. I drift to her other nipple, its perfect pinkness teased taut.

"Are you going to prove every comment wrong?"

"Damn right." I drift down beneath the sheet, my fingers finally finding the silky-soft skin between her legs. "And this? It can never get too wet. That's a goddamn compliment, and a man who doesn't see it that way isn't worth the title."

It takes us an hour to get out of bed. Jamie sits up, a flush of satisfaction on her cheeks, and sees my alarm clock for the first time.

"Oh my God." She throws the cover back and I get a glorious view of her nude body in the morning light. "It's past our usual workout time."

"Yes," I say. "Thinking about your family?"

She hunts for her underwear, finding them next to my dresser. I turn on my back and look at her shimmying them up long legs and hiding my new favorite place from view. "Yes," she says.

"What are your plans for the day?"

"Mom is meeting friends in the next city for lunch, and Emma and I will probably go to the beach. I promised her we'd bake this afternoon."

"Sounds nice."

She pauses, bra snapping around her chest. Hiding my second new favorite place from view. "Do you want to join us?"

"You and Emma?"

"Yes, if you want to."

"Yes," I say. "I want to."

A shy smile stretches across her face. "Okay. It's a date, then."

———

The next two weeks are the best of my life. I sail the new boat into the marina and both Hayden and my father are there to help tie it up at the dock. She's beautiful, and she'll need work, and she's all mine.

Hayden had crouched on deck and inspected one of the portlights. "Needs to be replaced," he'd said. And I'd grinned at him and he'd grinned back, and there's a reason he's my best friend and my brother in all but blood.

The yacht club has found its sea legs and runs smoothly under Stephen, Neil and Kristen's stewardship. I've had to put in another order for the caps, which apparently sold out after a local high schooler wore one to a party.

But what makes the weeks the very best is Jamie. The meltdown at the White Party seems to have broken through a dam and let out the fears she'd kept inside. Because the smiles she shoots me every time we're together make me feel ten feet tall.

It's not the teenage Jamie, occasionally defensive and argumentative and idealistic. And it's not the Jamie from this spring, with her guard up so tightly it was concrete-enforced steel.

It's a mixture of the two, and something entirely new, the image of the Jamie she is now. Grown, a mother, still strong and fierce but tempered the way a blade is, put through flame. She knows when to bend to avoid breaking now. It's become my mission in life to make her laugh as often as I can.

I'd surprised her one morning at work with a box, waiting for her in the back office.

"What's this?" she'd asked, running a hand over it. And then she'd seen the fruit symbol. "Oh. You got a new computer?"

I shake my head. "This is more of an investment."

"An investment?"

"Yes, in a talented graphic designer whom I hope the yacht club will work with for years to come."

Her eyes meet mine. Protest flares, then disbelief, and then surprised joy. "Parker, you didn't."

"I did."

"I can't possibly accept this."

"Of course you can. I've hired you to run the booking system, website, and the newsletter. Not to mention the store and all the merchandise. It was all your idea."

"But this is too much. I already have a computer I can use."

"Which is your mother's, and it's on its death bed. Won't this make your job easier?"

She looks down at the box. "Yes."

"Well, that settles it."

Jamie smoothes a hand over it. "I don't know how to repay you."

"You already have," I'd said. "Your help with the business has been invaluable." And that had been it. That evening she'd sent me pictures of the newsletter she was setting up for the yacht club on her new computer, with the logo as the header, informing the community about the seasonal menu items to be announced soon.

Her mother knows about us, too. We talk about it once when I go to pick up Jamie and Emma. They're coming with me to the docks to see the new boat and go for an evening swim. Vera is the one who answers the front door. She gives me a too-knowing smile. "Hello, Parker."

"Hi, Mrs. Moraine. How are things?"

Her smile widens, filled with insinuation. "We're all good, thanks. As are you, if what I've heard from my daughter is correct?"

I won't deny it. "I am, and your daughter has something to do with that, too."

She gives a delighted laugh. "And here I thought I would have to pull it out of you!"

"Oh, I'm an open book, Mrs. Moraine."

"Vera, please. I've known you your whole life," she says, waving a hand. "This is refreshing. I have to ask and ask and ask to learn things from my daughter, and even then, she tells me one thing and hides two."

"She plays things close to the vest," I say.

"She does. Always has. But not with you, I suppose. You know, she's happier than she was when she first got back."

My hand stills on my leg, from where it had been drumming. "I've noticed that too."

"I'm sure it's because of a lot of things... But some of it I think is your doing," she says. Then she looks over her shoulder, but Jamie and Emma are nowhere in sight. When she turns back there's caution in her eyes.

I know what she's going to say. So I save her the trouble. "I know," I say quietly. "I know, and there will never be any of that from me."

Her shoulders drop an inch. "I didn't know how much she'd..."

"Some," I say. "Enough."

"She mentioned that you're a lawyer?"

"A recovering one, yes."

"Good," she says, nodding. "Very good. You know, my granddaughter is the best thing that's ever happened to me after Jamie. Now, she's been saying great things about you. Crazy things too. You're a captain? I don't believe that. But it's important to protect her heart, too. Because if—"

Vera's words are cut off by a childish shriek and a jump as Emma joins us on the porch. She looks up at me shyly and then, overcoming it, raises her hands. I give her the double high five we'd started doing a few days back.

"Hi, kiddo."

"Hello!"

"I'm here, I'm here," Jamie says, digging through her beach bag. "We got everything... hi, Mom." She looks between us. "All good?"

"Yes," I say, at the same time her mother nods.

Jamie smiles, an exasperated one, and takes Emma's hand. "Shall we?"

Emma pauses at the top of the stairs and looks up at me. It's an expectant look.

"Ah. You want to ride high?"

She nods, her double ponytails bouncing. I crouch down and she scrambles onto my back.

"You're spoiling her," Jamie says, but the way she looks at me... *These girls are mine*, I think. It settles into place with a finality that feels destined, like a pattern finally discerned. I want to give them both what they deserve, I want to be a part of their family.

I want to be chosen by them in turn.

Emma loves the new boat. Jamie is more cautious, running a hand over the aged wood. "Are you sure it's safe? I know you want to take it out later this week, but are you *sure*?"

I grin at her. "How many years have I been sailing?"

"Since you could walk," she says, rolling her eyes. "I know you're capable. I just don't know if the boat is."

I catch her around the waist. "She's got stellar bones and shows great promise. All she needs is a bit of TLC and she'll do great."

Jamie raises an eyebrow. "Are you still talking about the boat?"

"Of course. I'd never call the woman in my arms anything less than perfect."

"Smart man," she murmurs, and kisses me. It turns into a long, heart-warming kiss, my hands tightening around her waist. *Mine*, my brain says.

There's an outraged shriek beside us. "Mommy!" Emma says, and then erupts in giggles.

It's the first time she's seen us kiss.

I lift my head and look away, running a hand over my mouth. Shit.

But Jamie only laughs and crosses the deck to her daughter, sitting on the picnic blanket she's brought, along with food. "I'm not allowed to kiss the captain?"

Emma giggles again and shakes her head.

"Why not?" Jamie sits next to her daughter, smiling. "Remember how I told you that I've become a very good friend of Parker's? We like each other a lot."

Emma looks at her mother with a challenging glare she's inherited from Jamie. "Yes, but we're on a boat," she says, like it's self-evident, "and you have to do what the captain says."

Jamie laughs. "So I can't distract him?"

Emma reaches for a grape and grins with her gap-toothed smile. She'd lost her first tooth last week and had been so proud when she showed me.

A calm settles over me, watching them. She's okay with it. They're okay with me.

I sit down opposite Emma. "You're right," I tell her. "Your mom distracted me, but she's allowed to as first mate."

Emma looks between us and breaks into giggles again. "Kissing!" she says, and keeps laughing.

Jamie joins in and I run a hand over my jaw, fighting a smile. "So it's okay if I'm together with your mother? You approve?"

She nods again and reaches for a grape. "Catch," she challenges me, before tossing it in my direction.

I guess children really are more adaptable than people give them credit for.

Two nights later they're at my house and I've gotten the papers prepared. An old colleague who works with family law had looked them over to make sure every loophole was considered.

Emma falls asleep on my couch to the soft sounds of a cartoon on the TV, and in my kitchen, Jamie is baking cookies.

"Didn't take me for a baker?" she says, smiling at me over her shoulder. I've been leaning against my kitchen island and watching her for the last half hour. The ease she shows in my kitchen, the happy smile, the small gestures that make my heart tighten.

"I remember a time when you swore never to do a domestic task in your life."

She chuckles, reaching for the sugar. "Yes, well, it's easy to have radical opinions when you're fifteen. Look at me being domestic now," she says, and slowly pours a cup into the mixing bowl.

"Gorgeous," I say.

She chuckles and shakes her head. "You're going to inflate my ego, you know?"

"It's a tough job, but someone's got to do it," I say. "Do you know how long it's been since someone baked in this kitchen?"

"No? How long?"

"Previous owner."

She rolls her eyes, but her face is open and soft. From the living room comes the muted sound of one cartoon character chasing another.

I clear my throat. "Remember what we spoke about last week?"

Her hand stops moving. "Custody?"

"Yes." The papers are in a folder, and I slide them across the island to her. All the preliminary paperwork. "There are a few things to do before you should officially file for single custody."

Her hand reaches for the paper. "Right."

"It's better getting ahead of this. Especially if you think he might... object."

I don't want to say *return*. I don't want to think about that man being close to my family. Since the text two weeks ago at the White Party, he hasn't contacted Jamie again. She never responded to it—but she's convinced he's not going to give up so easily.

"I'll read all of it. Should I hire a lawyer? What should I do?" She looks down at the folder. "He's not getting Emma."

I slide an arm around her waist and she leans against my chest. "He won't," I say. "I still have friends who practice law. Let me make some calls. Worst case, I can represent you. I'm not specialized in family law but I'm qualified."

"Parker," she whispers, and I hear what she can't say. The fear. Anxiety has been weighing on her for the past weeks. "I can't ask you to do that."

That makes me smile. *We're so past that,* I think, and kiss her temple. "Baby, I know you want to go slow. This isn't to pressure you... but in all the ways that matter, I consider myself yours."

There's an audible exhale of breath. "You do?"

"Yes. This, right here? The two of you in my house, the smell of cookies, you smiling in my arms... it's all I want."

She tilts her head back. Large, chocolate-brown eyes meet mine. "I come with baggage."

"I can carry a lot," I murmur. "You've seen my workouts."

She laughs despite herself and turns, wraps her arms around my neck. "I'm scared," she whispers. "About us, about him, about myself. I'll make mistakes, Parker. I know that. But..."

"But?"

Her lips rise in a smile. "Remember the girl who wasn't scared of anything?"

"Oh, I do," I whisper, bending to her ear. I'd been a little in love with that girl.

"Well," she murmurs, "I'm finding my way back to her."

24

JAMIE

I'm sitting crosslegged on the patio, watching as little Jamie and Emma run across the yard. They're racing, and Emma is winning with her longer legs, but Jamie has determination burning beneath his dark hair.

"They're still going?" Hayden asks me. He has a beer in hand and sits down next to me on the patio. From inside, we hear the calm sounds of Lily on the phone. A buyer has called her about the gallery, about a piece, and she'd pulled out her professional voice. I can't wait to tease her about it.

"Yes, they can't seem to stop. They're going to sleep well later."

"Out like two lights," Hayden agrees. His arms rest lightly on his knees, the beer bottle dangling from his hand. Despite the dark clouds, rain hasn't fallen yet, and we're taking full advantage of it. The scent of the grill being fired up is warm in the August air. "So… you and Parker, huh?"

I groan, and my best friend's husband laughs. He's been a constant presence in both of their lives since the age of eleven, and through them, also mine. We'd both been spectators to the Marchands.

Outsiders with one foot in, one foot out.

"You know I have to ask," he says. "He won't tell me anything."

"He tells you everything."

Hayden snorts. "Not this. I offered to start by talking about my love life, but he begged me not to. Was quite entertaining, actually. Seems he doesn't want to hear about me and his little sister."

I laugh. "Surprising."

"Baffled me. So, Moraine. Did you guys hook up in high school?"

"What? No, never."

He grins. "I always suspected you did, you know."

"Really?"

"Yes. If we'd be sitting on the quad and you'd walk by, he'd watch you like a hawk until you were out of view. I caught him at it several times and he always tried to play it off."

I roll my eyes, but my chest grows warm. "We were kids back then."

"So was I, and I was in love with Lily even so," Hayden says calmly, in that unwavering certainty he possesses. "Didn't you like him too? Lord knows you two argued enough for it."

I reach for my glass of lemonade. We're too old for blushing, and yet here I am. Maybe because this thing is new, and maybe because it's actually old, both true at the same time. And maybe because Parker had spent last night at mine for the first time, with my mother out of town... and helped make pancakes for breakfast along with a giggling Emma. She'd dared him to flip pancakes and he'd managed beautifully, capable of winning at any sport, and earned a round of applause from her.

"I did like him," I say. "But I never told Lily that."

"She knows," Hayden says simply. "You two never spoke of it, but she knows."

"Glad we were that obvious."

He grins and takes a swig of his beer, eyes on his son, running as fast as his bare feet can take him. There are grass stains on his shorts. "For what it's worth, I'm rooting for the two of you."

Maybe I would have rolled my eyes at that a decade ago. Now it makes something sting at my eyes. Having people interfere in your relationship can be annoying, and tough, and pressure-laden.

It can also be wonderful.

"Thank you," I murmur. "So am I."

He chuckles. "Does Parker know that?"

"Yes. You think he doesn't?"

Hayden shrugs, eyes dropping to the laces of his old sailing shoes. He runs a hand through his dark hair. "I don't know. But he's given both Lily and me pretty strict orders about not saying anything to you that might sound like pressure."

I laugh. "Of course he has. But I'm not going to spook."

"Spooking is fine," Hayden says, "as long as it's just a short thing. We all do it every now and then."

"Not you and Lily."

This time, he laughs. His son turns around to watch his dad, eyes looking to find what's funny. When there's no obvious reason, Jamie turns right back around and reaches for the hula hoop Emma is playing with.

"You think I haven't? You think she hasn't? You know us," he says, and reaches for his beer again. "Hell, when she told me she was pregnant, I spooked bad enough for the both of us."

That's news to me. "You did?"

He nods, a brief dip of his chin. "Yes. I didn't feel qualified to be a father. Now I know nobody does, of course, and it's still the best thing ever. You write your own playbook. But I didn't then."

I smile, watching Emma. "No. Nobody knows what they're doing. But it's the best winging it you'll ever do."

"Exactly," he says softly. "Just like in relationships. It's all winging it, Jamie."

The message is clear. But he says it differently than Lily, says it softer, says it layered. And I understand. I smile down at my lemonade, thinking that they're both looking out for us, me and Parker.

"Guys," Lily says. Her voice is back to normal now, her phone in her hand. "Have you heard from Parker today?"

I clear my throat. "He took the new boat out. Should be back soon, I think."

Lily frowns. "Do you know which direction he headed in?"

"No, I didn't ask."

"North," Hayden says. "That's what he told me last night, anyway."

She looks down at her phone and her frown deepens. "The storm that was supposed to pass us by has switched directions. It's heading here instead."

Hayden gets to his feet. "Try calling him."

"I've done that," Lily says. "He's not picking up."

Something cold wraps a hand around my throat. "I have his phone."

Two pairs of eyes turn to mine. "You do?" Lily asks. "Why?"

"He forgot it at mine earlier today."

Her green eyes lock on mine for a moment longer. "Well, I wish I could focus on that detail a bit more, but Hayden... what do we do?"

He's on his own phone. "We'll start by calling the yacht club and ask if he's already back."

But he's not. The new wood-and-navy boat with the cream sails hasn't returned to its spot next to the *Frida*. And they haven't seen it for hours.

It's fifteen minutes later when the rains hit.

It's like the sky opened its maws and released weeks' worth of moisture, cold drops assaulting the ground below.

Hayden turns off the grill and I grab Emma's sweater, forgotten on the patio chair.

"He would know about the storm, though," I tell Hayden. My voice is low and hard. "Wouldn't he?"

Hayden nods. "He's religious about checking weather. But if he didn't have his phone… and it was predicated to hit far north of here…" He shakes his head. "Things change fast at sea. Parker knows that too."

I try breathing through my nerves. "What's the latest prognosis on the storm? On wind conditions?"

The man next to me, who I never used to speak much to, who is Lily's soul mate and as much Parker's brother as his own, hesitates. Panic slides its icy grip around my spine. "I won't lie," Hayden says. "They're not good."

Somewhere during that dazed evening, I find my way to the couch, and pull Emma against me. Her eyes are on the cartoon Lily had put on for her and Jamie. On the mantel, the short hand ticks with steady movements. And still no news.

I barely register when the front door opens against the pouring rain. A gust of cold wind sweeps into the house, and then I hear Michael Marchand's voice.

"What's the latest?"

The family convenes in the dining room. I wrap my arm around Emma and fight against the fear in my chest. Not now, not when I've finally found him, not when I've finally created a life for myself that's safe.

"Mom," Emma whispers. "Is it the captain?"

I force a hard swallow. "Yes, sweetie. But he's going to be all right."

"He's at sea?"

"Yes."

"Oh." Emma relaxes underneath my arm, her eyes returning to the TV. "He's a good sailor."

I close my eyes. Yes, he is. But storms don't care.

Behind me, I hear Michael asks Hayden questions, sharing notes on wind conditions, waves, miles per hour.

"Good man," Michael says at one point, slapping Hayden on the shoulder. "Why weren't you out with him today?"

"I offered," comes Hayden's measured response, "but he wanted to take the new boat for a short spin by himself."

Michael's voice grows gruff. "Well. He's the best sailor on the East Coast, if not the whole goddamn country. He knows what to do."

When I turn, Lily has her arm around her mother, both looking down at her phone. "The coast guard," Eloise says. "Why aren't we calling them? Why aren't they looking?"

"They won't brave the storm," Hayden says simply. "Not right now."

Eloise looks at her husband with anger, but Michael nods, confirming it.

"So the only thing we can do right now is wait?"

"Yes. Unfortunately."

"Does he have a signal? Why isn't he answering his phone?" she demands, looking down at her own. Manicured fingers curl around the glass and steel. "He should pick up! He always picks up!"

"He doesn't have his phone on him," Lily says gently. She's been a quiet presence throughout this, soothing, making tea, lighting candles, kissing the top of her son's head over and over again. But the eyes that meet mine across the living room are strained. She loves all her brothers, the siblings close even when they're far apart. But Parker is her closest in age, the one she fought over chores with, the brother she sees weekly.

"Idiot," Michael curses. The word hangs in the space and no one contradicts him. It's laced with worry, at any rate, and not sincerity.

There's a tug on my free arm. Little Jamie climbs up on the couch next to me. His wide, dark eyes, so like his father's, look up at mine, questioning.

"Want a piece of the blanket? Here," I murmur, spreading the one Emma and I are using.

He nods and settles against my side, turning back to the TV. "Is my uncle all right?"

I wrap my arm around him too, and with all my might, I pour conviction into my voice. "Yes," I say. "He is going to be just fine."

Did you hear that, Universe? I think. *You owe me one.*

The evening turns to night. Night turns to two sleepy children, and me staying in the guest bedroom, texting my mother to be careful if she's out driving tonight. She's in a town over, and she sends back a bunch of hearts. I don't tell her about Parker. Not yet. Not as I lie in the dark, in Lily and Hayden's guest room, and stare up at the ceiling.

And when I creep downstairs at two a.m. and find Lily and Hayden in the kitchen, her head against his chest, we don't speak. She just pushes a cup of hot tea my way and meets my eyes with worried ones of her own.

When morning comes, and the rain has stopped, and there's still no sign of a boat... My fear settles into a painful realization, one I can't look at for too long. I care about someone that isn't my mom, or Lily, or my daughter.

I love him, and it terrifies me.

"Will you let me know?" I ask Lily. "As soon as you find out?"

Lily hugs me tightly. She smells like shampoo from the shower she'd just taken, and I feel the outline of her spine beneath her T-shirt. "Of course. You too. Okay?"

"Yes," I whisper, fear making it hard to speak.

All the things I hadn't said. All the things I hadn't dared to.

Emma has her hand in mine the entire walk back home. She's been quiet, and I know I should ask her why, but I'm too scared to hear the answer. That she's left afraid by this too. That she's grown attached to Parker too.

I'm focused on her hand in mine, and the careful way she avoids the puddles on the sidewalk on Greene Street, and don't see the person waiting in front of my mother's house until it's too late.

The tall shape. The dark hair. The backpack slung over a shoulder.

And under my breath, and within earshot of my daughter, I whisper the only thing that comes to mind.

"Shit."

25

JAMIE

"There you are." Lee's smile doesn't reach his eyes, not even as they drop down to Emma. "Hi, kid."

She steps behind my leg.

Adrenaline erupts into a steady drumbeat beneath my skin, a second heartbeat, warning me to flee. He's a black hole. I can't let us get sucked in.

"Why are you here?"

"Hello to you too," he says, and lets his backpack drop to the gravel path on Mom's front yard. He doesn't fit in next to Emma's pink bicycle and my mom's wind charms hanging off the porch. "You haven't exactly kept in touch."

"Neither have you."

"I think we both needed time," Lee says. "Some time to cool down and reflect on our actions."

"I've reflected," I say carefully. *On how I could be so stupid as to let him into my life in the first place.*

Lee nods. "I knew you would've, Jamie. Running away is beneath you. I've missed you this summer."

"You have?" I ask. But he doesn't seem to hear the disbelief in my voice, taking it for what it's not. Hope.

"Yes. The apartment isn't the same without you there. Without *both* of you." Lee extends a hand to the house. "Why don't you invite me in? We can have coffee and talk about us. It's time you came home. Both of you."

And I know I can't do that. Can't let him pour the poison into my ear, the slick reasoning, the slow breakdown of my arguments, of my self-worth. No one twists words better than he does.

"We don't have a future," I say.

His arm drops, and the smile turns into a frown. Brown eyes ice over. Disapproval, and despite the distance between us, despite the warmth, fear runs like a shiver down my spine. "Jamie," Lee says. "We have a child together. Please be reasonable."

I put a hand on Emma's head. Her arm is around my leg, a solid, warm weight against me. *I don't miss Daddy,* she'd told me.

Lee's frown deepens and he looks down at Emma briefly, as if he doesn't like what he sees. "Jamie, come to your senses. This has been a little experiment, but it's come to an end. I'll be here for as long I need to convince you I love you."

"You'll stay in town?"

"I've travelled a long way to get here." He looks at the tree-lined street behind me, at the large houses. "You're swimming in money now, it seems. I remember when you had to ask me just to buy groceries. Was it all an act?"

My breath whooshes out of me. I'd asked him because I hadn't been working, because *he* hadn't liked me working. Hadn't liked the supervisor at the restaurant I'd waitressed at. *He smiles at you too much.*

But then Lee's eyes soften. "That's okay, Jamie. I forgive you. I can be very forgiving, you know. I might be open to taking you back and forgetting this old childish tantrum. Why don't you unlock this door and let me sit down and have a beer?"

And I know, with a bone-deep certainty, that if I let him in he's never going to leave.

"We're not having this conversation in front of Emma," I say.

Lee goes still. "What?"

"Today's not a good time for me."

"It's not a *good time?*" he repeats, face paling. He never flushed with anger. He'd grown quiet, and white, all color leaking out of his cheeks. And he'd lash out with his words. "Why can't you ask your trophy wife of a mother to watch the kid? She's inside, isn't she?"

I shake my head. "That's not our house anymore. Mom sold it a few years back."

"You sold it," Lee says, and looks down at the child's bike on the lawn. But I don't let him call me on the obvious lie. I don't let myself falter either.

"I'll text you when there's a better time. Stay at the motel in town."

He rolls his neck, eyes on mine. He's annoyed, but he's also unnerved. I'm not reacting the way I used to. Any second now, he's going to start the old barrage… that I'm useless, worthless, that nobody would want me anyway, that he's the best I'll ever get…

"Fine," he says, and a smile sweeps across his face instead. "Text me tomorrow, then. I'll see you. I've missed you, Jamie."

I shift Emma to my left side. We leave down the sidewalk and I look once over my shoulder, over at Lee, still standing in front of my mother's house. His dark eyes watch me.

So I take Emma's hand and resist the urge to run the rest of the way down the cul-de-sac. We take the walking path between the houses, past the meadow, and onto Parker's street. Emma is quiet beside me, her legs moving fast, hand tight in mine.

She knows, I think. For all that I've tried to shield her, she knows, because she's too clever.

We stop outside of Parker's garage. A quick glance around

shows that Lee isn't following us, and I rush us into Parker's backyard.

"But he's not home. Right?" Emma whispers.

I nod and focus on sorting through the empty pots by the grill. He has the key to the garage in one of these, left for me if I ever wanted to work out when he isn't home… and in the garage, under the box with the extra sails for *Frida*, is the house key, hidden there if he ever locks himself out.

He'd shown it all to me.

Parker, I think, and bite down hard on my tongue to stop the tears. Here he is, saving me once again, and I don't know where he is.

He'd given me a job and trusted my skills when I didn't myself. He'd half-forced me into the workouts, helping me to build self-confidence without knowing just how nonexistent it was.

And now he doesn't even have to be here to save Emma and me from Lee.

I let us into his house and shut the door behind myself, pulling the deadbolt.

"Why are we here?" Emma asks. She's toeing off her wet shoes without me having to ask. "Is it because of Dad?"

I nod.

"Oh," she says, accepting it like she accepts everything. "Good."

"Good?"

"I don't think I like Dad anymore." She walks into Parker's living room and runs her hand along the wainscoting on the wall with every step. "Do we have to be quiet?"

"No."

"Okay. Can I turn on the TV?"

"Yes," I murmur. "Yes, of course."

The place smells like him. An old cable-knit sweater is tossed over the back of an armchair. I reach for it and pull it on. It's too long in the arms and I have to fold them up twice.

Come back, I think, looking at one of the trophies he has in his living room. I'd given him shit over them just a week ago. That he'd displayed them in the bookshelf, right next to a bunch of law textbooks and above a framed picture of all the Marchands on safari in Kenya.

"So boastful," I'd teased. He'd wrapped his arms around my waist, face against my neck. *Just wait till I get my trophy for winning you,* he'd said. *Watch me display it on the front lawn.*

Ridiculous nonsense, but the memory makes my eyes sting. I love him. I hadn't realized how much until he's gone.

Emma and I sit side by side on the couch and watch the first thing she finds. It's a cartoon she's watched before, and I pull her close to my side.

Lee is back.

Parker is gone.

But I still have her, and it's all that truly matters. Lee can't take her from me. The papers Parker gave me are in my mother's house, true, but they're there and they're all filled out. I'll file for single custody first thing tomorrow morning.

Lily and I text, but there are no updates. Nothing at all, not from the coast guard, not from the family. She tells me their father is moments away from grabbing *Frida* and taking the boat out to look for Parker himself, if he wasn't being stopped by Lily and her mother. Henry and Faye are on their way from New York. Rhys has been told.

Parker, I think. *Please come home.*

Emma is quiet beside me, like she often is. I didn't think she'd caught most of what was going on, not until the cartoon ends and she stretches on the couch. "Mommy?" she says.

"Yes?"

"Maybe we should bake the cookies he liked," she says. "With the M&M's. For when he comes back?"

I close my eyes to stop the tears. "Yes, I think that's a great idea."

While we bake, I put Parker's phone on his kitchen table, as if its very presence might force a call. As he might somehow call it himself. And we fill his kitchen with the smell of home-baked cookies.

Any updates? I text Lily.

None. Hayden and I are down by the marina, still no sign.

Emma eats two giant cookies and falls asleep on the couch. I spread the blanket over her and lean my head back. Close my eyes.

Come back, I think. *I'll do it all differently if you just come back.*

Between the soft sounds of Emma dozing and the scent of Parker on the sweater I'm drowning in, I drift into an uneasy slumber. My mind is filled with crashing waves. Him, his ship, Lee. Water filling up my lungs. Sea-salty hair. The way Parker looks when he swims, strong strokes through the water.

His voice cuts through my hazy dreams. *Jamie,* he says, and then again, softer. *Jamie, you're here?*

I squeeze my eyes shut tighter, fighting against half-sleepy tears. The past twenty-four-hours have been too much. I care too much.

"Jamie," his voice comes again, and then a hand lands on my shoulder. "Baby, wake up. Please."

There's a face bent over mine, beautifully familiar. A jaw with a two-day stubble and dark blue eyes.

"Parker?" I say.

He nods and puts a finger to his lips, motioning to the sleeping child beside me. I slide out from under the blanket and into his arms.

He gives a surprised *oof* and then his arms wrap around me, two steel bands that don't let go, my toes the only part of me still on the ground. The skin on the side of his neck is warm and salty and I bury my face against it. He smells like ocean, like seaweed and wind.

"Shh," he murmurs, hands moving over my back, and he buries his face in my hair, like he's breathing me in too. "It's okay."

I don't know when I start crying, but suddenly it's the only thing I can do, sobs racking my body.

"Jamie," Parker whispers. His voice is ragged and I tighten my hands around his neck. "Come here. Come, baby, let's not wake Emma…"

He walks me into the kitchen, away from my sleeping daughter. And the small act of thoughtfulness, such a contrast from Lee, makes my tears run faster, until I have to gasp for breath. And Parker holds me through all of it.

When I can finally shape words, I form the only ones I can think of. "How?"

His face feels rough from wind and salt between my hands. "Sheer luck, to be honest."

"We've been so scared," I whisper. "All of us. Your family…"

He nods. "I've heard. I'm sorry."

"How?" I repeat.

"I went too far north. She was flying beneath me, I swear, Jamie. Beautiful boat. But when I realized I needed to course correct, it was too late." He sighs, frustration marring his face, and I know it's his competitive nature playing into it. "It caught me two hours north of Paradise. I wasn't even far!"

My hands tighten on the collar of his shirt. "What happened?"

"I took down the sails, but the winds still damn near took the mast clean off. I anchored but soon realized it wouldn't help. The waves would just tear the boat apart, tugging at the anchor."

"So what did you do?"

"I let her drift."

I shiver, and he notices, his crooked smile appearing. "Good thing I don't get seasick easily."

"You didn't get swept overboard?"

"I strapped in," he says. "By nightfall I managed to motor into a small bay. There were rocks acting as a windbreaker, but it was a damn close thing. She might as well have gotten smashed on the rocks."

I close my eyes. "So you could have jumped off and swum to the shore at that point?"

"Probably," he says.

"Parker!"

He pulls me closer, tugging my head against his neck again. "I've weathered storms before," he says. "But trust me, the only thing I wanted was to get back home to you."

A noise escapes my throat, half pain and half despair. A large hand rubs a circle between my shoulder blades.

"I motored into the marina an hour ago," he murmurs. "Good thing I always stock my boats with extra fuel, just in case. Lily and Hayden said you were at home, and I went to your house."

"You did?"

"Yes, but you weren't there." His voice drops. "You were here, instead. On my couch."

I sniffle. "I used the key in the garage."

"I figured. And you've baked?"

"It was Emma's idea. She wanted... she wanted you to have your favorite cookies when you got back."

Parker's hand stills on my back and I can feel him swallow hard, the column of his throat moving. "She did?"

"Yes."

"Shit," he whispers, and pulls me closer. "Jamie, thank you for being here. You were the only person I wanted to see on that dock."

My tears speed up. "I'm sorry," I say. "Parker, I'm so sorry. For so many things. For... for..."

He leans back and puts his hands on my upper arms, steady eyes meeting mine. The state of him only makes me cry harder. There's a tear in his sleeve and a faint bruise at his temple. He's just survived a near-death experience and here I am, being comforted, when it should be the other way around.

230

"Jamie? What's happened?"

"You were gone," I say, "and I realized I'd never told you how I felt."

His eyes soften. "I know. Even if you don't tell me."

"But you shouldn't just *know*, you should hear it. I've been so closed off all summer. Keeping you at an arm's length, even when we've been spending time together. And I... kept telling myself it was because of Emma, because I couldn't have her get close to someone again only for it not to work out. But Parker, Emma loves it here. Emma embraced it all open-heartedly from day one. It was always me."

"You did what was right," he says, hands rubbing up and down my arms. "Is this my sweater?"

"Yes. It smelt like you."

A smile spreads on his face, golden and glorious, and I think my chest might break from how much I care about him.

"Okay," he says. "Baby, don't cry."

"You're hurt. Aren't you?" My fingers hover over the temple at his forehead. "What happened?"

"The beam. Almost knocked me out."

"You need to go to the hospital."

"No," he murmurs. "I need to be home, with you."

"Why is your sleeve ripped?"

"A cord snapped."

"Jesus." New tears bubble in my throat and I hug him toward me. I wish I could erase the past day, erase him at sea, erase Lee. Go back to my happy little bubble. "I never, ever, *ever* want you to sail into a storm again."

He chuckles hoarsely and kisses my temple. "James," he murmurs.

"Because I realized something earlier today, when I saw Lee. That I've been afraid for so long, and I don't—"

"What? Lee's here?"

"Yes. He came to town today."

Parker has gone still, his hands warm weights on my

shoulders. "Lee is in town," he says slowly. "That's why you're in my house. Did he do anything to you?"

"No. We spoke briefly, but I didn't want to have the conversation in front of Emma. He knows where my mom's house is."

"Is she home?"

I shake my head. "She's out of town tonight again, visiting my aunt."

"Good. Text her about him," Parker says. His voice has dropped into the steady, confident one. It brings back memories of him instructing junior sailors. *Strapping kids into life vests.* "Tell her not to come back home to the house until you give the all-clear. Okay?"

"Yes. Good idea."

"Did you sign the papers I gave you?"

I nod. "They're in my house though."

"We'll get them tomorrow," he says. A strong hand smoothes over my back. "Don't see him without me, James. Please."

A grateful breath escapes me. "You want to be there with me?"

"God, yes."

"Thank you," I say.

His eyes, thoughtful and sharp, meet mine. There's calculation there. "We can get ahead of this. Bluff about the custody papers."

There are dark shadows beneath his eyes. I smooth my hands over his cheek, against the stubble. "Thank you," I murmur. "But he won't bother us tonight. You need sleep."

"I need a shower," he mutters. "And one of these. Emma really wanted you guys to make them?"

I nod, watching him take a bite of the cookie. "You must be hungry."

"Starving," he says. "I don't know what I want most. A meal or sleep."

I stear him toward a chair and re-heat the dinner we'd had

a few days ago, still in his fridge. He eats while I put Emma to bed in his guest bedroom. She walks sleepily from the couch and murmurs something about not having to brush her teeth. *Not tonight, honey.* She smiles happily at the exception and snuggles into the guest bedroom.

"The captain?" she murmurs.

"He's back," I say. "He really liked your cookies, too. You'll see him when you wake up."

"Good," she whispers, turning into her pillow. "He makes you happy."

My heart is full when I rejoin Parker. He's heading to the shower and I join him, washing his hair beneath the hot water. He bends and rests his head against my shoulder when I dig soapy fingers into the tense muscles around his neck.

"Never stop," he says.

I don't, but I take the opportunity to notice the added bruise on his right arm, the cut along his left ankle. And when we're done, when we stand together beneath the hot water, I let it take my worries and fears with it.

Parker traces my collarbone with a calloused finger. "Thank you, Jamie," he says.

"For what?"

"For being here. For being you."

And tears blur my eyes again. I blink them away and tug him out of the shower. We towel off the bare minimum and pull back the sheets of his bed. Parker groans as he lies down.

"You're hurting," I say.

"Every damn muscle in my body," he mutters, and extends an arm to me. "Come here."

"I won't hurt you?"

"No." He curls his arm around me, pulling me against his body, and I tug the sheet up around us. Carefully, I put a hand on his chest, and he snorts. "I'm not close to death."

"No, but you're sore, and it'll be worse in the morning."

"Don't remind me." He sighs deeply and his eyes close. "If I wasn't about to pass out," he murmurs, "I'd spend the night showing you just how much I wanted to get back to you."

I press a kiss to his chest. "Sleep," I say. "No one is going to dispute your manliness."

"Good," he whispers. I listen to his breath evening out into sleep, the strong chest rising and falling steadily beneath my cheek, and I whisper the words into his skin.

I love you.

26

PARKER

Across the kitchen counter, Jamie's digging her teeth into her lower lip. She's reading through the document I've put together with a pen in hand. "This'll work," she murmurs. "It has to."

"It will," I say.

Behind us, Henry and Hayden talk quietly, sitting on Vera's couch. Giving us privacy.

Jamie had protested my idea first, when I'd suggested calling them. There had been embarrassment in her eyes. *Trust me*, I'd said. There's one impression I want her ex to have after today, one impression he'll carry with him out of Paradise and Jamie's life.

He'll never be able to fuck with her again.

He's never raised a hand to me, she'd reminded me quietly, in the early hours of the morning. I'd draped her over my chest and closed my eyes at the simple pleasure of her fingers tracing across my skin. A deep blue bruise had spread over my left shoulder from the beam, and she'd kissed it gently.

He hurt you in other ways, I'd said, eyes still closed. My anger leashed tightly. *And he never will again.*

Jamie had stayed close to me all night, and in the darkness

of my bedroom, she'd told me just how scared she'd been for me. That I wouldn't come back.

I haven't admitted to anyone quite how bad it got. Worse than I'll ever tell her or my family. The boat will need a few repairs to make it out of the marina safely again.

The ocean is a fickle mistress.

Jamie's thumb skims over the custody papers. "I'm ready," she says. "God, I'm so jacked up on adrenaline, I need him to come *now.*"

I round the counter to her. "You'll do great."

"There's so much I need to say... I don't know if I'll remember it all." She looks up at me and lowers her voice so the guys won't hear. "How are you feeling? Really?"

I lift a hand to smooth her hair back, ignoring the protesting muscles in my arm. "Don't think about me today."

"It's hard not to," she murmurs, "when you just almost *died.*"

I pretend to scoff. "It never got that close. The ocean and I have an understanding." I bend my head, brush my lips to the outside of her ear, and feel the same tidal wave of emotion as last night, when I'd found her and Emma asleep on my couch. She'd worn my sweater, and I'd never wanted her to take it off. "Just remember that you're Jamie Moraine," I murmur. "You're a great mother to the best kid, you're starting your own web design business, you go regularly to the gym, you have a very handsome boyfriend—"

She laughs against my cheek, breaking my stride.

I grin. "Isn't it all true?"

"Yes."

"Not to mention you have a lawyer, your friends, and an entire town on your side. This asshole doesn't stand a chance. So you don't believe a word he says. Okay?"

She nods, and I can see the steel she pours down her spine. "Not planning to."

When the doorbell finally rings, I walk her to the front door. I've agreed to stay out of sight until she calls for me. *I need to say a few things to him,* she'd told me earlier that morning. *Trust me, Parker.*

So here I am, my hands balled into fists as I hear the voice of a man I've dreamed of hurting far too many times. I've never considered myself a violent man. But here I am, brimming with it.

"Jamie," he says. "So this *is* your mother's house after all?"

The voice is smarmy, with an admonishing note. I lean my head against the wall in the hallway and look out the frosted glass window. The man is lanky and dark-haired. He stares at Jamie with uncomfortable intensity.

"Yes. I lied when I said it wasn't," she replies.

"Did you? You've picked up a lot of questionable habits this summer," he says. "I don't know if I like them, Jamie."

I remind myself to breathe.

"That's okay," she says. "You don't have to."

"Where's the kid?"

"She's with a friend," Jamie says. Emma is at Lily's together with Vera, both women fully aware of what's going on here.

Jamie had been embarrassed about that, too. *This is your family,* I'd told her. *These are your friends. We* want *to help.*

Let us.

And she has, my brave girl, standing on the porch now with steel in her voice.

"Oh? Hiding her from me?" Lee asks.

"You've never shown any interest in fatherhood, so I've been following your lead. Isn't that what you've always wanted me to do?"

"Jamie," he says, and there's clear displeasure in his voice. "When did you start talking like this? So defensive."

"I'm speaking my mind. I understand if that's a new experience for you, since I lost mine during the years I was with you."

"Stop this," he says harshly. There's thunder in the voice.

"This isn't you, this isn't the woman I love. I've told you I'll consider forgiving you if you come home with me, to our place, Jamie, but I'm going to change my mind if you keep acting like this."

"Good. I won't go anywhere with you ever again, and neither will Emma."

Lee scoffs. "So you'll stay here? With what money, Jamie? You'd live like a leech off your family or your old friends, and how long will that last? It's not like any of them actually want you here. You've been gone for *years*. They'll realize soon enough how worthless you are. How you don't fit in. Maybe they already have, huh? Haven't you started noticing the signs already?"

I grind my teeth together, my jaw hurting from the pressure, forcing myself to stay in place.

Not until she asks me to.

Then Jamie surprises both Lee and me. She laughs. "You really think that'll work on me? I left you and your poison behind. I'm not worthless, and you were always the leech. When I think of all the things I did for you, the paychecks you took right out of my hand..." She shakes her head with a dry laugh. "My only regret is that I didn't leave you sooner."

Lee narrows his eyes. "You think anyone else will want you? I know all your flaws, Jamie, and still I love you. I've forgiven you for all of them. And you'll throw that away?"

"What you felt for me," she says, "was never love. I know that now. Leave, Lee. And never contact me again."

His face goes bone white. I step toward the door. If he dares raise a hand—

"My daughter is in this town," he says. "If you think I'll leave without her, you've cracked your goddamn mind even worse than I thought. Is she inside?"

"No, she's—"

"Emma? Let me in, Jamie," he says, and tries to shoulder her aside.

I decide that's my cue and open the door. It would be

comical to see him halt, only inches from my chest, if I didn't see red.

Lee takes a step back. "What the hell?"

I've been in a fair amount of bars in my life, places where men with quick fists eye one another. Avoided them best I could, but there had been a fight or two in college. Stupid, drunken things. But I know what it feels like when a man sizes you up.

And I know how to do it in return.

So I let my eyes drift over the man in front of me, over his legs and the wiry arms. His face looks weathered beyond the years I know he has, and the eyes burn with indignation.

"Lee, is it?" I say. "Emma isn't here."

His eyes drift between me and Jamie, narrowing in anger. "Who the hell is this?"

"My lawyer," Jamie says. "Well, amongst other things."

A slow smile spreads across my face. "That's right. It's a pleasure, Mr...?"

"Thompson," Lee says. His gaze locks at my temple, where I have a bruise. "You're a lawyer?"

"Yes. Amongst other things." My smile widens. I know it's an unfriendly one. "So it's my duty to inform you that Ms. Moraine has filed for single custody."

Anger flashes in his eyes and he looks at Jamie. "What the hell? Have you completely lost your mind? What lies have the people here been telling you?"

"You've never wanted to be a father," she says. Her voice doesn't waver.

"Not true. Emma is the best damn thing that ever happened to me," Lee says.

Jamie laughs again. It's a chilling sound, and he stares at her like he doesn't recognize the woman he sees.

"What the hell has gotten in to you?" he says. "What has this asshole told you?"

"Asshole?" I say.

But Jamie is the one who answers. "You never took care of

239

her, you never read her a bedtime story, you never picked her up at daycare. There were weeks when you barely spoke two words to her."

"That's all that counts?"

I clear my throat. "Mr. Thompson, your ex-girlfriend and your daughter were in a different city for four months without you coming to visit. Is that not true?"

"I didn't know where they were."

"Yes, you did. You suspected they'd gone to Jamie's mother from the start." I raise an eyebrow. "But you waited four months. Doesn't show a lot of paternal affection, does it?"

The white of his face drains away to leave splotches of color. For a few moments, he can't speak.

"Jamie," he says, reaching out a hand to grip her arm.

I put a hand on his chest. "Back up," I tell him. "You don't touch her."

"Who the *fuck* even are you?"

"We've told you. I'm Ms. Moraine's lawyer," I say. As if on cue, Jamie leans into my side, closer than a friend would, and I can't resist adding the words again. "Amongst other things."

Lee's eyes darken on mine, and there's a hint of fear there. He's all bark and no bite. The kind of man who'd verbally abuse a woman—who'd abuse her in any way—isn't worth the ground he stands on.

"So you have rich friends now?" he asks Jamie, giving her a disgusted look. Like *she's* the one in the wrong. "Always knew you'd run back to your little trust fund upbringing. Where's the independent woman I love?"

"You know," Jamie says, her voice thoughtful, no sign of the rage I'm feeling at his words, "for all your big talk about sticking it to the elite, I've never once seen you volunteer for people who have it worse than you. And independent, Lee? You wanted me to serve you on my hands and knees. You're a hypocrite."

He looks between us again, and a light flicks in his eyes. "You want me to leave, Jamie? You want me to sign over custody and never bother you or Emma again?"

"Yes," she says.

Here it comes, I think.

"Well, what will you offer me in return?" he asks.

I laugh. It's so predictable. My reaction sets him off, because his arms tighten at his sides. But he ignores me and focuses only on Jamie.

"You left me in a bad situation when you took our money," he says. "I've been kind enough not to press you on it, but you know what you did. It was stealing."

"I took *my* money, from *my* account. It was money I'd earned from my last paycheck waitressing," she says. "That money was never yours."

"Mr. Thompson," I say. "No one is going to pay you a dime to stay away. That's not what's happening here."

"Then I'll fight custody. I'll fight it in court!"

I take a step forward, shielding Jamie behind me. "With what money?"

His eyes narrow. "What?"

"Lawyers charge exorbitant fees. I'd know, Mr. Thompson. Proceedings can drag on for months, if not years. You have a documented past of emotional abuse toward Ms. Moraine and Emma. We have texts and phone recordings, not to mention this four-month-long absence. Do you really want to go down that path?"

My question hangs in the air between us. There's a gossamer-thin veil of civility over my face, my words. If he tries to raise a hand, if he charges, I swear to God…

"Please," Jamie says by my side. "Let Emma live a good life. Don't turn her into a pawn in some game between you and me. She deserves better… and you never wanted fatherhood. You can be free of it. Of us."

Lee's voice falters, takes on a desperate edge. "I can still make your lives miserable. I could stay here. But I'll leave quietly if you give me something. *Anything.* You owe me, Jamie!"

He wants money.

How predictable.

I rap my knuckles against the closed door behind me, two sharp times.

They don't dawdle. Henry and Hayden must have been waiting in the hallway, because they join us on the porch right away. Hayden stands to my left and Henry on Jamie's right.

Lee takes a step back. "What the hell…?"

"I'll admit, these two aren't lawyers," I say. "But they are good friends of Jamie and Emma. Like me. None of us take particularly kindly to threats against either of them. Paradise is a small place. We take care of our own."

"And we're not going anywhere," Hayden adds, cracking his knuckles.

Lee takes another step backwards, eyes drifting to Jamie. "You've lost it."

"No," she says. "You've lost me."

A figure emerges from the bushes, as Rhys stretches to his full height. He brushes a leaf off his shoulder and walks toward us on the lawn. In his left hand is a film camera.

"Thanks for the show," he tells Lee. His voice is the slow, arrogant drawl I'd wanted to punch him for so often as a teenager. "The part where you demanded money in exchange for surrendering custody will play especially well in court. You're truly a devoted parent."

Lee's eyes drift across all of us. From Rhys to Henry, from Henry to Hayden, and then to me. Finally they land on Jamie, standing by my side, and the papers in her left hand.

"Where do I sign?"

He ends up getting money. The bus fare out of Paradise, in fact, in an envelope Jamie had prepared. When he's left she thanks each of my brothers with hugs. *I'm so sorry you had to do this, thank you so much…*

They each assure her they'd do it again in a heartbeat.

Henry dryly comments that all he had to do was stand there. *I never knew I could be so threatening*, he'd said, and Rhys and I had laughed. If there's one thing our eldest brother had always been good at, it was threatening us to obey.

We all end up back at Lily and Hayden's house. Rhys gives me shit about riding into the storm, but the arm he flings around my shoulders lies lighter than it usually does. "I'm not covered in bruises," I tell him.

He looks at my temple. "I don't believe that."

Jamie hugs her mom, and Lily, and Emma when we come back home. Mostly Emma. And she tells her mother that it's over, showing the signed custody papers.

There will be time for longer discussions when the dust settles. But for now, all I feel is a deep contentment, watching her smile at Lily and laugh with her daughter. It's the feeling after a fight, after the storm, when adrenaline and fear leaks out to leave only lightness behind.

Someone lights up the grill, and Henry recounts the story to his wife and Ivy. Faye protests at not being there and Henry lobbies the ball to me.

"It was all Parker's idea."

I pretend to grimace. "Sorry, Faye. But if we invited you there would have been bloodshed."

Her mouth drops open. "Excuse me?"

"You would have taken a swing at him," I say, grinning. "We couldn't have that."

Henry laughs and wraps an arm around his wife. "You are pretty fierce when you're angry," he says.

She pretends to grumble, but she's smiling, too.

At one point Hayden puts a hand on my shoulder, and his words catch me off guard. "You'll be a great father one day. You know that, right? I've always known it, but today... I can't wait to see it."

"Thanks," I say. It's unexpected and nice and I catch Jamie's eyes across the room. She'd heard, but she looks down at her lap. I can't wait to have her in my arms later.

Later that night, when the grill has died and the kids are half-dozing on the couch, I overhear Lily talking to Jamie. "I'm so glad it worked out," she says. "You know, Parker has a huge house. You two could move in there. I'm pretty sure he wouldn't mind."

I pretend not to hear and turn in the opposite direction, but I can't help grinning.

No, I definitely wouldn't mind.

27

JAMIE

Money.

That's what it all came down to. I struggle processing that for the first couple of days. That the only value Lee saw in our beautiful, happy, amazing little girl was the leverage she gave him over me.

But now she'll never hear him tell her that she's worthless. Never suffer his neglect and cold stares any longer. And she'll never have to hear him say those things to me, either. The relief is so big it's hard to feel anything else.

Emma starts school. My mother and I are both there on the first day of Paradise Elementary, watching as she disappears with her little purple backpack and braided hair. I cry as soon as she's out of sight.

Mom lowers her camera, having documented everything about Emma's morning until the very last step, and hugs me.

"I know, sweetie," she says. "It's the greatest and saddest thing you'll ever do, raising your kids only so they can leave you."

We have a heart-to-heart right there in the parking lot. "I'm sorry for leaving. I'm sorry for not coming back sooner. God, Mom, I'm so sorry I wasn't here when Grandpa died, and that I didn't come for his funeral. I can't believe I let myself... that I didn't leave Lee sooner."

"Hush," Mom says, and she's crying now too. "It's okay. You're home now. We'll always be family. You and me and Emma."

You and me and Emma.

It's what Lily had said. *You and Parker and Emma.*

The week passes in a blur, with Emma's school and my work and the newfound relief of the custody papers. But in the back of my mind is the niggling sensation that another shoe is about to drop.

I turn words over in my head. Lee's. Parker's. Lily's and Hayden's. *You'll be a great father,* Hayden had told Parker and afterwards he'd looked at me, happiness and hope in his eyes. Like I'm the one he wants to have children with.

And then Lily had said I should move in with him.

Is he expecting that? Are they all?

The fears turn over in my mind until it becomes a twisted knot I can't unravel.

On Thursday morning, after I've dropped Emma off at school, I join him in his garage. He's ordered some exercise bands for me and they're rolled neatly in a corner, along with my workout shoes. I'd left them here last time.

You and Emma should move in with him...

"Good morning," he murmurs, and kisses me hello. It's as soft and delicious as always, and my body relaxes. It's just my mind that can't.

He waits until halfway through the workout before he asks me. "So?" he says, lying on his back beneath the weight bar. "What's wrong?"

I bend at the waist to grab a kettlebell. "Nothing."

He does a few reps, voice calm. "Something's wrong. I've noticed it all week. Has he been in contact?"

"No. No, not at all."

Parker sets down the bar and sits up on the bench, running a hand over his forehead. "That's good."

I set down my weight, and slowly, unwilling to say the words, I look over at him.

"You can say it," he says, as understanding as he always is. I don't deserve him.

"Remember how you've been afraid I'll get spooked?" I ask. "Well, I think I'm spooked."

He gives a slow nod. "Ah. Right."

The words pour out of me. "I didn't realize how much I cared about you until last week. I mean, I knew I did, but I didn't realize just how *much* I need you. And it scared me."

He runs a hand over his jaw. "I can see why it would, yeah."

"Then I realized all the things we haven't spoken about, you and I, and it kinda overwhelmed me." I walk across the gym, to my water bottle, and take a deep swig. My fears have a solid grip around my throat.

"What things?" he asks. "You know we can talk about anything."

"Yes, well, maybe not everything. You know? We've just started dating, you and I. And I just got single custody of Emma... and I mean, I'm still living with my mom. I don't have everything figured out yet."

"I have space here," he says, calmly, and it twists in my chest.

"Yes, but we can't move in here. I'd be moving from Lee's to my Mom's to yours."

His eyes widen. "Right."

"Not that I don't want that—ever. That's not it. But I can't do it yet." I close my eyes, fear rising up. He's going to leave. He won't want to wait for me to sort myself out. *I won't be able to live up to his expectations.*

"I have to be my own person, after Lee, I have to figure out who I am. I have to do what's best for Emma."

"And that's not me?" he asks, calmly, quietly.

"No, I mean... I need to learn who I am when I'm just me again. Not me in a relationship."

"So you don't want to be in a relationship?"

"That's not what I mean either." I hang my head in my hands, cursing myself for bringing this up. For not knowing what to say to explain that I want *him*, but I don't know if I can be what *he* wants. "We've never spoken about kids. Do you want them? Because I don't know if I can give you that down the line either. Right now all I can think about is Emma."

"Jamie," he says softly, and I hear as he gets up from the bench. "We can sort all of this out."

"I won't be able to be the woman you want," I whisper.

Strong hands land on my shoulders. Hands I love, hands I want around mine for the rest of my life. And hands that deserve a wedding ring, a baby to hold, a beautiful wife at his side who knows how to sail.

"I want you," he says, "and I've wanted you for a very long time. I want you to choose me… to *want* to choose me. So if this is how you feel, that's okay. It's completely okay. It's been an overwhelming week."

I look up at his face, the strong jaw, the stubble, the steady blue eyes and the bruise already starting to fade at his temple. We'd almost lost him.

I don't know what I would have done if that happened, and it scares me more than Lee ever had.

"Maybe it's better for you to sort things out for a little while," he says. "I'll be here when you do."

"You'll wait?" I ask. It comes out choked, because I know what I'm asking for is impossible. He's in his mid-thirties. He's too good of a catch to wait for me to pull the broken slivers of my soul together.

"Yes," he murmurs, and kisses me again. It's a warm and urgent touch, and I cling to him.

"You're the best thing that's ever happened to me," I tell him. "It's important that you know that."

He smooths the back of his hand over my cheek. "Find yourself, Jamie," he murmurs, "so you can choose me."

When I leave his house and walk back to my mother's beneath the trees standing sentinel around me, I realize I forgot to tell him the most important thing of all. *I love you,* I think. *I love you, I love you, I love you.*

28

JAMIE

I finally see Lily's art gallery, a week and a half after the fateful conversation in Parker's garage.

"This is beautiful," I say, stopping in front of a charcoal drawing. Sharp lines depict a skyscraper, or, I think, a steep mountain. El Capitan or the One Trade Building. It's impossible to tell.

"Isn't it?" Lily comes to stand beside me. In her floral dress and long auburn hair, she's the picture of artistic elegance.

I wonder how proud the fifteen-year old Lily would be to know that she's here, back in her hometown, running an art gallery, painting full-time, and married to her childhood sweetheart.

"What's the matter?" she says, putting a hand on my shoulder. "Is the piece getting to you? It's such a great commentary on nature and industrialism."

I smile. "No. I mean yes, it is, and I can see why you bought it. But I was just thinking how proud I am of you."

Her eyes widen. "Really?"

"Yes. What do you think our kid-selves would say, if they saw us now?"

"Oh, gosh. That's a good question." Her face lights up in a

smile. "I don't think they'd be surprised to see us standing side by side."

"No, I don't think so either," I say.

"They'd be happy to see us both as mothers, I think." Her smile turns thoughtful. "How's Emma doing in school?"

"Oh, she's loving it."

"Really?"

"Yes. I was nervous she'd be overwhelmed, and she has been, but she's taken to it like a fish to water. Every afternoon she comes home and recounts everything they did that day. Some of it sounds unlikely. Apparently, they went to the moon in rocket ships during recess yesterday, but she's enjoying it, and that's what counts."

Lily's grin widens. "I can't wait till it's little Jamie's turn. I have a feeling I'll get a lot of calls about disruptive behavior."

I laugh. "He does struggle with sitting still."

"He's four," she says, "but I doubt it'll get much better in two years."

"Oh, a lot happens in those years."

We move through the rest of the gallery. She shows me the pieces she's especially fond of and the paintings she's done herself. They're beautiful, and really shows the growth she's experienced over the last couple of years. I tell her just how proud I am of her and Lily, true to form, brushes it off. But I can see that it pleased her nonetheless.

After the tour I pour myself a cup of coffee from the machine in the corner.

"So," she finally says, looking at me over the rim of her blue-and-white mug. "How's it been at work? With Parker?"

"Good, actually. We're still friends. Everything's amicable," I say. It's the truth. We say hello and goodbye, and we talk about the website when necessary. But every time I look at him it hurts a little in my chest. And I know I'm the one causing that, and causing the same longing in his eyes.

Lily leans against the desk she has at the back of the gallery. "I thought you were good together."

"We were, Lily... we are. It's all my fault. I'm the one scaring myself."

"You are? Tell me."

I sigh and look down at my coffee. "I see you and Hayden," I say. "And I see Henry and Faye, and Rhys and Ivy. I even hear my mother and her lovely, helpful, but also very annoying comments about how Parker's perfect. And he is, Lily—he always has been. And I want it. I want him, the life, all of it. But...."

"But?" she says gently.

"I don't think I'm good enough for him. I can't live up to what he wants, to what people expect. Not fast enough, at any rate." I look down at my shoes. "There are still days you or Parker or my mom don't see, when I struggle getting out of bed. When things feel dark again. I always get through them and I will get through them, but I have to *work* at it." I shake my head. "I've never fit into Paradise properly, Lily, you remember that. And Parker *is* Paradise. It's only a matter of time before he realizes I'm not capable of being who he wants me to be."

"Jamie," Lily says. "I know you don't believe in your ex's words anymore. But you'll also have to stop believing in your own."

I look up at her, meet the gaze that once steadied me daily. "I do?"

"Yes. So what if you don't want to move in together? If you're not sure you want to have kids? There's no rulebook."

"He told you?"

"Yes," she says, and closes the distance between us, putting down her coffee cup. "But only because he wasn't sure what to do. I told him you had to figure it out on your own and you will. Because you always do."

I whisper the words. "But what if we're not actually compatible?"

She laughs. "You and Parker? Jamie, my brother isn't a paragon of perfection. We both know that! Haven't you learned all his flaws this summer? I can list them for you if you don't already know. He can be too competitive, too bossy, a bit arrogant, he never washed behind his ears—maybe he's started now—and he can't cook at all."

I can't help but smile. "I think he washes behind his ears now, at least."

Her nose wrinkles. "Good. But he loves watching weird fantasy and sci-fi movies and he hated being a lawyer and he still wants to sail the world. He's not going to expect you to play at a housewife."

"Yeah," I say. "You're right."

"You used to be so full of rebellion," Lily says, gripping my hand. "Making your own path and deciding your own norms. When did that change?"

"I think it's because it's *him*," I admit. "I always had a crush on him. For years, and I never told you. Should I have?"

Her smile widens. "I forgive you for that. Especially if it means I get to keep you forever as a sister-in-law. And honestly, it was probably a good thing you never told me. Teenage me would probably not have handled it as well as I do now."

I squeeze her hand back. "You're still my favorite Marchand."

"Good," she says, and pulls me into a hug. "Keep it that way."

"I love you," I murmur. "And I love him, and I haven't even told him that."

"You should. Because I have to tell you, as his sister, that he deserves it."

A shaky laugh escapes me. "God, he really does."

He deserves love and so much more. A real relationship in every meaning of the word. I want to give him that. Maybe I won't live up to the ideals, either… but I can do my best.

And maybe that's the only thing any of us can do.

"Besides," she says, leaning back, "if you really want your

independence, you and Emma can move into our cottage. I'll even allow you to pay me a tiny amount of rent if it'll make you feel better about it."

"We can?"

"Of course!" she says. "Jamie, you have options!"

Options, I think. It might be the best word I've heard in forever.

29

PARKER

Slowly but surely, the boat is coming along. A few things had been broken or damaged during the storm, but the worst of it is now fixed. I'm sitting on her deck and working on changing a cracked portlight. It's a finicky process, but being on the boat and rocked softly by the waves beneath her is good for the soul.

For the mind, too.

Hayden had joined me earlier and helped with the hull, and we'd spoken about her. He'd heard through Lily that we're taking a break.

She's it for me, Hay, I'd told him honestly. *She's it.*

He'd nodded, commiseration in his eyes, and I knew he understood. That part he'd always understood. Because there's no one else I want beside me. No one else I can even imagine wanting. And if she needs time…

Well, I can give her time. I'm a patient man.

I've had to learn to be.

Across the docks, a figure approaches, silhouetted against the setting sun. It takes me longer than it should to see who it is.

I put the wrench down. "Jamie?"

She nods and shields her eyes from the sun with a hand. "Hey. Am I bothering you?"

"No, not at all. I'm just fixing some things." I wipe my hands on a towel and gesture to the deck. "Do you want to join me?"

It's not the first time we've spoken since the conversation in my garage. But they've mostly been quick exchanges at work, with other people around. Gone are the long workouts and evenings spent together. No early morning swims or weekend exploits.

"Yes," Jamie says. She steps onto the boat, feet firmly planted. A smile curves on her lips. "I was prepared to hate this boat after what it nearly did to you."

"The storm," I correct, putting a hand on the hatch. "This beauty saved me."

Jamie sits down on deck, crossing her legs. She runs a hand over the wood. "She's gorgeous, I'll give you that."

"Thanks."

"Have you named her yet?"

I rub the back of my neck. "Yeah, I have one in mind."

"You do?"

"Yes, although I was considering your name first. But I figured that might be too soon."

Her eyes widen. "My name?"

"Yes. But I don't want to spook you any more than I already have."

A flush rises on her cheeks. "You haven't, Parker," she says. "But you're right. It might have been... too soon. Not to mention there's already two Jamie's in your life!"

I chuckle. "Yeah, a third would have made my life even more confusing."

"That's right. So what did you settle on?"

"*Atlas.*"

Her eyes shine up. "Your old family dog?"

I nod. "He was a loyal dog, and she's already proven herself to be just the same."

"Hmm," she says. "An atlas is a map of the world, and a sailing boat can take you anywhere. Right?"

"Right," I say, smiling. "Good name?"

"Great name. Lily will love it."

I chuckle. "Yes, she will. How's Emma been?"

Jamie's face lightens. She tells me about Emma's new school, and how she's struggling with another loose tooth. I listen as a feeling of certainty settles over me. *My family*, I think. *If they'll have me.*

Jamie motions to the spot in front of her. I don't need to be asked twice and sit down. The boat sways softly beneath us.

"I went by your house first," she says. Her hands curl in her lap. "But you weren't home, so I figured you were here."

"I've been fixing her up most evenings this week."

"She looks good."

I nod. "But she'll look better in time."

Her mouth softens. "Oh, I'm sure she'll be the most beautiful boat in the marina."

"Will she?"

"Yes. You take good care of the things in your life."

I reach out a hand and smooth a lock of hair away from her forehead. She stays still, the smile soft on her face. Achingly beautiful.

"We've had fun together this summer," I say. "Haven't we?"

"Yes."

"There's something I want you to do for me."

"There is?"

I nod, letting my hand drop. "There's a security firm Hayden works with that installs security systems in houses. Sensors around doors, alarms, the works. I want your mom's house to have a system like that. You two will be the only ones with the codes."

Her eyebrows rise. "That's a good idea."

"Just in case. I doubt he'll come back, but I'd sleep better at night."

"So would I," she says, swallowing hard. "Thank you, Parker. For always looking out for us."

"I'll send you the details."

Jamie looks down at her hands. A faraway seagull cries out and the waves lap softly against the boat's hull. *This is it,* I think. She'll break or heal me right here.

"The last voice I needed to silence," she says, "was my own."

"It was?"

She nods and brushes a hand over her cheek. Her eyes are glazed and my stomach sinks, seeing it. "Yes," she says. "Last week, the expectations got to my head. That we would move in together, that we would have kids, all things you deserve, Parker. All things I... but it got to my head."

"I've never made you feel that way," I say. "Have I? Put any expectations on you?"

"No," she says, and laughs a little, wiping at her cheek again. "I realized that the last set were all my own. It's everything I want and yet, now that I could theoretically have it, it terrifies me. Maybe I don't feel like I deserve it or if I'd even get to keep it... and that if we fail, it'll hurt so much worse than anything with Lee ever did. If you were to get lost in a storm again..."

"I won't," I promise her. "Never."

Sincere eyes meet mine. "It was my own voice, in my own head. Reminding me of what I have to lose. *You.* What if I can't be what you want, Parker? What if I can't move fast enough for your liking?"

My hands ache to take hers. "You'll always be what I want, James," I say. "There's no timeline for us. Never has been. We've always defied it."

"I have baggage. A lot of it," she says.

"Everyone does."

She takes a deep breath and meets my eyes. "I love you," she says. "I think I always have, even back when you were someone I loved from afar, knowing we'd never make sense."

"Not true."

"A little true," she says, "and you know that, too."

"That was then. We're not the same people anymore."

"No," she says, and reaches for my hand. "We're not. I love you. I don't know if I can be what you want, but that won't change."

I love you.

The words send liquid warmth through me. Nothing else matters. "You are what I want already. All of it," I say. "What about what you said last week? About a relationship?"

She shakes her head. "I want to be with you, if you'll have me."

"Jamie," I protest, pulling her close. "You know I will."

She laughs softly against my shoulder. "I want to find my footing. I want to freelance with graphic design and I want Emma to properly start school and get friends. I want to move out of my mom's into a place that's just ours."

"Yes," I murmur. "I support all of that."

"I want us to be... equal. I can't live at your house rent-free. I can't put myself in a position like that again."

"Jamie, I understand. Trust me. And for the record? We are equal. We always have been." I take her hand and lift it to my cheek, needing her touch. "Whatever you want."

She takes a deep breath. "The last part. Kids? Do you want more? Because I don't know yet. I can't make any prom—"

I kiss her softly, stopping the words. Surprised lips open beneath mine. When I feel grounded again, I lift my head and rest my forehead against hers. "Jamie," I murmur. "If I'm an uncle and a stepfather all my life, that will be okay for me."

"It will?"

"Yes."

A sigh escapes her. "Oh. But don't you have wants, too?"

I can't help but smile at that. "Yes, I do."

"What are they?"

I brush her hair back. "I want to be the person you tell your fears and hopes to. I want to support your dreams. I want to spot you when you lift weights and get to know your daughter and help both of you grow. I want to be your safe harbor.

"But I also want you to tell me off when I'm doing something wrong and to argue with me and to never, ever be afraid of me, because I'll never be him. Hurting you would be to hurt myself. I can't promise I never will, because relationships are messy. But I will *never* do it deliberately."

"I know," she breathes.

I kiss her cheek, closing my eyes against the emotions. "You were my first crush and you're my greatest love. Just let me be with you forever. Here, in our home, with our families. That's what I want. The rest? We'll figure all of it out. Including the voices in your head."

Jamie kisses me, a soft brush of her lips against mine that I seize on. I pull her firmly against me and feel like I can finally breathe again after more than a week of fear. And when she gets cold, when we should leave the marina but can't bring ourselves to, I dig out the spare sweater I keep in the hatch and she pulls it on.

I tug her against my side. "You see me," I murmur, "in a way no other woman ever has. From the very start, all those years ago, you looked at me and you kept looking."

Not once had she thought the surface was all there was to me, and as long as I keep her clear gaze in my life, I'll be the luckiest man alive.

30

JAMIE

"Catch," Parker says.

"Wait!" I say. He doesn't, and I'm forced to jump to grab the rope.

He grins. "Nice."

"You're supposed to teach me!"

"People learn best under pressure," he says, moving along the deck to me. His footsteps are sure on the wooden deck of the *Atlas*. "And now what do you do?"

"I secure it here," I say, bending at the waist. I fasten it around a hook and focus on the knot he'd shown me last weekend. Up, and over, and across…

"Yeah, that's it," he says. "Tighten?"

I tug on the end of the rope and it slots into place beautifully, like a puzzle done right.

"Perfect," he says. "You sure you haven't been training in secret? Do you have another sailing boyfriend somewhere?"

I stick out my tongue at him and Parker's grin widens. The mid-October sun kisses his hair, tousled from the wind, and behind him the sail stretches taut. Without the motor on, the only sounds around us are seagulls and the waves cleaving beneath us.

"I'll make a sailor out of you yet," he says, and catches me around the waist.

"Aye-aye, Captain."

He rolls his eyes and kisses me. Once, twice, trailing along my cheek. I wrap my arms around his neck and breathe in the scent of him and salt and ocean spray.

"I'm so glad we took today off," I say.

"Mmm," he murmurs. "One of the many, many perks of working for yourself. I'm glad we both do."

"Sure you don't miss me waitressing?"

He chuckles. "Yes, even if having you around daily was a little bit distracting. But I still appreciate the shifts you take when someone calls out."

"I like doing it, every now and then," I say.

He shifts us to the seat, pulling me down beside him. The cushions here are waterproof and large and newly refurbished. "How are the websites coming along?"

"Great. I should be done with the one for your old colleague next Friday," I say.

My main job now is freelance web design. I'd showed Parker my own overhauled website a month ago. He said he'd send it to everyone he knew, and I thought he was exaggerating until I got *three* separate calls from small-scale law firms who needed an overhaul of their ageing websites. After a conversation with Ben of the Paradise Gelato Shop, I'm building them a website, too.

Four projects, and a job that lets me spend mornings with Parker in the gym, take Emma to school, and still be there to pick her up in the afternoons.

"Mmm. As long as you don't forget to check in with your first client."

I grin. "It's very hard to, when I'm also in love with him. Your newsletters will always come first."

Parker presses a hand to his heart. "That's my love language, baby."

Lily had talked our ear off about love languages last week

at dinner, explaining a book she'd just read in minute detail. She'd asked a frustrated Hayden, an amused Parker and me, mostly confused, what our languages were.

It made for an interesting dinner.

"I think I'm learning a new dialect in mine," I say, grinning.

"Oh? What is it?"

"Long trips at sea." I touch his jaw with my lips. "Who knew this was so nice?"

He chuckles darkly and curves his hand around my hip. "I did."

I rise up on an elbow. "Is this your move, then? Bring your girlfriends out on the boat with you?"

"This feels like a trick question," he says, still grinning.

"So you've done it before?"

"Yes, but it was a long time ago, and it was never anyone I cared for a lot. And it was never on my own boat."

"Good answer," I say.

He chuckles. "I'm learning what your love language is."

"Would you say that boats are your happy place?"

"In a way, sure. Although my happy place is where you are."

"Another good answer," I say. I scoot away from him on the bench and back up to the flat of *Atlas*'s deck. The wood is well oiled beneath me, in perfect shape after all the afternoons Parker's spent on refurbishing her. Emma has been along on more than a dozen occasions.

She's learning knots faster than I am.

"Why are you going further away?" he complains.

I smile. "Come here."

"There are cushions right here."

"Yes, but I can lie back flat here. Come on."

His eyebrows knit together, but he does what I ask, sitting down beside me on the deck. A gust of wind catches my hair and tugs tendrils loose from my braid.

"Okay," he says. "This is nice."

That makes my smile widen. I've been doing so much of it for the past weeks. I still struggle under the perceived ideals, ones I've internalized. But with my own business growing, with Emma loving her new school, with Lee gone for good...

I can just be me.

And I'm in love with the man beside me. "So if boats are your favorite thing—"

"*Second* favorite thing," he says.

"Right. I'm your favorite?"

"Naturally," he agrees.

I wrap an arm around his neck and tug him down with me. He braces himself on a forearm, surprise in his eyes.

"You've done a lot of things on boats, I'm sure," I say, bending my leg to twine over his. The October day is mild, and there's not another boat in sight. I feel wild, and teasing, and high on life. "But have you ever had sex on one?"

He lifts his head. Dark blue eyes widen, and he grows still. "Jesus. No, I have not."

"Well then," I say, and notch my leg around his hip.

Parker is perfectly still for another two seconds. And then he's kissing me, and I laugh against his eager lips.

"You're perfect," he murmurs against my ear. "You know that, right? Absolutely perfect."

I reach down for the button on his pants. "Maybe I just know you very well."

Ten minutes later I'm flat on my back on the boat and Parker is moving deep within me. His skin is sun-warm and his hair tickles against my forehead with every thrust. We're only partially undressed, but it's enough, and I bury my head against his neck. Hold him tight while we race to the finish line.

When the fire has passed, I look past his shoulder to the deep blue sky above us and keep my knees locked tight around him.

Tears leak down the outer corners of my eyes, dampening my hair at the temples.

"Jamie?" he murmurs. He's carrying most of his weight on his arms, and I tighten my grip on him. He relaxes with a grumble, letting me feel all of him. I'm pressed down against the ocean even as I stare at the sky. The sea around us is endless and boundless, but I feel anchored here, with his body against mine.

"I love you," I whisper.

He gives a huff at my ear. "I'll never tire of hearing you say that."

I wonder why I fought so hard against sailing when I was a teenager. Why I had to rebel at every turn, or why I needed to argue just to feel seen. It seems you learn some things too late, and others too early.

But some things? Some things you learn just when you need to. This is one of those things.

We are one of those things.

———

We have dinner at the yacht club that evening with the entire family. Kristen has added a few extra fall items to the menu, and in the Marchand family text thread, Lily had hinted at it being *necessary* to pull the entire family together.

"It'll be an announcement," Parker says on the way there. "You know it will be."

"Maybe," I say. I'd been working out of Lily's gallery the past week, sitting side by side with her when she takes calls and I design. She'd seemed completely normal. "But maybe it's for someone else? And she's throwing off the scent?"

He runs a hand along his jaw. "Could be. Emma, wait for us!"

My daughter stops ahead of us on the sidewalk, rocking back on her heels, and gives us an impatient look. "You're walking slow," she accuses us.

"Oh?" I reach out a hand. "Want to fly?"

She nods. With one hand in Parker's and another in mine,

we lift her high between us with every few jumps. I'd explained to her, after Lee left, that her father and I had come to an understanding. That he wouldn't be returning to us again.

I'd dreaded the conversation, my heart in my throat, waiting for her reaction. But she'd looked at me very seriously. "So he's never coming back?"

"Probably not any time soon, no."

She'd considered. "That's okay, Mommy."

"It is?"

"Yes." She'd looked down at her Play-Doh, and reached for the purple color. "I like you with the captain."

A breath escaped me. *Thank God.*

"So it's okay if I keep being with him?"

"Yes. He's going to teach me sailing when I turn eight." She'd wiggled from side to side, a little dance, and stacked her Play-Doh colors. "The square knot, and the thief knot, the clove… the clove knot…" she'd sing-songed.

So here we are, weeks later, walking with Emma between us toward the yacht club. My resilient daughter and our new life in Paradise.

The table Stephen has reserved for us is in the back of the restaurant, along the ocean-facing windows. Hayden and Lily are already there, along with little Jamie, who waves at Emma with a pack of crayons in hand. She takes off to sit next to him.

The rest fill up soon. Henry and Faye, and little Hazel. Michael and Eloise Marchand and then, late as always, Rhys and Ivy, coming hand-in-hand through the restaurant.

Halfway through the dinner, Michael gives Parker the ultimate compliment. "This is delicious," he says, motioning toward his chowder. "You've done a great job with this place."

Parker smiles easily. "Thanks, Dad." He drapes an arm over the back of my chair. It's without thinking, without asking, and I lean into his side. *We belong.*

Across the restaurant, a group of people I recognize follow Stephen to their table. It's Turner and Blair, and a few other people I remember from high school. People who'd moved in the same crowd as Parker and Hayden.

They wave across the restaurant. Parker raises his free hand and nods, never removing his arm from around me. And I find myself waving to them too.

The sound of someone tapping their fork against a glass silences the conversation around the table. Parker turns to me with a raised eyebrow.

Here it comes.

Rhys clears his throat. And, surprising us all, he starts to talk about Lily's wedding.

"I want to remind everyone just how great a time we had, celebrating Lily and Hayden. What a beautiful ceremony and delicious food. We partied late that night." He raises his glass to Lily, who lifts hers back, eyebrows raised.

"What the heck?" Parker mutters by my side.

"I'd also like to bring everyone's attention to Henry and Faye's wedding. Stunning New York location, a string quartet, excellent mingling opportunities. Hats off to the two of you, too."

Henry lifts an eyebrow in response. He has one arm around Hazel, who's falling asleep against his chest. "I had to show the rest of you how it's done."

"Right, right," Rhys says. "Exactly. I'd also like to humbly remind Mom and Dad how expensive weddings are."

Michael chuckles. "Where is this heading, huh?"

Rhys wraps his arm around Ivy, sitting by his side. She has a wide smile on her face. "Ivy and I have gotten married," he says.

"What?" Lily says. *"Rhys!"*

Eloise has her hands on her face. "You didn't!"

Parker's the one who grins, extending a hand across the table to his brother. "Congrats, man. And congratulations, Ivy. Couldn't ask for a better sister-in-law."

Faye pretends to gasp. "Excuse me?"

Parker laughs. "You're tied for best place! Both of you!"

It takes the family a solid ten minutes before they'll let Rhys and Ivy explain. I watch the two of them, their obvious happiness, and lean against Parker's side again. There really is no rulebook. Rhys has never followed one, at any rate.

Parker and I can do whatever we'd like.

Rhys and Ivy explain how they'd tied the knot, just the two of them and an officiant, on one of their trips. "We have pictures," Ivy says, almost shyly. "Would you like to see?"

Later, Lily makes a Hail Mary pass for a chance to celebrate them. "How about we throw a party for you two? Please, Rhys? Ivy? I can handle everything!"

Hayden clears his throat and puts a hand on her shoulder. "Can you?"

"Yes, of course I can."

"This is as good a time as any," he says.

"Right now?"

"It's what we'd planned," he says.

She nods, and smiles, and taps her fork against her own glass a bit sheepishly. That's how we learn that not only have Rhys and Ivy eloped, but Hayden and Lily are expecting another child.

Emma, oblivious to the cheers around us, tugs on Parker's sleeve. "Captain," she says.

He looks down to see her with an unopened lobster tail in hand. "Ah. Remember how I've showed you?"

"Yes, but it doesn't *work*."

"It does. Look here..." He cracks it open for her between strong fingers, and she giggles in response. I watch them with a warm weight in my chest. And when it's time to raise a glass to Lily and Hayden, and to Rhys and Ivy, I do so with my eyes on Parker.

"And to us," I mouth.

His smile widens. "Always."

EPILOGUE
PARKER

Two years later

"Dad?" Emma calls. "Where are you?"

"In the garage!"

"We have to *go*!"

"I'm coming!" I rummage around the box, searching for the gloves I'd bought for her first lessons. It hasn't gotten old yet, her calling me dad. She'd first started saying it a year ago. Casually, randomly, like it didn't upend my entire world every time she did it.

The first time it had happened, Jamie had met my gaze over Emma's head, oblivious in her play, and I'd seen she was just as shocked as I was.

From that moment on, Emma hadn't stopped using it. I'd told her earlier that she could call me whatever she wanted, and she'd been the one to settle on Dad.

"Here they are," I say, fishing out the pair. "Do you have your backpack?"

"Yes!"

I lock the garage and join her by my car. She's shifting from foot to foot, hair neatly braided. Jamie had done it this morning before she went to work. "Water bottle? Life vest?"

"*Yes,*" she says, our wannabe teenager, and opens the door to the car.

I grin at her eagerness.

We drive down to the marina, and she talks the whole way, all nerves and excitement. We've sailed a lot over the past year together, but this is her first proper lesson with other kids from her school and the area.

"What if I fall in?" she asks when we're down on the docks, watching the group by the training dinghies.

"You probably will, kiddo," I say. "But you'll be in a life vest."

"It'll be cold."

I chuckle and tug at the end of her braid. "Yes. But you know what to do. We tried this last summer, remember?"

She nods. "Yes."

Jamie and Emma had worked hard on her swimming skills all of last summer, and I'd been there to help as often as I could. They'd still been renting Lily's cottage then.

It's been seven months now since they moved into my house. Into *our* house.

"Mom will be here when you're done with the class," I say. "And I'll stay over here the whole time."

"You'll be watching?"

"If you want me to, kiddo."

She nods and looks up at me. Behind the hesitant expression there's determination in her eyes. She might be shy with strangers, but she's got a stubborn streak that's all Jamie. "Stay."

"Okay. I'll be right over there." I point to the benches along the dock. "Want me to introduce you to Neil?"

She shakes her head. "I can do it."

"Course you can." I adjust her backpack and nod toward the group. "You got this, skipper."

Her smile turns crooked. "I'm not a skipper, Dad."

"Not yet."

She snorts, steels her shoulders, and walks down the dock.

I watch her say hello and get welcomed into the group, the instructor fitting her with a life vest. I do just what I'd told her, and sit down to watch the lesson. They'll start with the basics, things she already knows.

I feel Jamie's fingers in my hair before I see her. She runs them along the nape of my neck, curling inside my shirt, and sits down next to me.

"Hey," she says.

I kiss her. "Hi, baby. How did it go?"

"It went great. Everything looks normal."

"And no ultrasound?"

She smiles. "No. That isn't until later. I just got some vitamins and a second check-up scheduled."

"I wish I could have been there," I say, and I mean it.

Her hand reaches for mine and threads our fingers together. "This was the earliest slot my doctor had, and Emma's been waiting for this class for years. She wanted you here, not anyone else."

"I know. But I'm not missing another doctor's appointment. Not for the rest of the pregnancy."

Jamie leans her head against my shoulder. "Good. I want you there, too."

"I know it's still too early to tell, but I wonder…"

"Boy or a girl?"

"Yes." I smooth my thumb over the back of her hand and breathe in the smell of her hair. Beautiful, and mine, and pregnant. It's unlocked a completely different side of me. There's something almost primal in holding her in my arms and knowing she's carrying our child.

"What are you hoping for?" she asks.

"Either. Both."

She chuckles. "Both? I'm not hoping for that. Can you imagine twins?"

"It'll be a lot," I admit. "Does this mean we can tell Emma soon?"

"Yes. But I want to be a little further along. You know she

won't be able to keep it a secret." There's a warm smile on Jamie's face as she watches Emma and the other kids across the docks. "When we tell her, we tell the rest of the family too."

I turn my face toward her ear. "I love you so much."

"Mmm." She nestles closer against my side and I wrap my arm around her shoulders. "You tell me that more often since I got pregnant."

"Well, I have to say it twice as often. I'm saying it to two people now."

"You're a charmer."

"Only for you." I kiss her temple. "I can't wait to marry you, James."

Her breath catches in her throat. It's brief, and then she's teasing me, like always. "I'm going to be pregnant in a wedding dress, and it's all your fault."

I chuckle. "Yes. But I feel more than a little proud of that. And you're going to look beautiful, baby. You always do."

"I've already said yes," she murmurs, smiling.

"I'll never stop complimenting you."

She runs a hand up my chest, stopping at the collar of my linen shirt. "I can't wait to see you in a tux, either. Or call you my husband."

"Lily's going to cry the entire wedding. I guarantee it. From start to finish."

Jamie laughs. "Yes, you're right, she will. But she's promised to throw a great bachelorette party."

"Hayden's trying to talk my brothers and a few friends into doing something for me, and I have a feeling it's going to result in beers at the yacht club and sailing," I say. "And I'm absolutely okay with that."

She turns her face up. Warm, open, teasing eyes meet mine, ones that haven't held the shadows of her past for months. One of her hands strokes along my jaw. "When this baby is born and a bit older, you and I are going on a honeymoon. A proper one."

"We are?"

"Yes. Remember how you've always wanted to sail in the Caribbean?"

"Really? You'd stay on a sailing boat with me for an entire week?"

Her smile widens. She's gotten used to regular trips with me, and she's learned, but she still doesn't need the ocean like I do. That's fine. As long as she needs *me* the way I need her, I don't need to get on a boat again for the rest of my life.

"Yes. Something that's just for you and me."

"Baby, we do things like that all the time."

She laughs. "When was the last time?"

I rest my forehead against hers. "The shower. Two days ago."

"Well, okay, if that counts, yes."

"It counts. I counted to two, even, for you."

Jamie rolls her eyes, but heat rises up her cheeks. "Did you add them to your logbook?"

I laugh, and kiss her. Asking her to marry me had felt harder than the conversation we had about children, before we started trying, and she went off birth control.

The child had been her idea. I hadn't wanted to pressure her in any way, and when she suggested we start trying, I'd damn near gotten on my knees. *Yes.* But when I'd asked her to marry me, fully expecting a *not yet* answer, Jamie had surprised me.

She started crying… and she said yes. So we ended up doing both at the same time, not quite following the rulebook, but fully adhering to our own timeline.

The way we always have.

"I wish I found my way back to Paradise sooner," Jamie says. "We could have been married years ago."

I tighten my hands on her waist. My soon-to-be-wife, the mother of my kids. Both of them.

"You got here in the end," I say. "That's all that matters."

AFTERWORD

Thank you for reading about Parker and Jamie! Their story is the final book in the Brothers of Paradise, a series I started over two years ago.

I'll be honest—every single book in this series has challenged me. From Rogue's frequent flashes into the past, to Rebel's constant travelling, and now in Hero, with Jamie's story arc. She's a wonderful protagonist and I wanted to make sure I did her past justice.

Emotional and financial abuse is a serious topic and I've tried to treat it with the delicacy it deserves. I hope I succeeded, but any fault in the depiction is mine and mine alone.

There are wonderful organisations worldwide that can help if you're looking to leave an abusive relationship. Most have excellent resources online, too, which can be a great place to start.

When it comes to the Marchand's, it's now time for me to leave them and their beloved Paradise Shores behind... I will miss them. Thanks for making a better writer by challenging me so darn much.

And just in case you're reading this and need to hear it—

you're not worthless. No one is, and especially not someone as kick-ass as you!

OTHER BOOKS BY OLIVIA
LISTED IN READING ORDER

New York Billionaires Series

Think Outside the Boss
Tristan and Freddie

Saved by the Boss
Anthony and Summer

Say Yes to the Boss
Victor and Cecilia

A Ticking Time Boss
Carter and Audrey

Seattle Billionaires Series

Billion Dollar Enemy
Cole and Skye

Billion Dollar Beast
Nick and Blair

Billion Dollar Catch
Ethan and Bella

Billion Dollar Fiancé
Liam and Maddie

Brothers of Paradise Series

Rogue
Lily and Hayden

Ice Cold Boss
Faye and Henry

Red Hot Rebel
Ivy and Rhys

Small Town Hero
Jamie and Parker

Standalones

Arrogant Boss
Julian and Emily

Look But Don't Touch
Grant and Ada

The Billionaire Scrooge Next Door
Adam and Holly

ABOUT OLIVIA

Olivia loves billionaire heroes despite never having met one in person. Taking matters into her own hands, she creates them on the page instead. Stern, charming, cold or brooding, so far she's never met a (fictional) billionaire she didn't like.

Her favorite things include wide-shouldered heroes, late-night conversations, too-expensive wine and romances that lift you up.

Smart and sexy romance—those are her lead themes!

Join her newsletter for updates and bonus content.
www.oliviahayle.com.
Connect with Olivia

facebook.com/authoroliviahayle

instagram.com/oliviahayle

goodreads.com/oliviahayle

amazon.com/author/oliviahayle

bookbub.com/profile/olivia-hayle